Coming Home to You

by

Barbara Lohr

Purple Egret Press

Purple Egret Press
Savannah, Georgia 31411

Cover Art: Kim Killion – The Killion Group
Editing: Nicole Zoltack

Print ISBN: 978-0-9908642-4-0
Digital ISBN: 978-0-9908642-3-3

For Parfait, Sasha, Brianna, Frida, Max and Lily—
pets who've shared our lives and brightened our days.

Chapter 1

The thumping started when Kate Kennedy reached Greta's Gifts on Red Arrow Highway. Cheese curls churned in her stomach as she tapped the brakes. Almost home but something was wrong with the kayak strapped to her roof. Gravel crunching beneath the tires, she pulled into Greta's and parked. The sun bounced off the hood of her SUV, but a cool May breeze bathed her face when she cracked open the door.

Welcome to Michigan. Her eyes felt grainy from fourteen hours on the road, but she was home.

Stretching, Kate breathed in the lake, damp and beachy. The tightness in her shoulders eased. Pine trees caught a high spring gust and the familiar rustle made her smile. Her stomach gurgled. Not much to eat the whole ride from Boston except peanut butter and jelly, plus bags of cheese curls washed down with coffee.

Looking up, she exhaled. At least she hadn't lost Gator, her green kayak. A red security tie flapped in the breeze. Must have lost the other strap along the way. Kate scrubbed her face with hands shaking from all the caffeine. A semi roared past, kicking up dust. She tugged up the zipper on her hoodie.

"Doggone it, Gator."

The kayak slid a bit farther. Too bad she'd left her small kitchen stepladder in the Boston condo, along with a lot of other stuff. When she yanked the remaining red band, it fell away in her hand. One frustrated shove and Gator retaliated, smacking her square in the chest before clattering to the ground. The pain bent Kate over like a paper clip. She almost didn't hear the door slam behind her.

Blinking furiously, she pulled herself up, grateful for the sunglasses. No way would anyone see Kate Kennedy cry. A man ambled toward her in work boots, worn jeans, and shoulders that tested the seams of a beat-up jean jacket. That walk looked familiar and her heart kicked up a beat. He wore aviator sunglasses, so no telling for sure. A black and white dog hung out of the pickup, Great Dane ears pricking forward. Big muzzle, big dog.

"Need some help?"

Yep, it was him. Kate's legs weakened. "No, I'm fine."

His eyes shifted to the kayak on the ground. "Doesn't look fine to me."

She fisted her hands on her hips. "I'm fine. And so is Gator." Her chest throbbed.

Blue eyes swept like a July wave over the tops of his sunglasses. "Gator?"

She swallowed. "My kayak. Seemed appropriate."

"I see."

But Cole Campbell had never understood why Kate wanted all her belongings named and in their proper place. Shoot. They'd been on the high school debate team together, and he didn't recognize her? Maybe it was her recent drugstore dye job. She'd had brown hair in high school. Now she ran a hand over blonde hair, crisp from two days of neglect.

He swayed back on his heels, a Good Samaritan with second thoughts. The two empty seats of the kayak stared up at them. "Lucky you didn't lose it on the road. Could have smashed into another driver. You need to batten it down."

"Thought I did. It was dark when I loaded it."

"Try doing it in the daytime. You could kill somebody."

"I left at midnight."

"Midnight?" He lowered the glasses and his eyes darkened.

Her chin came up. "Highway's quiet at night. Just the truckers."

"Exactly. Truckers. You think that's safe?"

None of his business. "I've, ah, probably got some rope in the back." She seriously doubted it.

"I'll be glad to help." Cole's attention shifted to her jeans. The corners of his lips lifted. "You saving that for something?"

Kate looked down. A cheese curl was caught in her crotch and she batted it away. No time for games. Especially not with him.

His eyes flitted from her to Gator and back. A stern mask slipped into place. Cole's teenage acne had left faint pockmarks that definitely didn't detract from his macho appeal.

Was he going to help her or not? Her chest throbbed. Could this day get any worse? The boy she'd lusted for in high school didn't even recognize her. Kate's throat closed. Nothing like feeling forgettable.

In two thrusts of his muscular arms, Cole had Gator back in the rack on top of her SUV. Disgusting how easy he made it look, but it gave her time to enjoy the view. Cole Campbell had definitely left "gawky" behind.

"Thank you."

Wheeling around, he caught her staring and grinned. "Got that rope?"

Her face burned. "Sure. I'll get it. Let me just check Bonita."

"Bonita?" He tilted his head.

"My car." One glimpse of the pretty blue SUV on the lot and she knew it was Bonita.

"Sure. Right."

Popping open the back gate, Kate launched herself into the tightly packed boxes and bulging trash bags. Her rear end felt big as a helium balloon.

"Finding anything? I might have something in the truck."

Feeling him hovering, she tried to squeeze her butt tighter.

When she heard the scratch of his boots, Kate thought maybe he was leaving. Her disappointment surprised her. After all, she wasn't at her best. If you're going to run into an old flame… well, a man you wanted to be your old flame… a girl should look hot, not sweaty.

Kate was sweaty. And not in a good way.

Finally, she climbed out empty-handed. Cole was ambling toward her with a roll of heavy gauge rope.

"That looks serious." Her mother wouldn't even be able to get a clothespin around this sturdy stuff, although she'd probably try.

"Want to stand on the other side and catch this?"

"Sure." *I'd hold anything for you. Like my breath.*

While Cole tossed a length of rope over the kayak, his dog

watched from the pickup with mild interest. Grabbing the rope, Kate threaded it back and he knotted it securely. "First, I like to tighten the bow and then the stern."

"You kayak?"

Whipping out a Swiss army knife, he cut the rope. "Way too much work. I sail."

Of course. She pictured an elegant yacht skimming Lake Michigan. Samantha McGraw would be rubbing her tan body against his. Kate didn't need the instant replay. Had enough of that in high school.

Cole worked with calm efficiency, the way he'd handled Student Council or Debate Club.

Oh, yeah. He'd handled their debate group just fine.

When he turned back, his eyes went to her hair. Smiling, Cole whisked something from the mess. Her breath left her body.

Maybe she was just tired.

Or maybe she was desperate for a man's touch.

He handed her a cheese curl. "You missed this."

"Great. Thanks." She jammed it in her jean pocket and then felt stupid. Was she going to press it in her high school scrapbook? Kate slammed her back gate shut.

Cole's eyes rested on the Massachusetts license plate. "Passing through or coming for the summer?"

"That depends." He still didn't know her? She edged toward the driver's door. "Thanks for your help."

Cole cocked his head to one side, like he was listening to her voice. "Sure. No problem."

"Got to get to an appointment." Maybe a shrink. She opened the driver's door so fast she almost cracked herself in the mouth.

"Ah, huh. Well, good luck."

"Right. Thanks." Kate needed more than luck this trip. Without looking back, she peeled out and did a U-turn on Red Arrow. In bad need of a friendly face, she headed into town.

Driving toward Gull Harbor, Kate passed the ice cream parlors, restaurants, galleries, and gift shops that lured tourists. Some looked closed, and she hoped that was just seasonal. Winters could be hard on businesses, and this economy didn't help any.

Clancy's grocery store sat at the main intersection of Whittaker and Red Arrow, just next to Dressel's drugstore. Kate ducked into the grocery, grabbed a cart, and zipped through the aisles, snapping up basic necessities like OJ, milk, bread and cheese curls. Stopping at the deli counter, she picked up some sliced turkey and cole slaw. Should hold her for a while.

After stowing the bags in her trunk, Kate glanced across the street. The Full Cup sign swung above the frosted glass door. A cheese crown called to her from Sarah's shiny clean case. Hardly any traffic on Whittaker in early May and she sprinted across the two lanes. Kate pushed open the door of the bakery and breathed in the scent of warm, fresh pastries. No need to begin sensible eating now. Sour cream donuts, almond braids, cheese crowns and frosted brownies were neatly arranged behind the glass.

Freshly perked coffee perfumed the air with a hint of hazelnut. Definitely not the roadside stuff. Everything about the place looked the same, just the way Kate liked it. Her irritation eased.

Would it be a cheese crown or a brownie? Kate was still deciding when Sarah whirled through the swinging door to the back, patting her brown curls. "Why, Katie Kennedy. Back so soon?"

"Couldn't stay away from your cheese crowns."

"I know. Me too." Laughing, Sarah wiped her hands on the apron around her ample waist. Miss Congeniality, hands down.

"Everything good? Boys and Jamie doing all right?"

Sarah had married Jamie Pickard, her high school sweetheart now serving overseas. They had two little boys.

"Yep, as far as I know. One cheese crown coming right up." Sarah handed over the largest pastry on the tray. She nodded toward the tables at the window. "Got time to chat? Coffee's free."

"Sounds like a plan." That run-in with Cole after all these years had left Kate's head fuzzy. She just wasn't ready to see her mom yet. After pouring a cup of hazelnut coffee, she slid onto one of the wire-backed chairs.

Sarah settled across the table with a sigh. "Your mother will be glad to see you."

"So you know about her stroke?" No secrets in this town. Today that felt good.

"How's she doing?"

"The therapists say she's improving."

"She'll be tickled to see you." Supportive to the bone, Sarah always had your back.

"Picked up groceries and thought I'd stop here." Kate's grin felt shaky. "Kinda tired. I started out late last night."

"A woman on the highway alone at night?"

"Cole Campbell already told me that was stupid."

"You're in touch with Cole?" Sarah's eyebrows lifted into her curly mop.

Kate brushed the crumbs from her jeans. "My kayak came loose, and he stopped to help."

"Really? Always so helpful. Cole's a mover and shaker here in town."

"Samantha must love that." Kate had heard Cole and Samantha married right out of college. By that time, Kate had been dating Brian for three years. High school friends pairing up had been old news.

But with Cole? Okay, the news gave her a twinge or two.

"They split up." Sarah stirred more cream into her coffee. "It's been tough for him the last few years. He has custody of their daughter."

Cole Campbell, a single father? "Thought the mom always gets the kids. Does Samantha live around here?"

"Nope. California, from what I hear. Anyway, Cole wants to move Gull Harbor ahead." Sarah glanced at the street outside. "Make some changes."

"Things look just fine the way they are." Kate took another bite of the sweet cheese.

"We've had a rough few years, Kate. Shops have closed or changed hands. Michiana Thyme was sold. Did your mom tell you?"

Kate shook her head, struggling to swallow. She always bit off more than she could chew. "Nope. She might be a little out of touch now." Craning her neck, Kate stared down Whittaker at the combination gift shop and diner on the main corner. Been there forever. Now it was sold? Her contentment at being home unraveled around the edges. "I was looking forward to their stuffed French toast."

"And I would have been right there with you, not that I need it. Loretta retired and moved to Florida to be near her son. No one wanted to take on the store."

"What's going to happen to the place?"

Sarah lifted a shoulder. "Town meeting pretty soon. Cole bought it. He's got plans. Your mom never said anything? She's always been so involved in Gull Harbor."

"She will be again. I have no doubt."

Sarah's eyes softened. "She'll be so glad to see both of you."

"Mercedes can't come. Too much going on with her company."

At least that had been the excuse. Kate didn't need to spell it out for her old friend. Eons ago, her older sister had borrowed an outfit from Sarah. The fluffy teal sweater and pants had been so pretty. After go-karting with friends, Mercedes returned it with oil stains. Never said a thing about it. Kate had been so embarrassed. Just another page from the book of Mercedes Kennedy. "I'm hoping Mercedes will be able to come soon."

"You Kennedy women are strong. Almost didn't recognize you, Kate. Like the blonde hair."

"What was I thinking? Crazy, right?"

"Maybe you need more crazy."

"Don't know if I'm ready for that." But change was bearing

down on her, whether she liked it or not. This two-block street was all Kate had ever known in Gull Harbor. They'd hung out here at the Swirly Top, eaten Loretta's special orange ricotta stuffed French toast at Michiana Thyme and grabbed pizza at Touch of Italy. All the local kids got part-time jobs in the shops during the summer. "I want it to stay just the way it is."

"I don't know if that's possible, Kate."

Her coffee had turned lukewarm. The cozy hazelnut flavor was gone and a chill stole through the glass window. "Boy, it's cold. When will spring get here?" Kate pulled her hoodie tighter.

"We had a long winter." Sarah gave her a wry smile. "The ice floes didn't melt until just a couple weeks ago. Beach is going to be wide this year. Hope people can afford to rent cottages."

By Memorial Day, families would be bustling from store to store with bulging shopping bags. At least, that's the way it used to be. "How's your business?"

"Not bad. Course I have been taking more day-old pastries to the soup kitchens. Might as well have someone enjoy them, right? Gonna be here for a while? I'm sure the girls would love to see you. You probably have to get back, though. Husband, job, and all that."

Kate sucked in a slow breath, not quite ready to share the news. "So much depends on Mom's condition. I'm freelancing now, you know. Healthcare blogs."

"Right, you told me the newspaper had a layoff." A silence stretched until Sarah carefully swept crumbs off the table and into a napkin. "Well, then. You always liked to read, Kate. Come to our book group."

"Anybody I know?" Last thing she needed was a bunch of strangers asking questions.

"Chili and Carolyn Knight, who teaches at the high school."

"Chili? Don't think I would have passed Spanish without her." Chili would quiz Kate about verb conjugations until she could recite them in her dreams. "You mean Miss Knight? Still single and teaching at the high school?"

"Yep and then Phoebe and Diana. Both new to the area. You'll enjoy them. Phoebe has a hair salon and Diana opened Hippy Chick, a clothing store. Kind of cute."

Being with other women might be good for her. "Maybe. Thanks for mentioning it."

Sarah looked pleased with herself. "Good. We're meeting next Wednesday. My house at seven."

Whoa. "But I haven't read the book."

"'Bridges of Madison County.' I'll get it to you next week."

"Oh, I can wing that one." An old favorite, the novel was packed up in the garage of the condo, waiting for a destination address.

The door to the kitchen slammed open, and two little boys tumbled out, barefoot with t-shirts untucked. "Mom, Mom!" the first little guy called out, running to Sarah. "Nathan won't share!"

"Mine! These are my dinosaurs!" The other boy clutched some plastic figures to his heaving chest. The unruly hair marked them as Sarah's children.

"Double trouble." Sarah stared them both down. "Justin and

Nathan, can't you say hello to Kate?"

The boys looked like they might consider it.

"Hello."

"Hi."

Sarah laid one hand on each boy's shoulder. "Where's Grandma Lila?"

Justin poked one finger back toward the kitchen. "Making something."

At that moment, a silver-haired woman appeared in the doorway, looking tired and more than a little frustrated.

"Sarah, I tried but they're bored." When Lila threw up both hands, white flour flew. "Hi, Kate. Good to see you."

"Boys, we're going to learn to share or your father will be very disappointed." Sarah wagged one finger before turning back to Kate. "Their daddy is a very brave soldier." The last was obviously said for their benefit.

"You must be so proud of him," Kate said. With his polished Italian loafers and weekly hair styling, Brian wouldn't have dreamed of going over to the Middle East. "Was Jamie in the reserves?"

Sarah nodded. "Called up, but he would have volunteered anyway. I've got a ton of chores ready when he gets back."

Kate checked the time. "I should get moving. Guess I'll take a cheese crown for my mom."

Shepherding the two boys toward their grandmother, Sarah bustled back behind the counter to retrieve Kate's cheese crown. "Mom, I think it's nap time."

Both boys howled.

Waving away Kate's money, Sarah squeezed her hand. "Oh, don't be silly."

"I'll see you…"

"Next Wednesday," Sarah supplied. "My house. Seven o'clock."

"Right." Slotting something on her calendar felt good. Almost banished the embarrassment from running into Cole Campbell.

After all, wasn't he the one who should be embarrassed?

Chapter 2

Tucked along Greenwood Road, Gull Harbor Care Center stretched long, low, and inviting. The nursing home had been a fixture in the community for over seventy-five years. Kate pulled into the parking lot, grabbed the bakery bag and climbed out.

Her mother could black top the driveway, trim the bushes, and replace rotted railroad ties on the beach path without pausing for breath. A whiz at crossword puzzles, she always had the Scrabble board ready. In a telephone conversation, Marianne, the social worker, had mentioned her mother's "resilience." Alice Kennedy had always been one tough cookie. Kate expected a quick recovery and she'd come as soon as she could.

Besides, she needed Gull Harbor. She needed home.

Purple and yellow pansies brightened the flowerbeds at the front of the care facility. The forsythia was starting to bloom, and the brown grass was reluctantly greening up. A hint of spring scented the cool air. As Kate tromped toward the front entrance, she passed an elderly man in a plastic lawn chair. The collar of his green wool coat was turned up and the ear flaps of his cap were pulled down. Typical for Michigan. Kate smiled and nodded.

"Hi, I'm Harold." His eyes were glued to the bakery bag.

"Hi, Harold. I'm Kate. Here to visit my mother. See you later?"

Kate hurried inside, wishing she'd grabbed a whole bag of pastries. She approached a young girl with bouncy brown curls sitting behind the main desk. "I'm looking for Alice Kennedy."

"Sign the visitor's sheet. Room 210. Left and straight back."

Kate smiled at the residents as she headed down the hallway, overhead lighting reflecting off the pastel blue tiles. The air smelled of freshly baked bread with an underpinning of lavender. During their tour, the marketing admissions director had made a point of mentioning the cookies baked every afternoon.

When Kate reached her mother's room, it was empty. An older lady in a bright purple top whirred toward Kate in a wheelchair. "Looking for Alice?"

"Yes, I am. Mrs. McGraw? Is that you?"

The woman squinted. "Katie Kennedy?"

"Aw, so good to see you." Bending down, she gave Mrs. McGraw a hug. "You look beautiful in purple."

"A girl still has to look pretty, don't you think?" Cole's mother-in-law patted her gray curls.

"Absolutely. Do you still make the rice crispy bars for Halloween trick or treat?"

"Of course. You always wanted more than one."

Kate blushed. How many times had she heard her mother explain that Kate was a *healthy eater?*

"You wore that cute orange clown costume with yellow polka dots."

"My mother made the costume." Every Halloween, their father had made the rounds of every house along Lake Shore Drive and all the side roads where they had friends. Finally, he'd wind up at the Roadhouse, his favorite bar out on the highway. Their mother hadn't been too happy about that, but the girls thought it was great fun.

"Alice is probably in therapy." Mrs. McGraw pointed down the hall. "Your sister coming too? Such a knockout, your sister."

Well, there you have it. "Mercedes hopes to be here for Memorial Day weekend." After saying good-bye, Kate followed the signs to Physical Therapy.

Sunlight beamed through a window onto the padded treatment table. A lady in a hot pink warm-up suit worked at lifting her right arm, enormous pink hoop earrings jiggling from the effort. "Just give me a minute, will you?"

No mistaking that voice.

Sinking onto a bench, Kate unzipped her green hoodie. When had her mother started wearing hot pink? Where were the beige elastic waist pants and baggy sweatshirts? Voice low and encouraging, the therapist took her mother through arm exercises. The right arm wasn't cooperating. "Darn thing. It's gone to sleep."

"In a way, it has, but you can train it to wake up," the physical therapist urged. "That's it, Alice." Her mom tried again.

"Can I help you?" Will Applegate took a seat next to Kate. The tall blond administrator always looked on the verge of a hug.

"I'm, ah, waiting for my mother."

"You're one of Alice's daughters."

"I'm Kate Bankoff, um, Kate Kennedy, I mean."

"Of course, I remember you."

Really? Usually Mercedes was the daughter everyone remembered with her blonde hair and blue eyes. Kate's hair might be blonde now, but her eyes would always be hazel.

"Just got in town. Long drive." Like that explained everything.

"Your mother will be so happy you've come." When Will smiled, his eyes formed happy faces. "You live in Boston with your husband, right?"

Kate sucked in a breath. "Right, I'm from Boston."

Will's eyes swiped her bare left hand.

Kate wasn't doing any explaining. "How's she doing?" Her mother was attempting a modified leg lift.

"She's a strong-minded woman. Lots of spirit."

"You've got that right." Spirit enough to hang her sheets outside to dry, even when the winter winds turned polyester to sheet rock.

"We're glad to have her with us. You might want to talk to Lisa later." He nodded to the physical therapist. "And Marianne, her social worker."

"Maybe tomorrow I could catch up." Suddenly, Kate wished Mercedes were here.

"Of course."

The session had ended. Lisa helped Alice into the wheelchair.

Kate stepped up. "Mom?"

"Mercedes?"

"No, Mom. It's Kate." She squatted so her mother could see her. "We talked yesterday about my visit."

"Well, of course I remember." Her mother's chin came up.

Yep, this was the mom Kate knew and loved.

"Katie, how nice."

Kate's eyes dampened and she gave her mom a quick hug. Her mother hadn't called her that in a long time.

Kate took the wheelchair from the therapist. "It's always wonderful when your daughter finally comes to see you." Alice's voice carried the staunch bravery that had been so familiar to Kate growing up. Stoic. Long-suffering. "She lives in…"

"Boston," Kate prompted.

"Bean Town," her mom had joked when Kate settled there. "My daughter lives in Bean Town."

"Like your outfit, Mom. You look good in pink."

With a pleased smile, her mother ran her left hand over her warm-up suit. "It's new."

"Did they take you on a field trip to go shopping?" How had they managed that?

"Heck, no. The shopping channel." Her mother looked at her like she'd just fallen off the stupid truck.

"I don't recall you shopping online before."

"Marie taught me. Easy peasy. I just work the remote with my left hand. Click, click, and it comes in the mail."

Was this really her frugal mother talking? The woman who even bought generic oatmeal? Head down, Kate wheeled her mother toward her room. Wait until Mercedes heard about this.

After she'd settled her mother into the blue vinyl chair next to the bed, Kate opened the white paper bag. The scent of pastry filled the room. "I brought a surprise for you."

"Saints be praised." Alice smiled while Kate broke the cheese crown in two.

As her mother began to nibble, Kate perched on the edge of the bed.

"Are you staying long?"

"For a while." She had no idea how long she'd be in Gull Harbor.

"I suppose Brian will want you home."

No sense putting this off. "Mom, Brian and I aren't together anymore."

Her mother's head jerked. "He left you?"

That was her first thought? "No, not really."

Kate's mother chewed slowly, as if digesting the news. "I always thought you two were perfect for each other."

"I did too. But we weren't. Not really."

Her mother brushed the crumbs from her lips with her good hand. "My goodness. He must have done something terrible."

Kate picked at the edge of the blue blanket. The fabric looked substantial but felt thin. Probably wouldn't keep out the cold but fine for summer.

Had Brian done anything? It was what Brian hadn't done. Like not telling her he didn't ever plan on fathering a child. How embarrassing that they'd never hammered out those details.

"I just want you to be happy, honey." Her mom's pale hazel eyes searched hers.

"I'm fine, Mom. Really. Just a little tired from the drive."

"Go home and rest." Her mother's forehead wrinkled. "Where

did you come from again?"

She kissed her mother's forehead. "Boston."

"Right. Bean Town." Her mom smiled at her own joke.

Kate handed her mother the remote. The shopping channel was extolling the virtues of a turquoise neck clip for reading glasses when Kate left.

Harold still sat guard at the door. "Bye, Kate."

"See you later, Harold."

Chapter 3

Turning off Red Arrow Highway onto Lake Shore Road, Kate opened her window. Her mom might be confused right now, but hopefully that would pass. She'd taken the news about Brian pretty well. Right now, all Kate wanted was a hot shower.

The sound of waves pounding the shores of Lake Michigan loosened the tension in Kate's neck. How often had that rhythm soothed her when she was growing up? When she failed to make the cheerleading squad like her older sister, when she studied for her SATs, when she waited to hear about financial aid for her college scholarship… those continuous waves told her everything would turn out all right.

For a short time, Kate was back in Gull Harbor, where things never changed.

She turned into the driveway leading to Breezy Point. A canopy of trees whispered overhead, plunging the winding road into shadows. Cracking the window open, she sucked in the damp lake air. Her shoulders sagged under a wave of fatigue. Bonita nosed into the clearing, and Kate could practically hear the water running in the tub upstairs, feel the steam and see the bubbles in the bath she was going to draw.

In back of the house sat her mother's trusty beige sedan. Parked next to it was a shiny green pickup truck. She'd seen that truck earlier today. What the heck was Cole Campbell doing here?

Kate wanted to bang her head on the steering wheel. Instead, she drew a deep breath. Birds chattered in the trees overhead. The whistle of an Amtrak train carried on the late afternoon air. Throwing back her shoulders, Kate shoved the door open and jumped out.

The pickup sat empty. No Cole and no dog. She hated dogs, and Cole's was giant size. Her father had always wanted a dog, but they shed hair and had accidents, or so her mother said.

 Kicking through damp leaves that needed raking, she walked around the side of the house. Kate had her work cut out for her. Usually her mom went crazy raking every spring. "You have to let the daffodils and tulips reach the sun, or they'll come up crooked." Not this year. The white frame house looked neglected, like an unshaven derelict.

Rounding the corner, Kate came to a halt. Cole's Great Dane was squatting on the front lawn, angling for position with delicate care.

"Stop! Stop that right now!" Rushing at the dog, Kate waved her arms like a windmill. The animal probably outweighed Kate by twenty pounds. Didn't matter.

Caught mid-squat, the dog looked insulted by the interruption. Its jowls trembled.

"Priscilla!" Cole came striding through the wild ferns with a swashbuckling gait. He'd grown taller since high school, with shoulders amazingly broad for such a slim waist. Even with a scowl, the man was too handsome for his own good.

Kate folded her arms over her chest. "You're on private property."

"Sorry. Prissy doesn't know that." Cole pushed his aviator sunglasses up. "Kate? So that *was* you?"

"Yep, it's me."

"I wasn't sure. The hair." But Cole wasn't looking at her hair. Smoky blue eyes did a sweeping figure eight.

Heat flared in Kate's cheeks and rolled downward.

"Good to see you." His hand shot out. She ignored it. Kate was being foolish, and she knew it.

Cole drew back those long fingers that drove home his point to win almost every debate on the high school schedule. "We went to high school together. I was in your sister's class. We were on debate team together, remember?" His eyes had turned wary, like the lake when it just might storm.

Apparently Prissy had finished, vigorously scratching the ferns with her hind legs.

Annoyance roiled in Kate's chest. Why was he here? Especially when she was looking so bad and he was looking, well, incredibly hot.

Today, Kate didn't want Cole to remember anything about her. She wanted a hot soak in the old clawfoot tub upstairs. "Debate Club. Right, I remember." *Way too much.* "In case you didn't notice, you're on my fa—mother's property." Her throat closed. Hadn't been her dad's home for a long time.

Cole tucked his hands into his jeans. She knew that look. He was sizing up the competition and planning strategy. "Think, then speak" had been their motto in Debate Club. Kate sure wished she could do that now.

When the sun came out from behind a cloud, the light found tiny lines bracketing his lips and fanning from his eyes. "Thought if that was you on the road, you might need help getting that kayak down to your boathouse."

"I can manage."

At the foot of the steeps steps sat a boathouse, dim and dank, cluttered with old inner tubes and beach toys. Made her tired to even think of hauling Gator down there.

Cole knew all this. "Just thought I'd help out if I could. With your mom's stroke and everything, I mean."

Yep, absolutely no secrets in Gull Harbor. "Thanks, but we've, ah, I've got it covered."

"As you probably know, your sister asked me to stop by."

Kate's mouth fell open. "She did? Why?"

Cole's glanced over Breezy Point like he appreciated the view. "Great piece of property. So you're selling the place?"

Breath whooshed from her body. "What? No way!"

"You're not even renting it out this summer?"

"Is there a sign at the road?"

"Maybe I misunderstood Mercedes."

"I need to have a talk with my sister." Kate's right eye started to twitch.

Cole scuffed one boot into the grass that hadn't been cut in ages. The Great Dane prowled, chewing the weeds.

She looked pointedly at the dog and the mess. Like her owner, Prissy assumed the property was hers for the taking. He hadn't come here to help her. "Don't suppose you've got a plastic bag to clean that up." Holy moly, she was riding high on her bitch horse today.

"Unfortunately, no. Priscilla, stop eating that grass. You'll get sick again."

"Priscilla?"

Cole finally looked uncomfortable. "I didn't name her."

They faced each other like strangers. Ten years had passed, but things hadn't changed. He was the basketball star, and she was the valedictorian. The difference felt wider than Lake Michigan.

Kate wanted Cole gone. She also wanted to strangle her sister. The wind rattled the tree limbs overhead, an eerie creaking. Dark clouds obscured the sun and the day turned cooler.

Staring down at the lake, Cole resembled a brooding Heathcliff. "Back home for a while?"

"Right. To see my mom." *To regain my sanity.* Following his eyes, Kate felt her shoulders relax. No way you could watch the waves on Lake Michigan and not feel peaceful. Why tear the guy's head off just because her own life was in shambles? "Sorry if I came on strong, Cole. Mercedes didn't mention anything to me about selling the house. It's premature to say the least, and I'll talk to her for clarification."

"Clarification." Business speak. Kate had heard enough of that kind of talk to last a lifetime.

"Good parcel of land here. Five lots?" His eyes resumed their roving.

"Yes, but they are not for sale." Tearing her eyes from the waves breaking below, Kate looked pointedly at the dog's mess.

"I'll clean it up, okay?" Cole walked toward his truck with a confident stride that took her back to high school. She'd trail down the halls behind him, keeping a worshipful distance. If she closed her eyes, she could smell Gull Harbor High School – the books, the gym clothes wadded in lockers, the bubble gum stuck under desks.

The clatter of tools as Cole rummaged through the back of his truck razored Kate's nerves. "Don't bother. I'll get it."

Head rearing up, Cole opened his mouth and then snapped shut. "Right." Jumping down like he was still eighteen, he slammed the back gate of his truck. When he yanked open the passenger door, Prissy leapt up onto the seat.

Pulling her phone out, Kate pretended to check her texts. Glancing up, she ran smack into those eyes. Cole hadn't given up.

"Some of the old-timers are selling. They're pleased with their decision. The recession is easing, and boomers are looking for updated summer homes. Just thought I'd mention that."

She'd forgotten the soft burr of his voice. Kate scrubbed the traitorous goose bumps on her arms, grateful for long sleeves. "Not. For. Sale."

Slamming his door shut, Cole started the engine and put the truck in gear. Prissy rested her chin on the open window and sniffed the air. "If you change your mind, give me a call." Reaching over his Great Dane, Cole extended a business card. "Good to see you, Kate."

Kate shoved the card into her pocket.

The man had a lot of nerve. Irritation hummed in her brain. She definitely had to talk to Mercedes, but Cole's receding truck sucked the anger right out of her. Robins chirped in the trees and the spring breeze soothed her. Grabbing the groceries from her trunk, she marched toward the house.

Although it needed painting, the white-sided cottage was pretty much the way it had always been. Faded blue shutters framed the windows, although the blue back door and window boxes needed painting. Kate held the squeaky screen door open with one knee while she fumbled with her keys and finally pushed the door open.

Inside, stale air greeted her. She swung the plastic bags up onto the counter. If Kate closed her eyes, she could almost smell her mother's apple crisp or the beef brisket.

White eyelet curtains sagged at the windows and needed laundering. Walking slowly over the hardwood floors Kate's dad had refinished, she entered the cool silence of the main room. Beyond the long table, a living room spanned the front of the house with bookshelves covering one wall and a fireplace at the other. Even in the half-light, she recognized each piece of furniture under the drop cloths.

When she opened the plantation shutters over the front windows, fading sunlight seeped into the room. After yanking off the white cloths, Kate balled them in her arms and chucked them in a corner. Later she'd tidy up. Now she only wanted to see the lawn-striped overstuffed chairs and the blue sofa that sagged in the middle.

French doors opened onto a porch that ran the length of the living room, but Kate took the steps to the second floor. Under a threadbare runner, the stairs squeaked. At the top was Mercedes' room. Nothing had changed. Her popular sister had never taken down the crumbling prom corsages pinned to her bulletin board or her cheerleading letters. Pictures of Mercedes with her friends formed a colorful collage, with Kate's sister in the center of each group.

Next was Kate's room, slightly smaller but very cozy. Her father had built bookshelves for her when she was in grade school. Tossing back beers while he worked, he'd nearly lost a hand to a buzz saw. Books still crammed the shelves, accenting the off-kilter angle of the wooden slats.

Kate hesitated before going into her mother's room. The four-poster bed faced the front windows, the best view in the house. From here, Kate could see the beach where she'd spent endless summer days. Sandals tossed into the dune grass, she'd shake out her towel and settle into the afternoon heat after slathering herself with coconut suntan lotion. In their early teens, Kate and Mercedes struck casual poses, angling for the attention of the boys tossing a frisbee in the shallow water, as if they didn't see the Kennedy sisters.

And they probably never did see Kate. It had always been Mercedes and her platinum blond hair they ogled, making fools of themselves to get her attention.

It didn't take Kate long to haul her luggage into the house.

Lugging her suitcase upstairs, she plopped it down on the window seat and collapsed across the chenille spread on her bed. Just a few minutes. That's all she needed.

The next morning she made a list while sipping coffee in the kitchen.

At the top of the list was "Call Mercedes." But first she needed more information about her mother's situation so she could update her older sister. She had to talk to Marianne and Lisa at the care center. And after that? "Run into Cole again." Did she want some answers…or did she just want to see him again?

Chapter 4

Cole waited for his daughter. Water dripped from the umbrella down his back. A jacket would have been a good idea. Finally, the bus pulled around the corner. Maybe he'd be able to get some work done after all. Diesel fuel cut the damp air when the vehicle came to a stop. With a whoosh, the doors opened and Natalie sprang out.

"Afternoon, Cole." Myra gave a wave.

"Hi, Myra." Had her hair been that red in high school?

Book bag in her arms, Natalie charged up Lake Shore Road ahead of him and the bus pulled away.

"Hold up, Nat. You'll get wet."

A gust caught her blonde hair when she turned. "Come on, Dad. I'm freezing."

They'd reached the driveway, and she galloped up the lane, hitting every puddle smack on with her tall yellow boots.

"Hey, watch it." Cole jumped into the next puddle with both feet, loving the way she squealed and laughed up at him.

She was going to be beautiful. Like her mother.

He was in for big trouble. "Wipe your feet on the mat."

Once they'd both scraped the mud off their shoes, Cole opened the door.

His daughter pushed past him, chomping on gum. "Where's your jacket, Dad? Don't you always tell me to wear a coat?"

"You look like a chipmunk, chewing like that. What if you get gum caught in your hair again?"

"Dad. I was four when that happened." She threw her bag onto the sofa. Prissy was batting her head against the kennel door, and Nat rushed to let her out. "Don't you think Prissy could be left alone when you go to the bus stop?"

"Nope. I don't. I've had to replace those door frames more times than I care to remember. She just eats right through them when we're out of sight, trying to get to us."

"Why don't you give her the medicine?" Natalie was scratching behind Prissy's ears in return for slobbery kisses. "The vet said the pills would help."

"Yeah, but I don't like the idea of doping her up. All she wants to do is sleep when I give her that stuff."

"Poor Prissy," Natalie crooned.

"How was school today?" Good day for a fire. Cole started to stack logs in the fireplace his father had built. His mom always told him how she missed the fireplace now that they'd retired to Naples, Florida.

Natalie slipped off her yellow windbreaker and hung it on the coat rack. "Fine, I guess."

"No detentions? No trips to the principal's office?" He turned on the gas and flicked the starter. The newspapers flared to life under the logs.

"Dad. That's so yesterday." She shook her head in exasperation.

So much for fatherly communication. The thought of puberty terrified him. "Hungry? Picked something up for you today."

Natalie put both hands on her hips. "Don't tell me. You got me another smiley cookie."

He gave a short laugh. "So that's a crime?"

Groaning, she rolled her eyes. "Dad, how many times have I told you I'm not a little kid?"

He handed her a tissue. Big sigh, but she got rid of the gum, foot stomping on the trash can pedal like she was giving it gas. In a few years she'd be driving. The thought gave him chills.

"But I thought you liked cookies." Lord Almighty, this was frustrating. He came home early so he could meet her bus, but he had to bring his work with him. He had to find a babysitter. Time was money, especially now. And this was the kind of grief she gave him?

But she didn't have a mother to wait for her. Not really. That sad truth made him clamp down on his tongue. He opened the bag and reached for a plate. Prissy bumped her wet nose against his thigh and sniffed the air. "Not for you, girl. Beside, you're in the dog house."

Hearing his tone, Prissy backed away, like *I really wasn't going to try, Cole.*

"What did she do?" Natalie slid onto a stool.

"Left a mess on a friend's lawn."

His daughter snorted. "Not much of a friend if he minds that, I'd say."

He let the assumption slide. "Maybe." Kate Kennedy may have

dyed her hair, but she sure hadn't changed that independent attitude. Made him smile.

Prissy laid her head in Natalie's lap. "Were you a bad girl today? I don't believe it. I think Dad's telling stories again." What a pair. Natalie paid more attention to the dog than to her own father.

"So I should eat that cookie myself?"

"No!" Natalie yelped. She grabbed the cookie and began to munch.

Cole poured a glass of milk. He should tell her to wash her hands after she touched the dog. But sometimes it was better if he just didn't say anything. He pretended he didn't see her slip chunks of cookie to the dog.

~~

"Francesca should leave that boring husband and go off with Robert Kincaid. You only live once."

Phoebe sure spoke her mind. Kate would have laughed but she was a visitor at Sarah's book club. Snugging her knees to her chest, she sipped her chardonnay and listened. "Bridges of Madison County" had always been a favorite.

Maybe she'd learn something. No way was she an expert on relationships.

"Oh, no, Phoebe." Chili shook her long, dark curls. A little plumper than in high school, she was still gorgeous with those fiery brown eyes. "Why would she leave Richard? He brought her to this country from Europe after the war!" Chili's grandparents had fled Cuba in the 60s.

Kate grabbed a potato chip and dug into the cucumber dip.

Had she forgotten to eat dinner again? The wine made her mellow. The past week had been filled with scrubbing, from the kitchen counters to the baseboards in the living room. She was her mother's daughter. Then she'd taken on the outside. Her back ached, and her hands had blisters from raking. Along with the chores, she continued to write pieces for the healthcare blogs and visited her mother every day. Tried to keep Mercedes updated. Exhausting.

"But wouldn't Richard understand?" Diana Palmer owned a shop at the end of Whittaker Street, or so Sarah had told her. Dressed in a blue tie-dyed skirt and tank top, she played with her long blonde braid.

Cheeks burning from the wine, Kate tugged at the neck of her Irish knit sweater. Why had she worn this thing? Made her feel like she'd dragged Boston back to the beach with her.

"After all, Robert seems like a rational man," Diana continued. "Couldn't they have joint custody of the children?"

"He's a farmer! A man of the soil," exploded Chili. "If Francesca leaves with Robert, they move from country to country, no? *Que lastima!* What Richard and Francesca have is special, raising their family."

"Boring," Phoebe threw in.

Chili pressed her full lips into a thin line. All through high school, the only thing Chili wanted was to marry Ignacio Rodriguez and have a family. She'd succeeded, and the girl radiated happiness. Chili had found the secret.

The Amtrak train rattled along the tracks not far from Sarah's house, its whistle echoing through the night. Kate sat there feeling like the girl who'd missed the train.

"Right, her family life is so special," Phoebe continued with a shake of her close cropped head, "that her kids go through all her personal stuff after she's dead, and guess what? They have no clue who their mother really was."

"Let's keep it down, okay?" Sarah glanced at the stairs leading up to the bedrooms.

Earlier, Nathan and Justin wandered downstairs with one excuse or another, so cute and cozy that Kate wanted to hug them. But now all was quiet up above and Sarah obviously wanted to keep it that way.

"Kate, what do you think?" Sarah turned to include her.

"Francesca and Robert are characters in a book. This kind of choice doesn't happen. Not in real life."

"You think men and women don't feel that kind of passion?" Carolyn Knight regarded Kate with thoughtful blue eyes. The soft-spoken teacher came to Gull Harbor High School to teach sophomore English Kate's senior year. Kate never got to know her.

Swallowing the hard lump in her throat, Kate slid her empty glass onto the coffee table. "The book is fiction, right?"

"But this happens every day." Sarah patted both hands on her thighs. "A man can be the most important thing in a woman's life."

Kate looked away.

"You're romantic, Sarah, and you're thinking about your Jamie," Phoebe said. "Understandable. After all he's been gone a while. You didn't have to divorce him to get some peace."

The words pierced Kate like a fish hook.

"Phoebe." Hoops bobbling, Chili shot Phoebe a warning look.

Phoebe drained her glass. "What? I'm telling you, so many marriages settle into meatloaf dinners."

Kate had never made meatloaf, but she sure had whipped up a lot of eggs and toast for herself. Brian often missed dinner. Always a business meeting somewhere and more billable hours.

"Maybe sometimes it's quesadillas and not meatloaf," Chili finally offered with a smile.

Giggles erupted, easing the tension. These girls didn't pull any punches and Kate was glad she'd come. Sarah poured more wine.

"Isn't there a difference between sex and passion? What are we talking about here?" Carolyn offered, as if she were leading a class.

"Francesca and Robert are soulmates." Chili dove right in. "Doesn't that mean both sex and passion? They're hot for each other, but they want to hang around later."

Laughing with the other women, Kate remembered how Brian would jump up to shower after they'd made love.

"Soulmates. Made for each other." Sarah's eyes turned dreamy.

"Don't know if I believe in that." Diana looked like a woman with stories to tell.

Phoebe took her keys from her purse and set them on the scarred coffee table next to the Fischer Price firemen.

Kate began stacking the plastic blocks the boys had left scattered on the floor. When she first read 'The Bridges of Madison County," she'd been in high school. Possibilities lay before her. That sure wasn't her life today. She sympathized with

Francesca. A lot.

Sarah clinked her wedding ring against her glass. "What do we want to read next time."

For a few minutes they discussed books, finally agreeing on a classic Agatha Christie mystery. The meeting wasn't for one month. Would Kate still be here? She could be back in Boston by then.

Getting up to leave, Carolyn yawned. "School tomorrow. And trust me, it's not nearly as much fun as this."

"Me too. Full day tomorrow. Lots of girls coloring their hair to get rid of the winter blahs." Phoebe had a hair salon in town.

After Carolyn and Phoebe left, the others lingered. "I'm in no hurry to get home," Chili admitted.

"Ignacio isn't waiting for you?" Sarah threw Chili a wicked smile.

Chili checked her watch. "I like to wait until he gets the kids in bed."

Their comfortable laughter made Kate feel like an outsider.

"How is your mother doing, Kate?" Chili asked.

"Doing great. I have a care conference tomorrow with the staff."

"I'm not surprised," Sarah clucked. "Has she run into Marie McGraw? She fell a few days ago and broke her hip."

"Marie just about met me at the door. She's taught my mother how to shop online Way too convenient. A few clicks of the remote have totally changed my mother's style." She gave them some details.

"Your mother's at the care center?" Diana's eyes sparkled. "So you get to talk to that yummy administrator?"

"Will seems like a nice guy."

Reaching for her purse, Diana laughed. "In a town this small, any single man stands out."

"Yes, and you've cornered the market on one of the best." Chili grinned at Diana, who looked away, a flush feathering her cheeks. "You and Cole make a perfect pair."

Kate's empty stomach lurched. Must be the wine.

"History. Old news." Diana played with her braid.

"Wow. When did that happen?" Phoebe looked amazed.

"Recently." Diana lifted a delicate shoulder. "Maybe we weren't soulmates, but we are friends."

"My homecoming surprise was finding Cole Campbell and his dog on our property." Kate's stomach didn't feel as jolly as her tone.

"Cole's company is very busy. Lots of plans for Gull Harbor," Sarah explained, her voice matter-of-fact. "But why was he at Breezy Point?"

"He was misinformed. Seemed to think the property was for sale."

"He's very active with real estate in this area. Right now Cole's helping with our fresh produce store. But I told him, we're not painting it pink like those cookie cutter condos next to the library. *Madre de Dios!*" Chili slapped her forehead.

"He didn't build those," Diana interjected in a proprietary tone.

When Kate was growing up, tidy homes on small lots lined the streets of Gull Harbor. Bikes littered front yards and plants spilled from porches in the summer. A lot of those homes had been taken down to make way for the condos. Stripped of all landscaping except for some struggling maple trees, the new pastel townhouses sat in neat, trim rows. The condos were nails across Kate's chalkboard. She wanted Gull Harbor to stay just as it was.

"When did those go up?" she asked.

"About a year ago. Good investments. You know, for the summer people." Diana's tapered fingers stroked her dangly turquoise earrings. "A lot of folks who use the marina bought them, although not as many as they'd hoped, or so I hear. Well, time to hit the road. Be around next month, Kate?"

"You never know."

Diana said good-bye, leaving the three high school friends. Kate joined Sarah and Chili in the kitchen to help clean up. Dishes dried and put away, Sarah took off the apron that said "World's Best Mom." "Kate, I don't know what you're doing with your time, but they sure could use some volunteers at the library."

"Truth is, I don't know what my plans are," Kate admitted. "But I can't clean the cottage every day, that's for sure." And the writing got lonely. She didn't need lonely right now. "Sarah, could I ask a favor? When you have pastries left over, could I take them to the care center? You know, for the residents?"

"Why didn't I think of that? I'll make sure they get there." Sarah looked up from sponging off the counter. "Must have felt strange to run into Cole."

"Like being sucked through a time machine."

Chili clapped her hands together. "What do you think happened to Cole and Diana?"

"Chili, let's not gossip." Sarah pulled out the lower rack of the dishwasher. "Cole's had a hard time the last couple of years."

Suddenly, Kate felt very tired. She grabbed her purse. "Thanks for inviting me, Sarah."

Sarah followed Kate to the door and gave her a hug. "Think about the library, okay? They could use you. And why don't you stop in the bakery soon? A chat would be nice."

"Are you mothering me?" Kate teased.

Her high school friend gave her another squeeze. "Maybe you need some mothering right now."

Maybe she did, although her mother had never been big on heart-to-heart conversations.

Her tires hummed on a quiet Red Arrow Highway as Kate drove home. Her mind chattered from all that soulmate talk. This Irish knit sweater was way too hot. What had she been thinking, dragging old stuff here from Boston? When she reached the stop light at State Road 12, she put the SUV in park and tugged off her sweater. Underneath she wore only a camisole. She rolled down her window. The light changed, and she drove home feeling the cool air on her skin.

She wasn't in Boston anymore.

Chapter 5

A care conference felt a lot like a parent teacher meeting, except the parent wasn't there. Kate had become the parent and new words came flying at her like frisbees. Range of motion, activities of daily living and length of stay. Led by Marianne, the social worker, the team discussed her mother's recovery.

Kate had been up since five, writing an article on TMJ for an orthodontist's website. Her own jaw felt like it might crack while she listened. Trying hard to take it all in, she wanted Mercedes here. Just for today.

Will Applegate straightened his red and blue silk tie. He always looked well turned out, as her mom would say. "The team will continue with therapy, Kate, but be aware that a time will come where she'll plateau…"

"And then?"

"Tara, our occupational therapist, will evaluate your house," Marianne said. "Make sure you have what you need. We have someone sit next to her during bingo, but Alice just isn't that interested."

Everyone around the table nodded. From the look in their eyes, if you weren't interested in bingo, something's amiss.

"Mom's never liked bingo. She kind of likes to do her own

thing, like crossword puzzles. How is Mom with the other folks here?"

Marianne jumped right on it. "She hesitates to ask for help."

"Kate, we're thinking that a roommate might be good for your mother. Kind of perk her up while she recovers." Those smiley faces danced across Will's face again. He was really very cute.

"Exactly." Marianne's head bobbed. "Sharing the room might have some advantages for your mother."

Her mother seemed plenty perky but they had a point. She'd been told that Medicare didn't cover private rooms. Still, her mother was so very private.

"I'll talk to her." Kate's sigh escaped.

Marianne smiled encouragement. "We were thinking Marie McGraw might be a good fit."

Hope glowed at the end of this tunnel. Her mom had known Marie for ages. The only thing they might argue about would be who got the remote.

After the meeting ended, Kate went to her mother's room to find her sitting in the blue vinyl chair.

"Hey, Mom." Kate kissed her mother's forehead. "Don't you look pretty."

"Thanks, honey. Do you like it?" Her mom smoothed a hand over a lilac top sparkling with green butterflies. "It's new."

"Pants too?"

"You bet." Gripping the arms of her wheelchair, Mom struggled to cross her legs, but the right leg wouldn't cooperate. "How does my hair look, Katie? The roots all right?"

Her mother had been blessed with thick hair. "Hmm, a touch up might be a good idea. I'll check to see when the hairdresser comes."

Pushing back the blue-and-white striped drape, Kate tried to get more light into the room. "You know, Mom, you might have a roommate coming soon."

Five beats of silence and then, "How duckie."

"You'd like someone to talk to, wouldn't you?" She wouldn't. They both knew it. Not the old Alice Kennedy. "Will Applegate mentioned Marie McGraw. What do you think?"

"She's a gossip, and she shops too much. She'll do fine. Can you pass me that clicker?"

Relieved, Kate handed her mother the remote. The screen flared to life, and a lovely tanzanite and gold necklace filled the screen.

"Do I look good in blue? Is that blue?" Her mom frowned at the screen.

"Yep, sure is. You look great in blue. But could we set a limit of fifty dollars?"

"Base price or payment?"

Oh, my. Kate choked. "Ah, total price, Mom. Okay?"

A grin lifted the left corner of her mother's lips. "Can't take it with me, right?"

"Don't be silly, Mom. You're going be around a long time." *From my lips to God's ears.*

"So there's no hope with Brian?" her mother asked above the description of the matching tanzanite earrings. "He's not coming back?"

"Mom, we're getting a divorce."

Suddenly subdued, her mother changed the channel and didn't ask any questions. Kate got up to leave. A quick kiss on the forehead and she sprinted down the hall. Inside the car, Kate hunched over the steering wheel. She couldn't go home. There was only so much cleaning a girl could do. She had dusted and scrubbed until her hands were raw. Instinctively, she headed toward town.

When she reached Whittaker, she made a right hand turn and took the last parking spot in front of The Full Cup. The bell jingled overhead when Kate entered the coffee shop.

Sarah came bursting through the kitchen door. "Hey, what is it?"

Kate pushed back a lock of hair. "Just wanted to thank you for taking the pastries over to the care center. They really appreciate it."

Sarah leaned on the glass. "Glad to do it. Everything okay?"

"Fine." Kate surveyed the case. "But I feel like living dangerously. How about a brownie?"

Brian had always been at her to lose weight. Now she didn't have to listen to his constant nagging. Brownies in hand, they both settled in at a front table.

Sarah looked at Kate like a wayward train had just crashed through the front window. "I don't want to pry, Katie. But if you need someone to talk to, I'm here. Your mother… the divorce. You've got a lot on your plate right now."

Grabbing her cup of coffee, Kate gulped it. Darn coffee was so hot it burned her tongue. "Thanks, Sarah. Things just didn't work out, if you're referring to my marriage. Time for plan B, I guess. In the meantime, I want to help Mom. Get her on her feet again, if that's possible. In all honesty, Sarah, I don't know if my mom's going to recover."

"Oh, honey, she's a survivor."

"You mean, considering everything she had to deal with."

Sarah ran one finger around the rim of her coffee cup. "Underneath it all, your dad was a good guy."

"Terrific guy. When he was sober."

Sarah didn't say anything. The drinking had been hard for her friends to understand while they were growing up. Didn't everyone have a few beers on the beach? But Kate's dad crossed the line. Mr. Wilkins coached their soccer team and came to every teacher conference. Kate's father always had some excuse.

"So hard for all of you."

Kate really didn't want to think about the past. The present was giving her enough trouble. "We all moved on, but now my mother needs help. Think I'll be here for a while."

Sarah's eyes lit up. "That's great, right?"

The sun had come out, warm and comforting as it beamed through the frosted window. "Maybe. Yes. I can write from Breezy Point. I don't have to go back to Boston. No Plan B," she finally admitted.

Her old friend smiled encouragement. "You'll think of one. Kate, don't forget the library. I can talk to Mildred. She takes care of the volunteers."

"Sounds good." She wanted to fill every minute.

When Kate reached the house thirty minutes later, she tossed her purse onto the counter and slipped out the front door. No need to lock up. Not in Gull Harbor.

The lake was calm that day, and the metal railing felt warm in her hand. Purple violets bloomed in the myrtle skirting the stairs. Once she kicked off her sandals, Kate raced toward the water, the dune grass tickling her feet.

Gosh, how she needed this. Waves soothed the shoreline with a comforting rhythm. Up above, gulls circled in a flock. At the water's edge, the damp pebbled sand felt cold underfoot. After that care conference, she needed a wakeup call. When could Kate and Mercedes walk barefoot along the shore? That was the day summer began for them.

Today, the soles of her feet protested. Pumping her arms, Kate picked up the pace. Soon perspiration dampened her hairline.

When she passed the Campbell property, Kate slowed, glad she was wearing her sunglasses. Not even five o'clock so Cole probably wasn't home. She didn't want him to think she was stalking him. Huge maples and oaks made it hard to see the house. Looked like the yellow frame house had been painted a sedate grey with black shutters.

Masculine. Imposing. Cole must have added the huge deck jutting out from the main building. My, the boy had been busy. Looking up, Kate felt her sophomore year come rushing back. She'd creep down here late at night, lurk in the shadows, and stare up at his house. Really stupid.

As if he'd know. As if he'd care.

Things had been so simple then, although she sure hadn't thought so.

She liked Cole's house better when it was yellow.

Just in case he was home, Kate walked a little farther before turning around. On the way back home, she played the old game of trying to step into her earlier foot impressions in the wet sand but the lines had been washed away. If they were still visible, heel to toe, her bare feet didn't fit. Her mind wouldn't stay focused.

Who was Cole now? Not the gangly basketball player or the skilled debate team member. His skinny neck and bobbing Adam's apple had been replaced by a neck strong as a tree and probably just as rigid. So he was working hard to get Gull Harbor on its feet? She wanted proof.

~~

Cole watched Kate pick her way down the shore. Had she come down this far for a reason?

"Dad, did you pick up any turkey?" Behind him, Natalie was rifling through the refrigerator.

A familiar guilt made his face heat up. "Sorry, sweetheart. Just had so much on my mind."

Natalie had that hands-on-her-hips thing down pat. "Did you get dog food?"

"You bet."

"Why do you always feed Prissy and not me?" But he saw the smile tweaking her irritation.

"Because I can't stand the look in her eyes when her bowl is empty?"

Grabbing Prissy's bowl, Natalie snorted. "Her bowl's never empty." His daughter zipped out to the garage where the huge bag of pellets was kept in a tall plastic can. He could hear the feed hit the metal.

Wandering back to the window, he checked out the beach.

And it felt empty.

Chapter 6

Bright red tulips greeted Kate when she pulled into the library parking lot. The third day of rain had darkened the gray brick structure but not the spring flowers. Slinging her purse over her shoulder, she scurried inside to the bright overhead lighting and the familiar smell of books. Didn't take long to discover that Mildred Wentworth, director of Gull Harbor Library, probably alphabetized her canned goods.

The main desk was kept neat as a pin. Patting the ridges of her tight gray curls, Mildred showed Kate around, although she could have given the tour herself. Fiction was shelved in alpha order with magazines and DVDs neatly arranged across the back. Felt like she'd come home, and Kate was glad Sarah had suggested volunteering.

In the right of the "T" at the end of the building was the children's area, furnished with small plastic tables and chairs in bright blue and red. The opposite end held the young adult books. Mildred shook her head at the dark covers picturing vampires and ghouls. "Dear me, what children read these days. It's a wonder they can sleep at night."

"Well, at least they're reading, right?"

Mildred tapped her powdered chin. "Excellent point. We don't like to see the books remain on the shelves, do we?" The older woman's impish attitude made Kate smile.

"I spent a lot of time here when I was a kid," she confided, following Mildred back to the checkout counter.

"Always helps to have a reader as a volunteer. Now here are the returned books." Mildred gave the pushcart a little nudge. "If you could just reshelve them?"

"Absolutely." Kate took it from there. Alphabetizing felt soothing after the research she'd done late last night on joint replacement appliances. Although she carried her electronic reading device everywhere, nothing beat the heft of a real book. Kate loved the clean papery smell, the feel of the spine, the whisper of page edges on her thumb.

Books stayed the same. You could count on them.

Unlike people. Especially husbands. When she left Boston, the lawyers had been drawing up the papers. Both Kate and Brian were goal oriented. Liked to check things off. But at their last meeting, she glanced over to find indecision clouding Brian's eyes. "This is the right thing to do, isn't it?"

Caught off guard, she felt her own resolve waver, as if Brian had tossed a stone into the lake and it rippled outward. Her eyes filled. But she knew. She just knew. "Yep, you bet. The right thing."

Brian's shoulders had visibly loosened, and Kate could have kicked herself for that moment of doubt.

She was reshelving Robert Ludlum when she saw the skinny blonde girl disappear into the young adult section. The hood of a bright yellow parka hid her face, and knee-high boots squeaked on the carpet. Craning her neck, Kate tried to get a better look. Yep, there she was at one of the tables, paging aimlessly through a book. When she shoved the hood back, long corn silk hair almost hid the delicate features of a cameo, an unhappy cameo.

The girl looked up and caught her staring, her eyes a startling shade of blue.

"Can I help you, ah, with anything?" Leaving her cart, Kate edged into the young adult area.

One narrow shoulder hitched. "Nope."

"Have you read any of these?" Kate motioned to Judy Blume and Beverly Cleary.

"Nope." The girl glanced at the book in her hands before slamming it shut. All these books and she looked lost.

Eyes raking the shelves, Kate searched for a book that might bring a smile. "You might like Beverly Cleary's stuff."

Shaking her head, the girl drummed her fingers on the closed book. Made Kate's heart catch to see the bitten fingernails. They looked like hers when she was about this age.

Kate began to stack books on the table. "Let's see. Ramona Quimby was a girl who, well, didn't really fit in. I kind of liked her when I was in grade school…" Kate bit her lip. No need to spill her own sad story of being tall, gawky, and invisible, or so it had seemed.

The girl eyed the books like they were broccoli. Finally grabbing one, she flipped it open and snugged her chair up to the table.

"You can take them out. Read them at home."

"Nah. That's all right. I'm good." With a sigh, she unzipped her glossy yellow slicker. A bright mauve top spilled out. What a startling color. Growing up, Kate had worn navy blue, always trying to blend in.

"Do you have a library card?"

"Nope." The girl's right leg startled to jiggle, like she had to be someplace.

"My name's Kate. I'm a volunteer and new at this, but I'm pretty sure we can fix you up with a card."

The girl's blue eyes got round as the bachelor buttons Kate's mother planted every summer. "You would?"

"Sure. No problem."

The whisper of a smile lifted her lips. "I'm Natalie."

"Hi, Natalie. Why don't we fix you a library sampler?"

Natalie smiled while Kate took two minutes to stack the books. Small success but it almost made Kate giddy. Natalie swept the pile into her arms like a favorite puppy and trotted behind her to the front desk. Kate almost felt her chest swell. Yeah, the library was a lot more fun than working at home.

"Mildred, we have a customer who needs a card," she announced when they reached the front.

"Isn't that lovely?" Mildred reached for the form.

"Guess so." Natalie slid three books onto the desk.

"Simple as pie." The librarian handed Natalie a form and a pen, eyes running over the girl as if she wanted to adopt her. Kate knew the feeling. "My, what a lovely top."

Natalie's face twisted. "It was a present." Enough said. She hated it.

Mildred's smile remained pasted on her face as her eyes lifted to Kate's.

Thunder rumbled in the distance, and more rain drummed on the rooftop, but all was right with Kate's world.

Finally, Natalie pushed the form back to Mildred, who quickly scanned it. "Well, Natalie, I will just add your information to our system. You can take these out today and here is your card."

"Really? Terrific!" She beamed at the green card.

Kate's heart broke just a little. Clearly Natalie needed some fun.

The front door flew open with a bang. Cole Campbell stood in the portal, rain dripping from a scowl. Looked like he hadn't shaved that morning. Her tumbling stomach told her that wasn't a bad thing.

But the scowl loosened with relief when he saw Natalie. "Natalie, honey, I asked you to watch for me."

Really? Well, of course. Those blue eyes. How had Kate missed that?

"Dad, it's raining. Now I couldn't stand out in the rain, could I?"

Mildred's mouth fell open.

"Suppose you're right, sweetheart."

She'd never seen Cole look so confused. He nodded to both Mildred and Kate. "Hope she wasn't any trouble."

"Your little girl now has a library card. Isn't that wonderful?" Disapproval darkened Mildred's words.

Cole's forehead wrinkled. "Really? Well, great."

Natalie let out a sigh that rivaled the wind outside.

Mildred reached below the desk and shoved an umbrella in Cole's direction. "You'll get drenched. Just bring this back when you can."

He grabbed the umbrella. "Thank you. Well, Priscilla's waiting in the car." His glance slid to Kate, and darn it, her cheeks began to burn.

Natalie tugged on her father's hand. "Dad, this is Kate. She helped me today."

Kate's blush deepened. "I'm a volunteer. First day."

A glint of mischief sparkled in his eyes. "Kate and I went to school together, Natalie. She's one smart lady. If you read all the books Kate picks out for you, someday you might be a smart lady too."

Always great to be branded as a geek. Head tilted, Natalie regarded Kate, whose face still burned. They could have roasted marshmallows on her cheeks.

"Thank you, ladies. Gotta run." Cole ushered his daughter to the glass door, one hand on her shoulder. Thunder rumbled outside, and water cascaded from the overhang at the front door.

"Dad." Natalie nodded to the umbrella.

"Oh, right." Took Cole a few seconds to get it open before they splashed out to the truck. Wrestling the door open, Cole helped Natalie in as if she were a priceless piece of china. Priscilla was seated on the front seat. Jowls trembling with delight, she gave Natalie a sloppy kiss.

"Poor man's really got his hands full," Mildred clucked as the pickup pulled away. "And he does so much for this town."

"Like what?" Kate stiffened, thinking of Cole surveying her mother's property.

"All these new condos?" Mildred's eyebrows rose. "Built by his company."

"I don't know how I feel about them."

"Neither do I, but Cole says progress is good for Gull Harbor. He wants to tear down this building and build a replacement."

Shock razored through Kate. "No way. What a hare-brained idea."

Mildred lifted a shoulder. "Cole says we need computer stations. Larger reading areas."

"Looks fine to me." But glancing around, Kate thought he might be right.

Shaking her head, Mildred went back to her work.

Before she left the library, Kate searched the audio books and picked out a couple by Mary Higgins Clark for her mother.

Kate stopped at Clancy's to pick up a few groceries, including more cheese curls. She needed them to write. Then she headed home. After parking in back of the house, she walked past the spring green shoots of daffodils and narcissus poking through the dark earth. Soon the trees would bloom. Was anything as hopeful as spring? For Kate, it had been a long time coming. The soft moist air caressed her cheeks as she lugged her bags up the steps.

After unlocking the back door, she slung her purchases onto the counter. Outside, water still dripped from the eaves. While she was putting the groceries away, the sun came out and beamed through the white eyelet curtains. The wet leaves on the lilac bush below the kitchen window gleamed. In fact, everything outside looked bright and new. Twinkling, in fact.

Like Cole's blue eyes when he saw her at the library.

Chapter 7

Writing from home and volunteering weren't enough for Kate. Not by a long shot. Not enough to stop thoughts of Cole Campbell from popping up way too often.

Today was moving-in day at the care center. She sure hoped her mom would get along with Marie McGraw. Cole's green truck sat in the parking lot when Kate arrived. Didn't help her tumbling stomach.

Whipping down the visor, she checked her hair and bit her lips for some color. Only here a couple of weeks and her Boston pallor was gone. Scooping up the two audiobooks from the library and an old CD player, she headed for the main door. Crocus brightened the planters with splashes of yellow and purple.

The unofficial doorman looked up and grinned.

"Afternoon, Harold. Still need that winter hat?"

"Summer's not here yet, I reckon." Harold might be missing a few teeth but he had a killer smile. "Sure like those sweets you're sending over."

"I'll tell Sarah Wilkins. She's the one dropping them off."

"That so? We like 'em. You're pretty as your mama, and that's a fact."

Surprise made Kate's skin tingle. Usually people said that about

Mercedes, not her.

The hallways smelled of cookies baking, and white narcissus stood in a tall vase on the reception desk, perfuming the air.

When Kate reached her mother's room, Marianne was just leaving. "I think Marie and your mom will make a great team."

"I sure hope so."

Kate peeked around the corner. Under Marie's direction, Natalie was arranging clothes in the dresser. Seated in a chair wearing a tiger-striped top and huge tortoise shell earrings, her mother watched with great interest. A sparkly black shawl was wrapped around her shoulders. Her mother's sequined splendor made Kate's navy sweatshirt feel downright dull. Looking totally useless and hot, Cole leaned against a windowsill with Prissy at his feet.

Kate snapped her attention back to the matters at hand. "Hi, Mom. Looks like your roommate has arrived."

Her mother's earrings jingled when she tossed her head. "You bet, and I gave her the bed by the window. You remember Cole?"

"My son-in-law," Marie interjected. "And my granddaughter Natalie." Kate didn't miss the pride in Marie's voice.

"Of course I know Cole from school." But the boy Kate remembered had been gangly and brashly overconfident. Now Cole carried a stillness, like the lake after a storm. Didn't matter. The man was too darn handsome for his own good.

She set the CD player on her mother's dresser. "And I met Natalie at the library."

"Hi, Kate!" Natalie's face brightened.

"Town feeling pretty small?" Cole murmured as he plugged the CD player into a wall socket.

"Just might be." Flustered, Kate turned her attention to Marie. Poor thing was hanging onto that walker for dear life, her knuckles forming a white ridge. "Looks like you've graduated from your wheelchair."

"Don't know as I'm ready." Marie swayed forward.

Cole was there in a heartbeat, shifting his mother-in-law into the wheelchair. Looked like he'd done this a time or two. "Maybe you should go easy on the walker."

"But I want to go home. And to do that, I have to be able to walk. You heard what they said."

"I understand, but let's take it one step at a time," Cole murmured.

Obviously relieved, Marie settled back in the wheelchair. "First they get you in hospital just cause you missed a step or two and broke your hip. Then they give you a new hip and ship you off to another hospital."

The two older women laughed, as if they shared a great joke.

"Like a merry-go-round, right, Alice?"

"Exactly right." Kate's mother nodded. "But this is rehab, Marie. We're breaking out of here soon as we can."

Cole covered his mouth with one hand.

Marie glanced around the room with satisfaction. "Don't know how long I'll be here, but Alice and me, we know how to have fun. Right, Alice?"

"You bet. Can you hand me that remote, Kate?"

Picturing the credit card bill rising, Kate scooped the remote from the bedside table. Her mother gripped it like a lifeline.

"As soon as you can learn how to handle the stairs, you'll be back in your own place," Cole assured Marie.

"Right, Grandma." Job finished, Natalie closed the last drawer. "Then I can stay with you while Dad's at work."

So that's how it was. School would be letting out for the summer soon. Was his mother-in-law Cole's only babysitter?

"Well, well. What a fine group." Will Applegate stood in the doorway. The smell of his soap freshened the room. "You two ladies look like double trouble to me."

"Got that right." Marie cackled boisterously.

Getting up, Prissy gave herself a backward stretch and then sauntered over to give Will a good sniff. Kate didn't know much about dogs, but Cole's Great Dane was a real beauty, lean and elegant.

"What have we here? A new resident?" the administrator joked.

Cole shifted in his work boots. "Hope you don't mind. Marie likes to see Prissy."

Will fondled the dog's head. "Pet therapy is great for the residents and word of your arrival traveled fast. Had to come see for myself. Beautiful dog."

Kate plopped the first disk into the CD player. "Maybe you ladies would like to listen to a book this afternoon?"

"I guess we can fit that in," her mother said. "I like to nap at three."

"That thing have a mute button?" Marie nodded to the plastic remote.

"I think so," Kate answered for her mom, who thumbed the plastic control like it was a genie's bottle.

Bending over, Natalie laid her head on Marie's shoulder. "Grandma, I brought home some books from the library. If I bring them in, will you read to me?"

The older woman melted like a popsicle in July. Did Natalie remind Marie of her own daughter?

"Must be nice to have grandchildren." Longing thick in her voice, Alice watched the two.

A hot flush worked its way up Kate's neck. When it came to adding to the family tree, she was way behind schedule.

"Gotta run." Will turned at the door. "Good to see all of you. We're having a family barbecue on Wednesday. Hope to see you all there."

"Cool." Natalie's eyes brightened. She looked up at her dad. "Do you think we can come, Dad?"

"I'll have to check the calendar. Busy week, sweetheart." He jingled the car keys in his pocket.

Natalie's face fell.

"I can pick her up, Cole." Kate turned to Will. "Can I bring anything?"

Will beamed at her. "Only your beautiful smile."

Oh, my. Kate blushed and Natalie giggled.

Cole stared at his work boots, jaw shifting.

"See you later." With a parting wave, Will was off, loafers clicking with authority along the corridor, greetings ringing out.

"Your face is all red, Kate," Natalie teased.

"They keep it pretty warm in here." Grabbing the AARP magazine, Kate began to fan herself.

"You know us old folks." Her mother settled the black shawl around her shoulders. "We need the heat up."

"I'm sweaty." When Natalie unzipped her navy windbreaker, the fuchsia top spilled out.

"Aw, sugar. You wearing that pretty blouse I gave you for your birthday?" Marie reached up and squeezed Natalie's hand.

"Yep." The blouse was the kind of clothing Samantha always wore. In high school Natalie's mother had been a walking parade of bright colors, tight pants and low necklines. None of the guys complained.

"It's beautiful," Kate said. "And you look really pretty."

Smiling, Natalie ran a hand down the gauzy fabric.

"Katherine, I certainly would like to go for a walk."

Katherine? Not a good sign.

Kate hurried to help her mother from the chair. Balance would be a problem until her mom regained use of that right leg.

"Do you think this place is getting too crowded?" her mother whispered once they reached the hall. The secretive, self-contained Mom was back.

For probably the tenth time, Kate wished Mercedes were here. Their mother always listened to her older daughter. "Mom, you've been lucky that you haven't had a roommate until now. Besides, you know Marie."

Her mom played with one of her earrings. "I forgot how Marie used to put on airs."

Hmm. And her daughter may have been just like her.

When they got back to the room, Cole and Natalie were saying good-bye. "Don't worry about me. I'll be fine." Marie waved her son-in-law toward the door.

"We'll be back soon, Nana," Natalie promised.

"And bring one of your books so we can read together," Marie called after them.

After settling her mom in the chair, Kate kissed her forehead. "Gotta hit the road, Mom. Got everything you need?"

"Could you turn on the TV, Kate? Do you mind, Marie?"

Marie huffed up her shoulders. "It's your room."

Her mother met Kate's gaze. "Katherine, if you please."

Grabbing the remote, Kate found the right station and turned it on low. As she went out the door, she could hear the volume rise. For a second, she hesitated but then decided the ladies could work it out.

When Kate reached the reception area, Natalie barreled past her, a box of Russell Stover candies in her hand. "Forgot to give these to Nana."

Kate laughed. "I hope she shares." A plate of cookies sat on a corner of the reception desk, and she couldn't resist that tempting smell. The oatmeal cookie tore off soft and the raisins were still warm and chewy. Almost as good as cheese curls.

"Everyone loves those," the receptionist told her.

Cole stood at the front door. "Think Marie and your mom are going to get along?" Next to him, Prissy danced anxiously, eyeing the plate of cookies.

"They have to, and that's that."

"Always so down to earth."

Cole's crooked grin made Kate feel sixteen again. His sudden moments of insecurity were oddly appealing. The longish hair was pulled back today. "The ponytail's a nice touch."

Cole cocked his head to one side. "You taking a subtle shot at me?"

"Of course not. My shots aren't subtle."

"Right. I remember."

They burst out laughing. This kind of banter had gotten them into trouble in Debate Club.

"Good to have you back, Katydid." That nickname really made her mad in high school. Now it tugged her home to Gull Harbor in a comforting way. "How long you going to stick around?"

"Until my mother's back on her feet." The last few days had made it clear that it would be a while. Kate felt fine with that.

His gaze fell. Was Cole looking at her bare ring finger? Kate shoved her left hand into the pocket of her jeans.

"Not married?" His brows drew together over laser blue eyes.

"Not anymore."

Cole's eyes seemed to soften. "Sorry."

"No need, but thanks. I'm sorry about Samantha. Natalie seems like a great kid." No details had been given and this sure wasn't the time to ask.

Natalie's tennis shoes squeaked as she barreled to her dad's side. "Grandma says thanks."

Looping one arm around her shoulders, Cole squeezed. "Pain in the patoot most of the time, but I have my girl."

"Oh, Daddy." Natalie socked him gently in the arm and then sniffed. "Boy, those cookies smell good."

"Have one." The receptionist nudged the plate closer.

Sweeping a cookie from the plate, Cole held it out to Kate. "You always had a sweet tooth."

"I already had one." She sucked her stomach in. These jeans felt tighter every day.

"Since when were you known for restraint?" His warm breath was more enticing than the fresh cookies and those blue eyes knocked every bit of sense out of her head.

What the heck. Kate took another cookie. Oatmeal raisin cookies had never tasted this good. Chewing had never been so slow and sexy. Next to them, Natalie munched away with a pleased smile.

A crash and a screech from the receptionist made Kate turn just in time to see Prissy slurp up a cookie or three and gallop toward the door. Collateral damage, the vase of flowers had shattered on the floor.

"Priscilla Campbell, if you don't beat all!" Face flushed, Cole looked totally overwhelmed. Kate loved it.

Prissy settled at the door, licking her lips and staring into the distance. *Don't know a thing about it. I just got here.*

The receptionist brought out a roll of paper towels. Kate and Natalie each grabbed a handful and got to work.

"You two stay away from the glass." Still muttering, Cole began picking up the larger pieces. "This isn't funny."

"I'm not laughing," Kate protested but when she met Natalie's eyes, they both burst into giggles.

~~

Night falls in slow motion during a Michigan summer. That evening, Kate took a peanut butter and orange marmalade sandwich down to the beach and perched on the last railroad tie of the steps. Her favorite time of day. She stretched her long legs out. Some evenings, the lake could be crazy wild, slapping the shore with angry, gray waves. She never ventured into the water on nights like those. Tonight was peaceful, timid waves lapping the shore and releasing quiet ripples. A green pail and one blue frisbee had been left on the sand. Didn't bother her a bit that people had used their "private beach," as some Gull Harbor owners referred to the strip in front of their house. People could get crazy trying to keep renters off their square of sand. Not the Kennedys. Her parents had always felt the beach was for everyone.

Kate licked one final blob of marmalade from her thumb and adjusted her sunglasses. The light could be blinding as the sun sank. Looking at the water restored her sense of calm. Might be a good time to introduce Gator to Lake Michigan. The boathouse smelled musty when she wrestled the kayak from the dim enclosure. Grabbing the tow handle on the stern, she dragged Gator to the water's edge before running back for the life vest and lightweight paddle that had cost her a fortune.

How Brian had complained. Golf was his game. Better for developing business relationships. At least, that was his excuse for spending wildly on golf equipment.

After snapping the paddle together, Kate zipped up the vest. She pushed the kayak through the cool shallow water, jumped into the back seat, and grabbed the paddle. No need to drop the rudder on such a calm night. The rowing rhythm came back so naturally, right to left and back again. Took so much work to kayak in Boston. She bought the two-seater so Brian wouldn't feel overlooked, but he never took to it. Her friend Lisa ended up going with her most of the time.

But here in Gull Harbor, she could just grab the boat and go. Settling back in the webbed seat, she chuckled at the gulls circling and diving for the last bites of dinner before settling in clusters along the shore. Today's cookie fiasco at the main desk came back to her. The look on Cole's face made her laugh until she had to set the paddle across her lap to wipe the tears from her eyes. How amazing. She'd never liked dogs.

Out past the sand bar, Kate turned north. The easy paddling settled her mind and she was glad she'd come home. The whine of a motor drifted over the water from a speedboat heading toward the Gull Harbor Marina. Was that where Cole kept his sailboat? Wasn't that what he'd said that first day as she wrestled with Gator? He preferred sailing.

They'd all learned to water ski on this lake. Back then, Cole had cut quite a figure. He'd also been an idiot, spinning out way too close to boats, even trying to ski on his bare feet. Kate would crouch at the top of the stairs, spying on Mercedes and her friends. In their boat Sea Mischief, Jamie Pickard's older brother Ryan would circle back again and again until Mercedes was on her feet. Kate's sister would give that girlish squeal, as only Mercedes could. Sometimes Cole would be in the boat, tan as all get out, tall and skinny as a rail back then. Standing, he'd pull in the tow rope and spin it again like a lasso to the next person waiting on the sand bar.

She'd wanted it to be her, but that didn't happen until she was a freshman.

Well, Cole's skinny days were obviously over. Kate shivered as a cool night breeze whipped over the water. Time to turn around. All the way back, she battled the whitecaps that had come out of nowhere and thoughts of Cole Campbell that were just as disturbing.

Chapter 8

"Leave the umbrella on the porch. So it's raining. What do we care, right?" Sarah's cheerful voice met Kate when she arrived for book club.

Shivering from the rain that gusted onto the porch, Kate plopped her Monet umbrella next to the porch swing and rushed inside, glad to be here. Her divorce papers had come. She'd signed them and took them right back to the post office. Now it was time to move on.

"What you need is some hot tea." A warm hand on Kate's back, Sarah guided her into the living room.

Light glowed from two stork neck lamps Kate recognized from their childhood. Stepping into this room was like entering a time machine. Sarah's green plaid sofa and brown overstuffed chair were just as Kate remembered, maybe a little worse for wear.

"Glad to see you again, Kate." Carolyn gave her a sweet smile from where she sat in the blue bean bag chair.

"We were afraid we'd scared you off." Phoebe giggled.

"New hair color?" Kate could swear Phoebe's curls had been blonde.

Phoebe primped her mauve hairdo. "Always. Stop in, Kate. I could do the same for you."

"Maybe I will." Kate sank onto the sofa next to Phoebe and fanned the pages of her book, yellowed at the edges. "Do you believe I actually found a copy of 'And Then There were None' on my book shelf? Even has notes in the margins."

"Short chapters. Lots of dialogue." Light brown hair in a ponytail, Carolyn looked girlish. "I teach a class called The Novel for juniors and seniors. Some of my students aren't great readers, but they like this book."

How old was Carolyn, anyway? Since Kate was nearing thirty, she'd become sensitive about age. Had Carolyn ever been married? Was it hard to date in Gull Harbor?

She glanced around. "Where are Diana and Chili?"

"Oh, Diana had something to do first. Tea or coffee, Kate?" Sarah asked. "Chili should be here any minute. Kids, you know."

No, Kate didn't know. A hole opened in her heart. "Tea sounds great. Especially if it's decaffeinated."

"I have a great peach tea. Very comforting on rainy nights." When Sarah bustled back into the kitchen, Kate jumped up and followed her.

"Mom! Mom!" A little voice sounded at the top of the stairs. With his dad's curly blond hair, Justin was terminally cute. "Nathan says he's the boss! Tell him *I'm* boss."

"No, Mom. *I'm* the boss, right?" Older Nathan fisted his hands on the hips of his dinosaur pajamas. He reminded Kate of Mercedes, smug in the role of first born.

Justin wasn't having it. "No, me. *Me.*"

Sarah pumped one arm like Rosy the Riveter. "Boys, don't

make me come up there!"

"Okay." Nathan backed away, followed by his brother.

"Sarah, how do you handle all this?" They drifted into the kitchen.

"You do what you have to do." Sarah's gaze drifted to the photos of Jamie on the refrigerator. Dressed in uniform, he had one foot on a tank and the other on his rifle. Kind of like their senior yearbook, only then his foot had been on a basketball. Fierce. Proud.

Pictures of their little boys with Jamie formed a patchwork on the harvest gold refrigerator. Dishes crowded the sink, but two pairs of tennis shoes sat neatly at the back door, jackets hung on hooks above. Smelling of tomato soup and grilled cheese, the cluttered room felt comfortable and very Sarah.

"Can I help you with anything?"

Sarah nodded to a box of pastries while she plopped a tea bag into a mug and poured the steaming water. "You could take those out and cut them in quarters. You know where the plates are. I never changed a thing after we took this house over from my folks. Boring, right?"

"Not to me." With a knife, Kate sliced cheese crowns and sticky pecan rolls into quarters. An enticing wave of sugar made her stomach rumble. Often dinnertime came and went, but she just wasn't hungry. She grabbed a hunk of pecan roll.

"Feel free to take more than one. Since just about everyone is on a diet, I cut the pastries into easy bites."

"Works for me. I can't believe I've gained three pounds since I got home."

Home? Was Gull Harbor home now, not Boston?

"Kate, you needed a little extra weight," Sarah chided, handing her the mug.

The doorbell rang, and Carolyn called out. "I've got it, Sarah."

The sound of Chili's voice bubbled from the living room.

Sarah scooped the plate from the counter. "How is your mother doing?"

"She has a roommate now, which might help. Cole's mother-in-law."

Sarah's eyebrows arched and she handed Kate a small stack of napkins. "Should be interesting."

Kate smiled. "Oil and water, those two. At least, they used to be. Now? I don't know. Anyway, I just want Mom to be able to come home."

"Of course you do and that will happen." Plenty of troubles of her own but Sarah's eyes brimmed with compassion.

The two trailed back into the living room. "Hey, Chili." Sarah slid the platter on to the coffee table, and Kate placed the napkins next to it, nudging the Fisher-Price toys to the side.

"Treats," Phoebe crowed, reaching for a sticky bun.

"Calories. Let's get to it. I have class in the morning." Carolyn slipped a pair of readers into place.

"First of all, I think the idea of a murder taking place on an island is downright scary." Phoebe dove right in.

Carolyn smiled. "My students would agree."

"And the guests get killed off, one by one," Kate added. "Not exactly party perfect.”

"The more murder, the better." Carolyn's mouth twisted. "High school kids love it."

"I only read half the book," Chili admitted. "We're crazy busy with plans for the vegetable stand. Where's Diana? Not coming?"

"Oh, she'll be here," Sarah assured her. "Dinner date, you know."

"No, I don't know," Carolyn burst out with a little laugh. "Not in this town."

"Is it tough being single in Gull Harbor?" Kate tried to keep her tone casual.

"Not exactly a mecca for single women." Phoebe took another sip of her peach tea. "But I'm pretty new at this divorce thing."

"Me too," Kate said quietly, cupping her warm mug. But she didn't want this to become a pity party. "So, who's the first guest on the island to get knocked off?"

For a while they discussed the classic murder mystery. They were arguing about one of the "red herrings," misleading clues, when the doorbell rang. Diana swirled through the front door in a wave of perfume. "Sorry I'm late." The pretty blonde carried the excitement of a woman who'd been on a date as she shook the raindrops from her long hair.

"So, did you have fun?"

Trust Phoebe to get to the heart of the matter. Kate liked her candor. She pictured women gathering in Phoebe's hair salon, talking about a lot more than hairstyles.

A secretive smile danced across Diana's lips as she sat on the floor, pulling her legs under her. "Yes, we did."

"So who's the lucky guy?" Phoebe closed in for the details.

The apples of her cheeks reddening, Diana never answered Phoebe's question.

"We're talking about how Agatha Christie builds suspense," Carolyn began in her teacher-like voice. Had Diana even brought a copy?

"Oh, that." Diana began to root around in her multicolored bag. "Thought I threw my reader in here somewhere."

"Maybe you were preoccupied." Phoebe's eyes sparkled.

"Phoebe, you are a dickens." Chili shook her head.

"Hey, I like the way Diana is building suspense a lot more than Agatha Christie's techniques." Phoebe threw them a defensive look.

Everyone laughed but Diana. Obviously not a woman to be intimidated, she whipped out her reader. "That island bit. So scary."

"So lonely." The words were out before Kate could call them back.

"You can always work more hours in the library," Sarah suggested, handing Diana her mug of tea.

Kate thought of Natalie, looking so lost in the stacks and wearing that blouse from her grandmother. "I enjoy the library, always have, but it's pretty quiet. I might have to do more than that…"

"Sounds like you'll be here for the summer?" Phoebe pressed her.

"Oh, please say yes." Chili clapped her hands.

Gull Harbor felt safe for Kate right now. If she returned to Boston, she'd have to find an apartment in the summer heat. Since she hadn't heard from many of their former friends, she figured they'd sided with Brian. Kate's face heated up, remembering the silent disapproval.

Here, no one seemed to judge her. Books had closed, fingers tucked in to hold the place. Outside, a tree branch knocked against the gutters.

"Ignacio is opening a vegetable stand," Chili said. "He's looking for workers."

"Me too," Sarah added, her voice matter-of-fact. "I'm thinking of hiring someone this summer myself, but I won't be able to pay that much."

"I work in Clancy's deli every summer," Carolyn said in a quiet voice.

"Aren't you embarrassed to see your students in that store?" Diana looked totally horrified. "Everyone shops there."

Carolyn waved the comment away. "My students all have summer jobs. Why shouldn't I?"

"Any chance we can keep you here for the whole summer?" Chili turned to Kate.

She swirled her tea bag in her almost empty mug. "Looks like I'm going to be around. My mother can't manage for herself yet, and Mercedes is busy with her company."

"I'm excited we'll have you a little longer." Reaching over, Sarah gave her arm a squeeze. "Mercedes coming to visit soon?"

"Memorial Day." Kate had a few issues to settle with her sister.

"Think about the vegetable stand." Chili nibbled on a tiny cheese pastry. "Ignacio would love to have you there, and Cole is helping him set up shop."

Excitement kicked up in Kate's chest. "Where are people getting their flowers now that Joe Jackson's is closed?"

She'd been looking for some flowers for the house, but they hadn't been easy to find. Jackson's stand had closed to make way for more condos, but then the recession hit and that project was abandoned. Now the town had no vegetable or flower stand.

"Good question," Diana said, scanning the circle. "I miss those fresh bouquets of snapdragons and bachelor buttons."

Chili's eyes lit up. "Why don't you open a flower stall, Kate? You know, with us. People would have two reasons to stop."

"Where are you planning to open your store?"

"Remember the Dairy Queen near St. Mary's Church? Right across the highway, there's an old cinderblock gas station. Cole's going to help Ignacio convert that. How hard could it be to add a flower stall?"

"Please. Let's not talk about Cole Campbell as if he's the second coming, okay?" Diana raked long nails through her hair.

"But, Diana, he's done so much for Gull Harbor." Chili put her mug down.

"That's your opinion, Chili. I'm glad he's helping Ignacio with the stand, but he's making other changes that, well, I'm not sure are in the best interest of Gull Harbor."

Sarah's chin was cradled in her hand. "Then you should come

to the town meeting next Tuesday night. Speak up.”

“Already on my calendar.”

“Like what changes, Diana?” Kate cringed when she thought back to finding Cole on her mother’s property.

“Michiana Thyme. The buyer is Campbell Construction.” Diana’s face flushed, while Phoebe and Carolyn grew pale.

“Cole always has the good of the town at heart,” Sarah persisted. “You know that.”

“I think Cole always has Cole in mind.” Diana was not backing down.

“Oh, Diana.” Sarah gasped.

A cold hand squeezed Kate’s heart. Was this sour grapes or did Diana know something?

Diana grimaced. “Word is that he’s going to tear down the buildings. There are three lots in a row you know. That was a big shop. People say he wants to put up a hotel.”

The only sound was the howling wind outside and the clink of Carolyn’s spoon as she stirred more sugar into her cup.

“That will radically change the look of the town.” Kate’s eyes circled the group.

“But a hotel might bring more people to Whittaker Street. More foot traffic.” Sarah always saw the glass half full. The others didn’t look convinced.

The thought of a hotel looming over the street sent nausea swirling through Kate’s stomach. “Might accommodate more summer people. Those who haven’t bought the condos and want to sleep off the boat for a couple of nights.”

"Yeah, the summer people will be here soon." Sarah's eyes gleamed with anticipation. Her bakery business picked up when the tourists arrived.

"Summer people need a reason to come into town, and that means shops." Diana took a sip of her tea. "We don't need a small hotel that will have trouble filling rooms every winter. We need reasons to explore, shop and spend."

Their discussion wound down and Carolyn offered to have the next gathering. Determination throbbed in Kate's temples as she drove back to Breezy Point that night. She hadn't come home to have the Gull Harbor she knew and loved disappear before her eyes.

Debate points were lining up in her head. And this time, Kate and Cole wouldn't be on the same team.

Chapter 9

After the bus picked up Natalie, Cole grabbed a mug of coffee and was out the door. He was late. Priscilla jumped into the pickup next to him. "Be a good girl, you hear? No more cookie capers."

Priscilla's forehead wrinkled. *What? Me, Cole?* Then she returned to licking her paw. Poor neurotic dog. Prissy had been Cole's attempt at filling the hole left when Samantha left. Votes still weren't in on how that had worked out.

Moisture beaded the windshield, and he turned on the wipers. Man, summer couldn't come soon enough. So many projects but he had the best crews in the area. Recently he'd brought Kevin Corbin on board to help out as a project manager. Marie's broken hip had left him without a babysitter. Always something.

He downed another slug of coffee and cracked open his window. About time it smelled like spring. White dogwoods had started to bloom behind his house. Samantha used to float them in a shallow green bowl they'd picked up at a gas station.

A bad memory in a lot of ways.

Those were her better days.

Still early and not many cars at the main stoplight on Whittaker. What was he doing in a one-stoplight town? And now he'd never leave. Someone had to watch out for Marie, and she'd never leave

Gull Harbor. Besides, this was the only home Natalie had ever known.

The light changed, and Cole hit the gas so hard, coffee slopped over. Prissy reared up. "Easy, girl. Easy." She circled the seat twice, bopping Cole with her rear end and making shifting impossible. "Down, girl. Everything's fine."

Prissy settled. Raised her brows. *Cole, let's remember. You're the one who tried to burn me with coffee.*

"Sorry, Prissy." He fit the mug securely into the console and rubbed her neck.

Ignacio's shiny red truck was already there when Cole pulled into the deserted gas station. His boots crunched on the gravel as he got out, Prissy bounding down behind him. Suited him just fine. At least the Great Dane listened to him sometimes, which was more than he could say about Natalie. Lately, everything he did was either "stupid" or "lame."

Rocking back, Prissy put her head down and gave herself a good backward stretch.

"Those yoga nuts don't have anything on you," he told her.

You're telling me. One sniff and his dog danced off into the tall grass along the parking lot.

Ignacio would have to cut those weeds back. Place had to look trim, businesslike.

Morning sun warm on his shoulders, he surveyed the empty structure while traffic rumbled past on Red Arrow. If anyone could make a go of it here, Ignacio could. The summer would tell the tale. The tourist trade was always a testing point for Gull Harbor.

"Priscilla, get out of those weeds!" The last thing he needed was for Natalie to catch poison ivy from the dog again.

Head down, Prissy came trotting toward him.

"Hey, Cole." Ignacio banged open the front door, hand extended with Chili right behind him.

"Sorry I'm a little late. Natalie decided she wanted braids this morning. I was the wrong man for the job."

"You are the right man," Chili told him. "Such a good dad."

Shrugging, Cole felt pleased. Not many awards being given out for fatherhood these days. "So what are we going to do here?"

"Come on inside." Ignacio crooked a thumb toward the door.

Leaving the sunshine, they entered the damp interior. White paint was peeling from the gray cinderblock walls. Floor only had a couple cracks, but the oil spots had to be sanded out or painted over. A fuel smell hung in the air.

"Can you get some fans in here?"

Ignacio nodded. "We're going to hose it down, dry the place out, and start painting, one end to the other."

"When you open, I'd leave the big doors up. Let people see what you have."

"Of course. One has a broken pulley, but I'm repairing it."

"Can't you just see it, Cole?" Chili's hands flew as she talked. "Fruits and vegetables in the middle. A little counter on the side for baked goods. Maybe a cheese cooler."

Ignacio gave his wife a little hug. "Chili, *por favor.* This is a vegetable stand not a deli."

"But so much room. *No?*" She gave her husband that little smile that had socked it to Ignacio in high school. Time hadn't changed that.

Some day, Cole wanted a woman to look at him like that. But now, about that ceiling. No stains but some damp spots for sure. "What about the roof, Nacho? Got a ladder?"

"Follow me." Ignacio led him out the back door to where a ladder leaned against the building.

The wooden ladder was about as old as the building, but Cole clambered up, boots scraping the worn rungs. He liked working with the guys he'd grown up with. They understood each other.

Up on the roof, he tested the gritty shingles before giving them his full weight. Seemed solid, but some of the patches had worn through.

"I think we're good," he hollered down. "Just a few spots need attention. I'll drop off some shingles." Up here, the air smelled clean, and moist from the lake. When he turned north, he could see Gull Harbor and the yacht basin.

"You're in a good traffic pattern here," he told Ignacio, making his way down the ladder.

Priscilla nosed his leg. *Thought you got murdered up there, Cole. Thought you were never coming back. Phew!*

He couldn't be out of the dog's sight for a second without her going nuts.

"So what do you think, Cole? Good place for a business, right?" Chili narrowed her eyes, sun bouncing off her dark curls. She hadn't changed a bit since high school, except now she was a wife and mother. Three kids. He should be happy for them.

"Let me sketch out some ideas. Meet you back inside." Prissy on his heels, Cole zipped back to the truck to grab a yellow pad. As he slammed the door closed, a blue SUV pulled up. He was getting used to seeing Kate's bright vehicle around town. What did she call it? Bonita? But he wasn't used to the strange feeling in his chest every time he ran into her.

Kate jumped out in snug jeans and green hoodie the color of spring leaves. Her hair bounced over her shoulders as she approached with her long-legged stride that tightened his throat. She'd always been a knockout, even when she was a pesty sophomore who never bothered with much makeup, if he remembered right.

Same girl but different. And it was more than the blonde hair. Seeing him, she shrugged in that restless way she had now, almost like she was shaking him off.

"Had to stop and say good morning to our mothers." She fell into step next to him, the breeze having a field day with that blonde hair.

"Were they playing nice? Sharing their oatmeal?" He loved his mother-in-law, but she could be a real handful.

"I just hope they get along." Her wry expression told him they were on the same page—holding their breaths and hoping for the best.

"Here to see Chili?" He held the door open and bathed in the citrusy smell of her hair as she whirled past.

"I'm here on business." Her green eyes flicked up, suddenly reserved. He felt a chill that didn't come from the cinderblocks.

"Kate!" Pivoting toward them, Chili threw her arms open and Ignacio smiled.

"Sorry I'm late." Kate gave each of them a hug. "Got hung up on research about diabetic neuropathy for an article I'm doing, and then I stopped to see my mom."

"You work too hard." Chili clucked.

Kate did look tired. The lines at her eyes and mouth—exhaustion or stress?

While Chili and Kate were doing their girl thing, Cole slapped his yellow pad onto an old table. "Let me show you what I'm talking about." Taking out a pen, he began to sketch out some rough ideas to change the empty structure into a vegetable venue. He liked working on this type of project. Repurposing buildings would be the future of Gull Harbor.

After he gave Ignacio some estimated numbers, he felt Chili at his elbow. "Cole? We have one other favor to ask, *por favor?*"

Behind Chili's shoulder, Kate's cheeks got red. She was really pretty when she blushed.

"Favor?" The color faded, and Kate frowned. "I'm not really asking for any handouts, Chili."

"No, no. Kate's right, of course." Chili's hands fluttered again, like she was erasing those words. "Kate is going to help our business… with her own flower stall."

"But I'm doing this myself." Kate's pointed chin came up. "Sort of, I mean."

Cole looked from Chili to Kate. He'd never understand women.

~~

Kate hated how Cole studied her—like she was a charity case. He looked like he'd just tumbled out of bed— another strike against him in her mind. The dusting of a five o'clock shadow accented his square jaw. His dark hair was tied back in a low ponytail. Smoking. Hot.

But time to focus. "The flowers would be an add-on to Ignacio's vegetable stand. An additional point of purchase." Did that sound businesslike enough? Not just some flighty idea from her book group.

Cole's blue eyes darkened. "You're going to operate a flower stand?"

Her skin flushed warm. "Anything wrong with that?"

"Just surprised, that's all. Boston College and everything."

"Summer work." Did she have to explain herself? Cole's eyes stayed murky.

Chili's head pivoted between them, like she was watching a tennis match.

With a shake of his head, Cole shoved his sunglasses back in place and walked out, his long-legged stride outpacing her.

Was that a muffled giggle behind her? Kate threw a frown over her shoulder at Chili. Another choked laugh was the answer. Great. Maybe high school friends always acted like teenagers together. Kate and Cole had gone head to head in high school – well, most of the time—and now they were at it again.

Beginning with the door, Cole paced off lengths, setting the flower stall far enough from Ignacio's store to give Kate "growing room," but close enough so customers had to walk right past her stand.

His comments still rankled. "So you think I'm just doing this on impulse?"

A grin tweaked Cole's lips. "Kate, when did you ever do anything impulsively?"

Heat flooded her face. She could think of one time. With him.

"Oh. Right." His lips rounded. A muscle moved in his throat, right near the pulse throbbing at the base of his neck.

So he remembered too?

Chili and Ignacio had followed them outside and they exchanged a glance.

"Where you going to get your stock?" Serious again, Cole forged ahead.

"A farm up on Red Arrow Highway." But Kate heard her own hesitation. She still had to talk to the people.

"Kalamazoo has some growers," Ignacio piped up. "In the beginning, I was thinking of doing the flower part myself, but I've got my hands full, especially if Chili wants to make this a delicatessen, eh, *mi amor*?" He pulled his wife closer, a cuddle that made Kate look away.

Cole turned toward her. "Sounds like you might be in Gull Harbor for awhile?"

Chili and Ignacio did their visual telepathy again.

"For summer, at least. Until my mom's on her feet."

"Terrific. I mean, ah, good for the community."

"Maybe. I hope so." The flower stall might be frivolous and

fun. Right now, she needed fun.

As the three of them continued planning, Kate enjoyed the excitement bubbling in her chest. Gave her something else to think about besides divorce and her mother.

Cole's dog had been lying in the tall grass, eyes closed and drinking in the sunshine. Now she got to her feet and came over to snuffle his hands.

"Lie down, Prissy," he told her, giving the Great Dane a stern look.

The huge black and white dog settled at his feet with an aggrieved sigh. Kate fought a laugh and wondered if Natalie obeyed Cole like this. Somehow, she doubted it.

"Your dog's pretty well trained. Well, sometimes," she added.

"Actually she is. That day at your house? An exception."

"If you say so." She couldn't help smiling. Cole just had that effect on her. Then she remembered the rumors about the changes he'd bring to Gull Harbor, and her smile froze. Things were different now. *They* were different. She had to remember that.

Ignacio excused himself and went back inside. Dragging her feet, Chili followed her husband, throwing Kate a questioning glance.

"Business," Kate mouthed to her while Cole sketched.

Chili mouthed back, "No way."

Chapter 10

With a toss of her head, Kate snapped her attention back to the yellow pad.

"Looks good. Nice touch." She pointed to a sign he'd added that read "Kate's Blooms."

"That's just a place holder."

"I like it. You always were good with words."

Cole's eyebrows lifted. "Are you kidding me? You could argue points around me in Debate Club."

When Cole raised a brow, he could have just stepped off a pirate ship.

Kate shook off a rogue shiver. "That's not how I remember it. Wasn't that why you were elected president of the club?"

"For that year. You were only a sophomore. Heard you followed in my footsteps."

"Big shoes to fill."

"Not for you, Katydid. You'd take on anything. Anyone." Cole's playful grin faded. "Thanks for helping Natalie pick out some books. I'm no good with that stuff."

"I enjoyed it. She's a special little girl."

"She's a lot like her mother." Cole's tone sounded matter of fact, not nostalgic.

"Natalie has some of Samantha's features. But her expressions? Strictly Cole Campbell."

He looked downright pleased. "You think so?"

"It's the truth." She stabbed one toe into the gravel.

Grinning, he ripped his sketch from the yellow pad and handed it to Kate. "Let me know if you need anything else." He paused, like he wanted to say more.

She studied her beat-up tennis shoes. "Sure. Thanks." Why was it so hard to accept anything from Cole?

"Priscilla." Cole snapped his fingers. When he opened the passenger door of his truck, the dog leapt inside, a graceful streak of black and white. Cole closed the door and Prissy rested her head in the open window, giving Kate a sad look, like *I really wanted to stay for some girl time. You know that, right?*

Kate walked to her car, digging in her bag for her keys. Sometimes Cole could take her right back to high school, wondering why the guy she'd made out with one night had invited another girl to prom. Now that painful memory had started to dissolve, like invisible stitches. After all, it had been so long ago. What did it matter?

Cole threw his pickup into reverse, hesitated at the highway, and then hung a right.

Chili had wandered back outside. "Nice guy."

Kate slipped her sunglasses back in place. "Yeah, I guess. Why is he still single?"

"Maybe he's just busy with his daughter… and his mother-in-law."

What did Kate care? Closing her eyes, she drank in the warmth, imagining sand warm against her back. *Come on, summer.*

"Cole's different now." The sadness in Chili's voice made Kate open her eyes.

She stared down the empty highway. "Can't imagine how that would feel—losing your wife when you have a little girl to raise."

"I guess Samantha's living in California."

"Yes, but people talk about her as if she were dead."

"Might as well be." Chili pulled her head into her orange sweatshirt like a turtle.

"Okay, Chili. What are you not telling me?"

"It's more than Samantha eating away at Cole," Chili finally said. "He wanted to go to Afghanistan, like Jamie, but he couldn't because of Natalie and Marie. So he took on the renovation of Gull Harbor. Sometimes I think all that energy is, well, frustration."

"He always did want to be in the thick of things." Kate's phone rang. Pulling it out of her pocket, she checked the screen. Mercedes. She tucked the phone away. Her sister could wait. Mercedes never picked up when Kate called.

"We've got folks lined up for this weekend. What do you think of these colors for inside?" Chili pulled some paint swatches from her pocket.

The two of them began planning. What fun to be involved in paint and flowers, instead of interviewing a doctor about a new cardiac unit. At times Kate's writing for health care blogs drained her. Working around the complexities of physician and hospital schedules was never easy. Selling flowers felt simple.

This summer, Kate was all for simple. "Chili, thanks for including me."

"We're the lucky ones. Your flowers could be the eye candy making people stop. In fact, maybe *you'll* be the eye candy." Her infectious chuckle made Kate smile.

"Cole suggested I call it Kate's Blooms." Felt funny, him suggesting a name. Bold, invasive, exciting.

Enough. She was sick.

"I love it." Chili walked Kate to her car. "So Cole came up with that, huh? For you?"

"It's not a marriage proposal, Chili."

Tossing her head, Chili kept that silly look on her face.

When Kate opened her car door, a welcoming wave of heat greeted her. "Thank God summer's coming."

Frowning, Chili glanced around. "So much to do. Memorial Day is only two weeks away."

"I'll be here tomorrow. Help in any way I can."

"I can always count on you." One more hug from Chili, who always smelled like patchouli, and Kate jumped into the SUV.

Today she was volunteering at the library. Only one other car in the parking lot when Kate pulled in. After turning off the engine, she sat staring at the tidy stone building. Did it need to be replaced? Maybe Cole was right. How she wished she could stop thinking about his broad shoulders, deep-set eyes, and the fresh smell of spicy aftershave. Maybe she should turn on the air conditioning.

Then she remembered her sister's call. Gritting her teeth, she hit a button on her phone.

"Just wanted you to know I'm coming in the Friday of Memorial Day weekend." Mercedes came right to the point. That flirty cheerleader giggle she sometimes used? Her sister kept it for special occasions. This wasn't one of them.

"Need a ride from the airport?" Kate was equally short.

For a second, they talked details.

"Mom's doing fine," she finally offered, although Mercedes hadn't asked.

"Well, I'll be there soon." As if that would solve everything. As if Mercedes would just walk in and like magic their mother would be making spaghetti in the kitchen.

Still, their mom would be thrilled to have Mercedes visit. Truth was, her older daughter had always been her favorite. An old bruise ached in the vicinity of Kate's heart.

She was wrapping up the call when Mercedes added, "I was hoping we could talk about the property when I come home."

The property? Not Breezy Point. Not their home but "the property." Like Breezy Point was already listed.

Anger tightened Kate's throat. "I'm not changing my mind, Mercedes."

"This isn't up to you, Katie."

Katie? Sure. Keep me in my place. Was Mercedes working on their mother with some crazy scheme? Kate wouldn't be able to hold off the two of them. She knew that from experience. "We can talk about it when you get here."

After the call ended, Kate had to practice her deep breathing for a couple minutes. Didn't work. Finally, she got out and locked the door. After all, she wanted it to be here when she came out.

But that would never happen in Gull Harbor. Kate was used to locking everything up tight. Boston habits died hard. Pressing another button, she heard the lock click open and smiled.

~~

The community room was jammed the night of the town meeting. Kate had to crawl over people to reach a middle seat in the back row. People lined the walls, voices rising in the low-ceilinged room. Up front, Cole was talking to a man who looked like he was in charge. The Gull Harbor Town Council reclined in their seats at an eight-foot table. Displays were set up in the front.

"Kate! Kate!" Chili waved from a front row. Next to her, Ignacio held an official looking roll of papers in his hand.

Business was happening tonight. What was Kate doing here? She'd come home to help her mother in the Gull Harbor she knew and loved. The town represented the last outpost of sanity in her life. She perched on the metal chair.

The mayor had just called the meeting to order when Diana Palmer squeezed into the seat next to Kate. "Quite a crowd."

"More than usual?"

"Oh, yeah. For sure."

Tonight reminded Kate of her first years at the newspaper. In her community beat, she'd covered more meetings than she cared to remember. New parks. Dog control. Traffic signs. Pages of notes that had nothing to do with her. This gathering felt different.

Personal.

The gravel rapped. "This meeting will be called to order."

The next few minutes were filled with the details of government— reading of minutes, all stuff that made Kate yawn and papers rustle in the audience.

"Up late last night?" Diana asked in an undertone.

"Don't I wish. Breaking my back to get my flower stand ready." She'd been at Ignacio's almost every day since their planning session. Her back and shoulders ached, and the smell of paint clung to her clothes.

"Can't wait to see it."

Ignacio was up next, whipping up the sheet covering one of the easels. "I wanted to give you an update on a new venture that will benefit everyone. Hopefully keep visitors in Gull Harbor so they don't go farther up the road to Sawyer or Stevensville for fresh produce."

The crowd nodded. They knew Ignacio and were receptive to the points he laid out for them.

"Great work," one man called out when Ignacio wrapped up.

The mayor stood. "Any community enhancement is good for all of us. Cole Campbell is going to take us through another project to help Gull Harbor prepare for the future."

Not that there was any bias on this project. The two men grinned at each other, like they golfed together once a week. Wasn't until he smiled that Kate recognized the mayor as Billy Cramer, a total cutup in high school.

"Thanks, Bill." Eyeing the crowd, Cole didn't need any notes.

He knew how to make any speech personal. Obviously, his debate skills had stayed with him. "As most of you know, Loretta has decided to retire, giving us an exciting opportunity to update the look of Whittaker Street."

Update. *Change.* That's what Cole was really talking about. Kate's shoulders stiffened.

A restless shuffle rippled through the crowd. Cole whipped a sheet from an easel and flicked on a laptop. "For some time, we've needed an upscale hotel to accommodate tourists as well as boat owners who come into harbor."

"Thought we already had that," called out a man in the middle.

Bill was on his feet in a minute, chest puffed in what he no doubt thought was a mayoral stance.

Cole waved him aside. "That's all right, Bill. Sure we do have some small hotels, Jeremy, but we've also had two go belly up along Lake Shore Drive. The backers were from outside the area and didn't know the territory. Two weeks here during the summer and they dove in without a needs assessment. Do we need another outsider coming in to Gull Harbor? We need a tasteful hotel we'll design and build ourselves. Right?"

"Damn, he's good, isn't he?" Diana whispered.

"Yep." Kate assumed Diana was talking about Cole's presentation.

As Cole held the audience's attention, Kate marveled at how he could sound so objective, as if he were totally impartial to this project. Her cheeks burned. A three-story building would stick out like a sore thumb on their small main street of two-story buildings.

What was he thinking?

When Cole finished, Bill entertained questions. That's when it really hit the fan. Diana joined the line in front of the mic to ask a question… something about the restaurant in the hotel taking business away from Hannah's across the street from her shop. "Hannah's draws traffic to Hippy Chick. You put in another major restaurant, and well, I have some concerns."

Diana wasn't shy. Cole swatted her objections away like they were playing badminton. Hand on one hip, Diana served shots right back at him.

Kate could hardly stand it. Her head pounded. But if she joined that line of people behind the mic, she might make a fool of herself. She'd been gone for so long and didn't know all the issues. She pressed her lips together so tight they pulsed.

Just when it seemed like everyone had said their piece, she jumped to her feet. Heck with it. She had to speak up. Diana's brows rose as Kate stumbled over her. Hands shaking, Kate sucked in a deep breath as she took the mic and introduced herself.

"What we have in Gull Harbor is really special," she began, hating the quaver in her voice. She took a steadying breath. "I'm visiting from Boston. You probably know that. You know my mom Alice. I grew up here."

Some heads were nodding. She was going for the yes. Get the crowd to agree and then slide into the trickier points.

"I can tell you that Gull Harbor has something rare, a small community feel worth preserving."

"Cold winters and high fuel bills, that's what we've got," one voice piped up.

Kate's confidence wavered.

Cole held up a hand. "Let's let Kate talk."

"Thank you." She widened her stance, aware of the paint spots on her tennis shoes. In Debate, Cole and Kate used to challenge each other during practices before competitions. Facing him felt familiar. She wanted that brash high school confidence back.

Her stomach was threatening to do an elevator dive, like when she lost her job. When her marriage broke up.

Didn't matter. She pushed ahead, sucked in her stomach, and dove back in. "You tear down a historical building, and you can't bring it back."

The only sound was the whirr of the overhead fans.

Cole didn't look pleased. "The plans for the hotel would have every modern convenience but retain that old fashioned charm."

How strange for him to fall right into her point of differentiation. "Exactly," she shot back. "But the people who visit Gull Harbor don't come here for modern. They come here to escape the city. They come for old-fashioned. They come for the arched windows, etched glass, beaten tin ceilings and crown moldings. They come for what we have now."

She was driving home her points with the parallel structure Theodore Sorenson had used writing John F. Kennedy's speeches. They'd both studied Sorenson's style, and now Cole paled.

Kate wasn't finished. "They come for the plaque that says 'Built in 1925.'"

That's when it hit her. The historical society. Lifting her hands, she glanced around at the others in appeal. A slow boil of murmurs simmered among the crowd.

"The latest features can have that appeal, Kate." Cole was losing them, and he knew it. The words *historical* and *plaque* were being whispered, persistent as sand gnats. A grin tickled Diana's lips.

"Table this motion!" a man shouted. "Send it back to the Downtown Development committee."

We have a Downtown Development Committee?

People applauded in agreement. Face hot, Kate walked back to her seat, shoulders straight and stomach shaking. She hadn't meant to make a spectacle of herself, and embarrassing Cole in public sure hadn't been her goal.

But someone had to say something. Maybe that person was her. Ten years back, they'd let Ned Ransom put up a cinderblock beach shop, and three stores had been demolished for that project. It still stood out like a sore thumb. She didn't want to end up with a whole string of architectural abominations like that.

The committee agreed to send Cole's proposal to the Downtown Development group. An update was scheduled for July. Head down, Cole shoved papers into his briefcase. She slipped out of the room before the meeting ended and dashed to Bonita. The breeze caught her hair, and excitement fired her blood. This called for action. The entire community needed to understand why bulldozing Michiana Thyme was exactly the wrong thing to do.

Flyers. Yes, flyers for every home and every place of business.

Frustrating Cole almost felt like old times.

Chapter 11

The plane was late. Sitting in the airport in South Bend, Indiana, Kate could hardly hold her head up. She took another slug of coffee. Memorial Weekend and she'd need more than caffeine to make it through three days with Mercedes.

The past week had been crazy. When she wasn't talking to her floral sources, she was helping Chili and Ignacio paint the walls or visiting her mother. She'd put her writing on the back burner, except for the flyer she pulled together after the town meeting. "Save Gull Harbor… protect history for future generations." Mercedes would call it overly dramatic. No sense soft peddling it.

Whatever. Kate was sleeping better than she had in months.

The weather had turned warmer. Purple iris pushed through the damp earth outside Breezy Point and opened, lush and velvety. She threw open the French doors and windows to banish the stale winter smell. The gust of winds that blew through the house that day stoked Kate's energy.

Did her restlessness have anything to do with seeing Cole so often? His truck showed up a lot at Ignacio's, although he must have higher priority projects. She knew the sound of his pickup, the squeal of the driver's door, and the spring of Prissy's padded feet on the gravel. In college, Kate had studied Pavlov's response.

Every time Cole's dark green truck pulled in, a tingling broke out in her chest like clockwork.

Crazy. How could she be disgusted with and long for something at the same time?

Waiting for her sister's plane to land, Kate stared out the plate glass window. Dusk was falling. Her mind felt just as murky. All of the divorce self-help books said she was in a state of transition. She'd leave it at that.

Memorial Weekend and flight delays were announced with annoying regularity. Kate considered flipping up the arm rests and stretching out on the hard black vinyl cushions to snooze. Finally, Mercedes's flight number flashed to "landed" on the Arrival and Departure board. Kate pitched her coffee cup into the trash and joined the others crowded behind the roped off area.

Within minutes, a stream of travelers burst through the doors. Lots of hugging and excited conversations. The burr of rolling luggage wheels abraded Kate's nerves. So much depended on this visit. The two of them had to get along, never easy.

Not hard to spot Mercedes. The sleek black trench coat, dark stockings, and expensive heels set her apart as she took the hall with long strides.

"Mercedes! Over here!" Kate waved.

Her sister looked more annoyed than delighted to see her. "Feel like I've been to hell and back on these damn planes," she mumbled, offering a cheek. A whiff of Tresor tingled in Kate's nostrils. "They route you from New York City all the way to Atlanta and then back up again. Makes absolutely no sense."

"Where's your carry-on?"

By then, Mercedes was three steps ahead of her. "I'm not dragging around any luggage. That's what we pay the damn airlines for."

Okay. Happy to see you too. Kate caught up with her, sandals feeling heavy. She'd be damned if she'd trail behind her sister. Did enough of that growing up.

"So how's Alice?" Mercedes always called their mother by her first name – except to her face.

Where to begin? "Think I mentioned she has a roommate."

"When did that happen?"

"Right after I got here. I told you about it in a phone call. Marie McGraw." Her sister often had selective memory.

Mercedes sliced her blonde bob with manicured fingernails. "Sorry, Katie. My mind is on autopilot. I appreciate everything you've done with Alice. Really I do. It's great that you can be here."

Head down, Kate kept walking. She had to buy new sandals.

"You're staying for a while, right?" Mercedes prodded.

"Is a bluebird blue? Of course I'm staying… for a while." *Because my life isn't working out. You're the successful sister.*

Her sister cut her a narrow glance.

Kate sighed. She'd promised herself that even when her sister behaved like a bitch, she wouldn't be one. "Sorry, Mercedes. It's late. I'm tired. I wasn't planning on staying here all summer, but now I am."

Thank goodness they'd reached the baggage claim where luggage was already thumping onto the conveyor belt. No ragged yarn or ugly bungee cord on her sister's bag, only a discreet red tag on the handle. Probably to match the soles of Mercedes' shoes. Grabbing the suitcase, Kate wrenched it from the spinning turnstile.

"I'll take it, Katie."

"No, you must be tired." After yanking out the handle, Kate headed for the door. Her breath tightened like an annoying allergic response.

The night air blew cool against Kate's cheeks when they exited the terminal and headed for the parking lot. When they reached the SUV, Kate stowed the bag in the back.

"Nice car. Blue, huh?" A frown appeared like an exclamation point between Mercedes' eyes.

"Awesome, right?" Kate couldn't resist. Her sister always bought black cars. "Bonita."

"What?"

"My SUV. I named her Bonita."

With a snort, Mercedes yanked open the passenger door. "You and your names."

"It means pretty." Kate slid inside. She could practically taste the cloud of Mercedes' expensive perfume.

"I took Spanish too, Katie, remember?" Mercedes ripped out the seat belt and clicked it shut.

The three-day weekend began to feel eternal.

"How's work?" Mercedes asked. Then the light went on. "Oh, that's right. You lost your job."

No *I'm sorry, Kate. How do you feel?* "That was a while back. I've been freelancing."

"So are you going to take a vacation, a marriage break, and then go back to Boston?" Mercedes was chuckling at her own joke. "You always liked it there, all those museums."

Kate started the engine and put it in reverse. Thank God for backup screens, although she was ready to run someone over. "I'll be working, not vacationing. No need to get back because my marriage is, well, over."

The bomb dropped so easily. She liked the way Mercedes' mouth fell open.

"Wha-what?"

Ah, now she had her sister's full attention.

"Brian and I. Over. *Finito.*"

Her sister was gasping like a beached fish.

Kate swallowed a chuckle. "I'm setting up a flower stall with Chili and her husband Ignacio—you remember Chili from school?"

Glancing over, she saw Mercedes' eyes had widened. That bright green must be contacts.

"Flower stall?" You would've thought it was a bordello.

"Right. Where I'll sell flowers. Part of Ignacio's large produce establishment." Sounded much more glamorous than the abandoned gas station.

"Well, I…" Mercedes at a loss for words? Priceless. "Oh, I suppose you need that time off. Sorry. I wasn't thinking."

Kate was having trouble keeping her eyes on the road. Selling from a stand for eight hours a day hardly seemed like "time off."

"Gull Harbor needs a vegetable stand, and everyone needs flowers."

Okay, that sounded corny. Kate didn't care.

"Sure. Right." Fanning out one hand, Mercedes studied her nails in the darkness. "Wish I could have had my nails done before I left, but it was so damn busy."

Her sister was an expert on moving beyond things she didn't want to understand.

"I'll be working at the flower stand a lot this weekend. Sorry about that. But there's nothing I can do. Memorial Day should be busy. You can drop me off at the stand, er, store in the morning and use the car. I'm sure you want to see Mom."

"Right. Good."

Kate glanced over. Her sister was silent, gazing at the dashboard like it held the mysteries of life. "Everything okay? Business good?"

"Fine. Great."

Mercedes turned to look out the window.

The rest of the ride was quiet. Kate snapped on some jazz and let the mellow saxophone soothe the tension in her shoulders. She didn't want to get into it with her sister. It was late. They were both tired.

When they reached Red Arrow Highway, the four-lane highway was dark and silent except for the Chicago people whipping off Highway 94, eager for a holiday weekend. Next to Kate, Mercedes sat strung tight and awake. Trees rustled overhead and the light glowed over the back door as they approached the house on the winding driveway. Thank goodness she'd left that back door light on. Darkness in Michigan could be so absolute. Kate hoped the peeling paint wasn't obvious. She wanted the house to look welcoming. Almost felt as if she were staging it for showing. That thought rankled, and Kate struggled to erase it from her mind. Mercedes had to see Breezy Point as their home, for cripes' sake.

Once inside, Kate snapped on the kitchen light and heaved Mercedes' bag into the center of the room. The roller wheels scraped on the gray linoleum. Turning, she was shocked by the dark circles ringing her sister's eyes. Then again, Mercedes had always worked punishing hours.

"You okay? Want some coffee?"

"I drank enough coffee in Atlanta between flights." Mercedes' hand shook as she unbuttoned her coat and took in the room. "My God, hasn't Mom gotten rid of those white curtains yet? Eyelet? Really?"

"She loves those curtains." Kate had washed and pressed them two days earlier.

"And that refrigerator? Archaic."

"It runs fine, Mercedes. Refrigerators can be very expensive."

"Still, we should have bought her one last Christmas."

"Mom wanted a new fuzzy robe."

Her sister's mouth opened in a huge yawn.

"You must be exhausted. I'm just going to lock up."

"See you in the morning." Mercedes dragged her suitcase over the rag rugs in the living room and headed for the second floor. Her suitcase bumped against every stair. Mercedes never lifted anything if she could help it.

That day, Kate had opened the windows in her sister's bedroom wanting to freshen things up. As she slid the bolt on the door leading to the screen porch, she could hear Mercedes slam the windows closed.

Chapter 12

The cooing of the mourning doves woke Kate up the next morning. The eight-thirty alarm hadn't gone off yet. Stumbling, she pulled on jeans cold from the floor and her green *Say Yes to Michigan!* sweatshirt. Tiptoeing into the bathroom so she wouldn't wake up Mercedes, she yanked her hair into a ponytail, brushed her teeth, and splashed water on her face. Then she eased herself down the stairs.

Coffee was perking on the stove before her sister made it downstairs dressed in designer black jeans, black boots, and a black hoodie that probably had a designer label.

"Thank God." Mercedes grabbed the carafe and an empty mug.

"Cereal?" Kate held up her box of Kashi.

"I'm on a diet. The coffee keeps my metabolism up. Such a struggle." She sighed, as if staying slim was as serious as the war against hunger.

Tugging her green hoodie over hips that suddenly felt big as a sand dune, Kate grabbed her keys. "I'd like to get to the flower shop. Then you can drive on to visit with Mom."

Mercedes rubbed her fingers into her eyes. "Maybe I'll swing back to put some makeup on before I do that."

"Mercedes, this isn't New York."

"What does that have to do with it?" Her sister rummaged in one of the cupboards "Didn't we have some travel mugs?"

Reaching around her sister's head, Kate snatched one from the top shelf. She was taller, not a benefit in grade school. Then she filled out.

With a sigh, Mercedes transferred her coffee, and the two of them were out the door. Chilly late spring air greeted them. Moisture beaded on the hood of her blue SUV.

"Good morning, Bonita."

Mercedes gave an exaggerated sigh. She'd never even named her dolls.

They got in and Kate revved the engine. She tapped the brakes all the way down the driveway, loving how her sister's head jerked. "Sorry, Mercedes. I'm having trouble shifting."

"You should get an automatic."

"I did."

Silence. Big sigh. "Cut the crap, Katie."

The smile would probably stay on Kate's face the entire day.

Red Arrow Highway didn't have much traffic this early. Summer people usually slept in, with the exception of the folks who walked the beach early, gathering stones and driftwood with plastic buckets.

When they reached the main intersection of Whittaker Street and Red Arrow Highway, Mercedes glanced both ways. "Amazing. Nothing ever changes here."

"Pretty great, right?" Then Kate's delight crumpled. "But Michiana Thyme has been sold. Do you believe it?"

"About time. The clothes were about ten years behind. All those long skirts and beach hats." Mercedes shuddered.

The light changed. Kate stepped on the gas, and the car lurched forward.

"The tourists like long skirts and sun hats, Mercedes."

"That kind of stock will never bring in the right kind of people."

Irritation churned the coffee in Kate's stomach, but she buttoned her lips. She needed her sister's cooperation.

When she pulled into the empty parking lot, Cole was there with Bob Burns, her flower supplier. The two of them were heaving containers from a flatbed while Prissy sniffed each one.

"My word, what is that thing?"

Kate followed Mercedes' eyes. "My flower, er, stand." She'd almost said shop but that might be a stretch.

"No, that animal. Looks like a starving cow."

Funny how that stung. "That's Prissy. Cole's dog. She's sweet." *Did I really say that?*

Mercedes swiveled to stare. "Since when are you a dog lover?"

"I'm not." And why were they here? Didn't Cole have his own projects?

She waved. Three long tables formed a U under a snappy white tent. A sign in bright pink and green lettering was posted on one of the support beams.

"'Kate's Blooms'?" Her sister's tone snapped something inside Kate.

"Maybe a little cutesy, but I like it." The "right kind of people" would probably never stop at a shop called Kate's Blooms.

"My, oh, my. Is that Cole Campbell?" Mercedes lowered her sunglasses.

"Yep. He's helping Ignacio and, well, me."

"What's this? You never mentioned you'd hooked up with him again."

Kate bristled. "I haven't 'hooked up' with him. We're both working on this project. He's helping Ignacio with… stuff."

Cole's navy jacket was thrown across one of the tables. In a gray T-shirt that looked so soft, his muscles corded when he hoisted boxes of flower pots like they were lettuce. No wonder her sister was staring. Yep, this was going to be a long weekend. Cole looked up, and Mercedes inched down, like she didn't want Cole to see her without makeup.

Kate grabbed her purse and a work apron she'd found in a drawer. Her mother always wore full-length aprons, not "those sissy kind." Her very words. Kate jumped out. "I'll text you when I need to be picked up. Probably stay until my stock runs out."

"Got it." Somehow Mercedes crawled into the driver's seat without getting out.

"Oh, and Mercedes?"

Her sister looked up, still slouching.

"Careful with that shifting now."

Her sister's lips moved furiously behind the window. Kate recognized some of it, but Mercedes always brought back colorful new terms from New York. Poor Bonita.

"Ready for the holiday weekend?" Cole asked as she slipped

into the apron.

"As ready as I'll ever be." Maybe Mercedes had a point about the makeup. Kate nipped her lower lip.

"Nervous?"

"Not at all. Should I be?" She tied the apron strings in a tight bow in the back. Yep, definitely had to go easy on the cheese crowns.

"Just meant first time and all that." The sun danced off Cole's dark hair, and his blue eyes glinted. "But that's right. Only a sophomore and you were always prepared for every debate. Even with Michigan City while the rest of us shook in our boots."

Her eyes fell. He'd shed his work boots for cowboy boots that looked hand tooled. Hand tooled and hot. "You never looked nervous to me. None of the seniors did."

"Looks can be deceiving. But you? You were the real thing, Katydid. Always hit your mark."

"If you only knew." The morning of every debate, Kate got the dry heaves, hanging onto the toilet bowl until Mercedes hammered on the bathroom door and screeched in a voice she never used at school.

"Got something for you."

"Really? What?" Her curiosity turned to an amazed chuckle when Cole handed her a large bag of cheese curls. "You shouldn't have, but I'm out. Thanks. Giant size?"

"Yep. That's me, ah, it. Giant size." His face had colored. "Special moments have to be remembered."

Special? Really? Blushing, she tucked the bag in an open box under the counter. "I'll save these for later."

Cole studied her, eyes blue as the sky above. Made her feel the sun was shining just for her.

She had to get out of here. "Guess I'll check in with Ignacio and Chili."

Inside, Chili stood at the register along with one of Ignacio's cousins. Produce and fruit were heaped in varying shades of green, red and yellow on the counters. Cheese and sauces along with who-knew-what else filled the refrigerator cases. Place looked pretty darn good. Tension and excitement hummed in the air.

Cole disappeared, and she circled back to the stand outside. Cars arrived and couples got out, shopping lists in hand and skin pale from the winter.

Dressed in khaki shorts and bright polos, the summer people snapped up cantaloupes and green beans, zucchini and spring lettuce. Chili told Kate later that customers assured her the vegetable store was "quaint," just what the area needed.

At Kate's stand, bouquets of snapdragons, calla lilies, and even some lilies of the valley and peonies were displayed in old mason jars. "I should have more in a couple of weeks," she told one couple. It was a little early for the sturdy annuals.

"Are you going to handle perennials too?" asked one father with a two-year-old in his arms.

"Sure. Why not?" she assured him. "You might check back later." Jotting down notes, Kate would call her suppliers.

By the time the noon sun had climbed high and hot in the sky, she was sold out. Her mason jars held only water. Empty flats were stacked below the table.

Her legs felt rubbery. Kate plopped into a folding chair and reached for the bag of cheese curls. First day and she'd sold out. Who would have guessed?

"I need more stock," Kate whispered to Chili when she went inside in search of a soft drink.

"Told you so." Chili beamed and rang up the next customer. Then she reached out and wiped something from the corner of Kate's lips. "Cheese curls?"

"Of course." Kate took a deep swig of cold root beer.

"So good to have you here, *amiga mia.*" Chili swept away a hank of Kate's hair.

But Chili had work to do and Kate sauntered back to her stand. Memorial Weekend. She felt confident, even a little cocky. Maybe she should have worn red, white, and blue today. Her green sweatshirt felt heavy, like last summer. After all, Memorial Day Weekend always promised three months of carefree, fun-filled days. Throwing her head back, she yanked the rubber band from her hair and shook it out. The shiny green pickup turned in from the highway.

Stepping down from the driver's seat, Cole came toward her. Prissy trotted at his side. "What? Everything's gone?" When he swiped the dark glasses from his face, his blue eyes danced, like he was happy for her. Not that she was reading too much into it.

"Looks like it."

"Don't sound so surprised."

She had to laugh along with him.

"Kate!" Natalie stuck her head out the pickup window. The breeze snagged her blonde hair, and Natalie swept it away from her shy smile. She was going to be so gorgeous.

Kate walked over. "Finished the book yet?"

"Yep. You going to be at the library next week?"

Kate thought ahead. "Let's see. Maybe late Wednesday?" She hated to give up volunteering.

"Dad, I can go to the library Wednesday after school. Can't I?"

Pulling out his phone, Cole jotted something into what must be a calendar. "Sounds good."

Natalie drummed her fingers on the edge of the open window. "Be sure you get it in right, Dad. Not like the parent teacher conference. Pretty please?"

His cheeks colored a ruddy red. "Natalie, I try."

Reaching out, Natalie patted his arm. "I know, Dad. I know."

The role reversal choked Kate.

Keeping his head down, Cole pocketed the phone. Arms crossed, he turned to study the vegetable stand. Cars continued to turn in, spewing out families with lists. "This is great, Kate."

"Thanks for your help. Ignacio and Chili really appreciate it."

His steady gaze found hers. "We help each other in Gull Harbor."

"I can see that. I think." But was he helping himself more? Suspicion darkened the edges of the bright day. She hardly felt any guilt about the bright yellow flyers in the back of the SUV.

"You *think*? What does that mean?"

One searing look from Cole and Kate swore her soul felt

stripped bare. Never good at hiding her feelings, she dropped her head. "Nothing."

Chili would kill her. Cole had been nothing but helpful. He'd made time for them, not easy with all the projects on his plate. But were the local people easily led? She didn't know the answer and she didn't want to see one more building knocked down in the name of progress.

The crinkle of plastic made Kate turn. Prissy was tussling with the bag of cheese curls, snapping them up as soon as they hit the grass.

"Prissy! Bad, bad girl." Cole advanced on his pet.

Dropping the bag from her huge jaws, Prissy skirted the scene of the crime until she sat at the door of the pickup, incriminating orange splotches dusting her white and black coat.

While Natalie and Cole fussed over the dog, Kate tried hard not to laugh. Cheese curls littered the area. Good thing Cole bought the large bag. Also good that Kate got to them first or she'd be plenty ticked. Natalie began to clean up while Cole got Prissy in the cab of the truck.

"You coming to the Memorial Day barbecue on Monday?" He closed the truck door.

"Wouldn't miss it. How do you think our mothers are getting along? I mean, your mother-in-law."

Cole's dark brows knit together. "In a lot of ways, Marie is my mother, especially since my own folks moved to Florida. She seems to be getting along just fine with your mom. They have a history."

"Like a lot of folks in Gull Harbor." The words just slipped out.

Really. Kate meant nothing.

Cole registered no response and she exhaled.

Maybe best not to go there. Kate needed the arrangement with Cole's mother-in-law to work out until her mom came home.

Natalie had climbed back into the pickup. Prissy's head hung out the window, nose sniffing the air as if searching for cheese curls. One hand on the driver's door, Cole turned. "Guess I'll see you Sunday?"

"But I thought the picnic was on Monday."

"Right. I meant that meeting with you and your sister. Sunday, right?"

Kate felt the day dim.

"Anything wrong?"

Would be a cold day in hell when Kate would admit her sister had said nothing to her about Sunday. "Not at all

. See you then." She could hardly get her mouth around the words.

Cole wasn't even out of the parking lot when Kate pulled out her phone to give her sister a call.

Chapter 13

Sunday evening Kate and Mercedes sat on the blue couch in the living room, drinking peach tea. Kate's throat felt scratchy from trying to reason with her sister. She drummed her fingertips on her mug in time to the beats of the clock on the mantel. They'd only been waiting for Cole for ten minutes, but it seemed like forever. Kate set her cold tea down on the coffee table. "Think I'll wait outside."

"Is he always late like this?"

"I have no idea. He has a little girl."

Mercedes looked up from paging through the latest issue of *Vogue* she'd brought with her. "So this is what kids do to you, huh? Make you late for meetings?"

"Meetings?" Was there more to this than Mercedes had admitted?

"Conversation. This is only a conversation, Kate."

"It's a lot more than that, Mercedes, and you know it. Mom should be here for any discussion about Breezy Point." Anger tightening her chest, Kate stomped out the front door onto the porch. She let the screen door whap shut behind her. Pretty juvenile and she couldn't stand herself. She'd come home to find peace, the security she'd lost somewhere in Boston. But had she been detoured into unwanted conflict instead?

The sounds of happy families drifted up from the beach. Summer days were long in Michigan. Families didn't pack up and leave the sandy shore until the light dimmed from the sky. Below, children laughed, calling to each other as they splashed through the shallow waters. Kate should feel happy. Her first weekend at the flower stall and she'd sold out of stock. Instead of talking to Cole about their property, she'd rather be online, hunting down other resources for perennials.

This wasn't just a friendly talk. It was a meeting. She'd had her fill of them, including the town gathering where Cole made his presentation.

The slam of the pickup truck door put a cap on her thoughts.

Tennis shoes kicking through the tall grass, she rounded the corner. "Hey, Cole."

He looked great. Again. His dark hair gleamed in the dusk, kind of smoky, like his eyes. The jean jacket looked so soft, so crushable. She had to fight the urge to reach out and run a hand over his broad shoulders. Definitely had a thing for the way time had changed her Debate Club buddy.

"Hey, Katydid. How's business?"

"Blooming."

A grin tweaked one corner of his mouth. "Still so quick with words."

"That would be me." But not when it counted. She'd seen Cole in action at that meeting, and it scared her how persuasive he still could be.

As she told him about her weekend success, she realized he probably thought in terms of five or six digit returns, not the meager dollars from a flower stand. She didn't care. His grin widened while she talked. So easy to forget and let him be the same enthusiastic president of Debate Club from so many years ago.

"Where are Natalie and Prissy?" she asked.

"With a neighbor." His smile turned sheepish. "Folks in my neighborhood are always glad to help out. Besides, I didn't know if they'd be welcome."

"Of course they are. I locked up the cheese curls." She wanted no distractions during this conversation.

"Hey, Cole." Mercedes appeared in the back door. Her black jeans and boots were her uniform, but the stylish trench coat had been replaced by a black leather jacket. Had she slipped that on after Kate stomped out of the room?

The two shook hands. Seemed like Mercedes held on longer than necessary. The rush of resentment made Kate's head swirl. If Mercedes thought she was in charge of this conversation, she was so wrong.

Cole looked from one sister to another. "Maybe I should ask why I'm here today?" Each word was edged with caution.

When Mercedes shook her head, her hair shimmered like a whip. "Just wanted to talk about the property. Want to walk around?" Flattening the violets still in bloom, she pivoted toward the front.

"I believe Cole's already seen the property."

Cole's face flushed. "As a matter of fact, I have. Stopped by after your call, Mercedes, a little while back. Beautiful setting. The five parcels of land make it especially valuable."

"Love to hear it." Mercedes led the way until they stood at the point where they could look down and see the water rolling into shore in glittering waves.

Kate felt strangled. Growing up, she'd played hide and seek with Mercedes in the tall ferns her sister was trampling. But she refused to let Cole see how mad she was. This was family business and private.

Cole nodded slowly. "Yep, breathtaking view."

His sunglasses gave no clue about how he felt. Probably pleased. She could only imagine what he would clear from a project like this. Condos? Another hotel? Chickaming County was casual about zoning. She ducked her head and slammed a lid on her uneasiness.

With Kate trailing behind, Cole followed Mercedes as she walked the broad front of the land, the parcels that had given the family so much privacy growing up. The property had been given to them when Grandpa Clarence died. Their mom had been an only child.

"Are you thinking of selling the five lots as one piece?" Cole gave no indication that he might be the buyer. "Or will you section it off?"

Mercedes looked like she might be frowning. Hard to tell with all that Botox. "Why don't you give us some figures for both scenarios? All hypothetical. Just for the sake of discussion," she added, eyes sliding in Kate's direction.

"Sounds good. Just want to grab a pad of paper from the truck." Cole took off in that long-legged stride.

"Meet you inside," Mercedes called over her shoulder. She wiggled her brows at Kate. "Pretty hot."

Kate was boiling. In silence, the two sisters tramped into the house. Kate took a seat at the long pine table in the dining room area. Chairs were tucked in, as if they'd just left a family meal. How she wished their mother would come through the door with a platter of pot roast and brown potatoes. Make this all a bad dream.

"You could lose the attitude," Mercedes said as she sat down.

Kate's tongue swelled. If she said anything, she'd burst out bawling. She was just that mad. This whole scenario felt so familiar and frustrating. Whether it was Barbie dolls or borrowing the family car, her sister always had the upper hand.

Cole was back within minutes, slapping his legal pad onto the table just as he had with Ignacio not too long ago. She'd liked him better then but not by much. "As you might know, the property runs at a premium, even though we're still climbing out of this recession. Let me just go through some of the hot buttons."

Oh, he was pressing her hot buttons all right. While Kate knotted her hands so tight she thought her knuckles might crack, Cole launched into a rehash of the merits of their property. Mercedes' eyes glowed. Amazing that she wasn't openly salivating. Using the calculator on her phone, Mercedes ran some figures, smile broadening. When he finished, Cole sat back. His poker face had always been so hard to read in any debate. Probably served him well in situations like this when he was trying to finagle people out of their property.

Mercedes continued to tap on her calculator. Kate studied the blue placemat, her fingers rolling a corner. Somewhere during the discussion, she'd forgotten to breathe. Now she sucked in the air. Still smelled and tasted sour in the house from being closed up during her mom's hospitalization.

"All very interesting." Mercedes reached for Cole's figures. "Mind if I take this, Cole?"

"Whatever you need." Cole ripped the sheet from the pad.

Sure. Right. Kate felt like her skin was peeling off along with the page of figures. Maybe her older sister was a changeling. Maybe Mercedes in all her blonde perfection had fallen from a planet of aliens.

Kate refused to say a word. The silence became uncomfortable.

Cole shoved back, chair legs scraping the floor. "Guess I'll hit the road. Questions come up? Give me a ring. See you at the picnic tomorrow?"

"Picnic?" Mercedes set her phone aside.

"The Memorial Day picnic at Gull Harbor Care Center. I mentioned it Friday." Kate worked to buff the impatience from her voice. "Mom was excited you would be here for it."

"Oh, right. What time is that again?"

"About four or so."

"No problem. I've got a late flight."

While Kate worked at the produce stand that weekend, Mercedes had visited with their mother. Kate wondered how that went. Seemed like most of her sister's visit to Gull Harbor had been spent barking out orders on the phone to her assistant.

Mercedes lived her business. Was it any wonder that she didn't have time for a relationship? Remorse stilled Kate's mind. After all, she herself was divorced. Maybe Mercedes had been wise not to dip her toe in the matrimonial waters.

"Great, see you tomorrow then." Cole had reached the back door. He was looking around, probably taking in the dated kitchen. Figuring how much it would get on the market.

She wanted to strangle someone. At this point, either Mercedes or Cole would do.

"Sure. Can't wait. Thanks for coming, Cole." Mercedes walked Cole out to the truck, Kate trailing behind. A sense of déjà vu washed over her. This was just how it had been in high school when she was a sophomore and they were seniors.

Cole swung up into his truck. Kate hung back, but Mercedes grabbed the open door. "Gull Harbor is lucky to have you, Cole." Good lord, she was practically purring, hanging on the door like a cat in heat.

Kate kicked at a dandelion in the gravel. "This is Cole's job, Mercedes. Buying and selling Gull Harbor property."

That's all they were to him. Owner of a great parcel of land.

She had to have more yellow flyers made.

Mercedes was blinking up at him as if he was still the star forward on the basketball team and she was the cheerleader. "But isn't the development of Gull Harbor, well, a noble cause?"

"Some of us see it that way, Mercedes." Cole never blinked.

Kate's snort ended in a strangled cough.

Mercedes' attention remained with Cole. "See you tomorrow, Cole."

"Tomorrow." But his gaze brushed Kate as Cole slammed the door and started the engine. The suspension of his truck squeaked all the way down the driveway.

"Too many tree roots in that road," Kate murmured. "We should have it paved." But city driveways were paved, not beach properties. She gave the poor dandelion another frustrated kick and headed to the house. Maybe she was foolish to want to hang on to Breezy Point when so much needed work.

"So you two are an item?" Mercedes twirled a length of hair around one finger.

"What? No. We most definitely are not."

"Katie, I sure felt something back there. Weren't you two in a club together or something in high school?"

The screen door squealed when Kate yanked it open. "Debate Club."

"Oh, right. That." Her sister wrinkled her nose. After all, Debate Club wasn't exactly cheerleading. It was more like National Honor Society. Not enough popular kids in that group for Mercedes.

Chapter 14

Memorial Day and the sun beat down, warmer every day. When Kate was growing up, this day held excitement and promise. Today, it only held questions. What would summer bring?

"Bratwurst, hot dog, or hamburger?" A blush stained Will Applegate's cheeks. The administrator was seriously cute standing over that barbecue grill.

But "cute" had never done it for Kate. "Bratwurst, of course."

"Of course?" Brandishing a fork, Will plucked one from the grill.

"Summer days call for bratwurst loaded with ketchup and onions."

Her sister gasped behind her. "Onions? Really?"

"Lots of them. Load it up, Will. So you're chef for the day?"

His flush deepened as Will plopped a bratwurst into her open bun.

She held up the other plate. "And a burger for my mother, please."

"No bun?"

"Something about sensible eating and a diet."

"She certainly doesn't need it. And that runs in the family."

Now it was Kate's turn to blush. The ridge of Mercedes' plastic plate dug into her back.

"Like your sweater. Very patriotic." He nodded to her red-and-white striped sweater with blue stars spangling the lower right hip.

"Thank you." Another nudge from Mercedes, who wasn't used to being upstaged. "You've met my older sister?"

All through high school, Mercedes had liked being called the older sister. Apparently, those days were over. After darting a sharp glance at Kate, Mercedes turned her full attention to Will. "Of course we've met while I was visiting Mom. What a lovely picnic. Such a great idea for the families."

Grab a shovel. Mercedes could really pile it on. While she jabbered with the administrator who seemed dazzled by her blonde beauty, Kate squirted ketchup on the brat and burger. Then she heaped mustard potato salad on both plates.

"So what's the deal with Will Applegate?" Mercedes asked as they walked toward the gazebo where their mother sat waiting.

"What do you mean?" Kate worked at keeping both plates balanced.

"Just asking." Mercedes gave a casual shake that made her blonde hair shimmer in the sunlight. Kate's own dye job still looked and felt like straw. Maybe her box from the drugstore was the difference. She'd have to set up an appointment with Phoebe.

Once while she was visiting her sister in New York, Mercedes had dragged Kate to her hair salon. Kate quickly realized she could only afford a manicure. Of course, Mercedes had offered to pay. No way was Kate accepting her sister's charity.

Was Gull Harbor working its magic on Mercedes? Kate hadn't

seen her sister this relaxed in a long time. She hadn't checked her phone for at least ten minutes.

"Kate, wake up. What's the deal with the administrator?"

"Will? Nice guy."

"Married?"

"I don't see a ring. Interested?" Kate wheeled around. Will hardly seemed like her sister's type.

"Just asking."

"Seems sincerely interested in the residents." Kate's tone was objective, as if they were critiquing a teacher. When Mercedes raised her eyebrows, she chuckled. "And okay, he's looking good today."

Goody-two-shoes hot. But she kept that to herself. Brian had exuded confidence when Kate met him. Cole had some of those same traits and she guessed Will was probably a bit meek for her own taste.

Giggling together, they could have been back in study hall under the watchful eyes of Mrs. Werner, who handed out detentions like they were birthday treats. Even though Mercedes had been two years ahead of Kate, Gull Harbor High School was small. A study hall pulled from all grades. Some of the clubs, like Debate Club with Cole, had the same kind of mix.

Debate Club. Where it had all started and ended. But Kate wouldn't let that spoil this day.

Clouds scudded overhead. Red, white, and blue banners fluttered from the eaves of the gazebo. The day felt perfect, the first day of a summer of possibilities. Mercedes was home. The weight of responsibility for their mother felt lighter on Kate's shoulders. Their disagreement about the property? Mercedes could be difficult, but she'd never been totally unreasonable.

"One hamburger straight from the grill." Kate set her mother's plate in front of her.

"I could've gotten it myself."

Of course, no way could her mother manage her walker and the plate. Kate exchanged a look with her sister.

"Like your red sweater, Mom. Is it new?" Mercedes asked.

Their mother shook her left hand. "The Internet is a wonderful thing. Click, click. Only three monthly payments."

Mercedes' jaw dropped.

"Internet shopping," Kate murmured, setting the plates down. "I told you about it."

"Right." They shared a smile and for a second Mercedes was the sister who'd taught Kate how to pluck her eyebrows. How Kate had looked up to her big sister then, so beautiful, so popular.

Now they had to find more serious solutions together. The social worker had indicated her mom would be coming home soon. Her recovery had "plateaued." That was Medicare language for "we aren't going to cover any more treatments."

"Your mother, well, she might not be the same," Marianne had told Kate. "You'll have to accept that."

But Kate couldn't. Alice Kennedy's life had been defined by a flurry of activity. After their father left, Kate would wake up to the buzz of the lawn mower. Or she'd find her mother weeding the garden with a vengeance. Alice didn't just clean. She did battle with the vacuum, that whined when it caught a throw rug until she ripped it free. When she canned, steam converted their kitchen into a sauna. The shelves of the basement larder groaned under the weight of her efforts.

Now she'd "plateaued." The lines had been drawn. Kate was ready to do battle. Mercedes might take off for New York but Kate was staying right here in the trenches.

But there were complications. Breezy Point had no first floor bathroom and the stairs were sharp with a difficult turn. They couldn't afford private duty nursing, and Alice Kennedy would never accept an aide. A crazy idea had formed in Kate's head.

"Mom, I'm really busy at the vegetable stand right now."

"That's wonderful, Kate." Her mother struggled to open a bag of chips.

Reaching for the bag, Kate ripped it open. "I've been thinking. Cole Campbell is looking for a companion for his daughter, Natalie."

Mercedes threw her a cautious glance.

Her mother put her burger down. "What's that got to do with us, Kate?"

"What would you say to having Natalie spend some time with you? Didn't you always say the happiest years were when we were kids? Natalie loves to read. Our shelves are stuffed full of books."

"That's an interesting idea, Kate." Mercedes sounded cautious, like she was waiting for the other shoe to drop.

Kate watched her mom process all this. "I didn't want to say anything to Cole until I spoke to you. What do you think?"

Her mother's faded hazel eyes focused and then gleamed. "Marie might not like this. I'd really hate to hurt her feelings."

Somehow, Kate doubted that. Excitement brought a rosy splash to her mother's cheeks.

"Marie probably won't mind. She might be here for a while, and this is just for the summer. What is it with you two anyway?"

Her mother fingered the star pattern on the plastic tablecloth. "Oh, we go way back. Silly, really."

Okay, so she was going to be mysterious.

"Mind if we sit with you?" Cole's voice made Kate jump.

When she turned, her breath caught in her throat. The man could turn a blue chambray shirt and jeans into a fashion statement. Cole had charge of Marie's wheelchair, with Prissy dancing at his side. Standing at her father's elbow in a bright red top that sparkled with sequins, Natalie shot Kate a shy smile. That little girl was such a sweetie, although she certainly knew how to ride herd on her dad.

"Have a seat." Kate moved the chairs over.

"My daughter's here," Mom chirped to Marie, a proud lift to her chin. "Mercedes."

Kate swallowed hard. Some things would never change.

"Marie and I chatted a couple of times this weekend, Mom," Mercedes said quietly. "During my visits?"

"Right. Of course. Guess it just slipped my mind." A slight frown wrinkled their mom's brow.

Yes, it was good that Mercedes had come. Kate's older sister had to see the situation for herself. Frustration followed on the heels of that relief. How would her mother ever be able to have a discussion about Breezy Point if her memory was so jumbled?

"How's your reading coming, Natalie?" She patted the chair next to her, and Natalie sat down. Cole seated himself on the other side of his daughter.

"Fine." Natalie bobbed her head, and the sun caught the sparkles in her tortoiseshell headband. Behind her ears, the thick hair was a mass of tangles.

"That hair needs a good brushing." Marie threw Cole an incriminating look. "When we get back to the room, I'll tend to it."

"No." Natalie's hands flew to her headband. "You always hurt me."

Marie fell back. The muscles worked in her throat, and Kate felt like there was baggage here, more the steamer trunk type than a duffle bag.

"Conditioner might help." Kate aimed the comment at Cole. The guy who'd had everything under control in high school, from a basketball to his prom date, seemed helpless in the face of an eight year-old's hair.

Everyone at the table became very involved with their food. Patriotic music blared from speakers, and the resilient brass eventually lifted the mood at the table. Sometimes mothers and grandmothers just said stupid things. No harm intended. But she could forgive Marie a lot easier than her own mother, who was gazing at Mercedes as if she were the second coming.

Mercedes had brought Mom a red zipped hoodie with "I Love New York" scrawled across it in white. The new addition was draped over the walker. Kate was still trying to acclimate to this vibrant version of her mother whose wardrobe had mainly been denim and beige.

"What did you think of Ramona in the library book?" Kate asked Natalie.

"She was great. Finished the book." Natalie's eyes sparkled. "Ready for another one."

"Come on Wednesday about four o'clock if you want some help."

"What about your flowers?" Cole asked Kate around bites of his potato salad.

Kate hitched up her shoulders. "The flowers are sold by that time."

"Who did you say is working with you?" her mom asked.

"Ignacio and Chili. Remember them, Mom? They dated in high school and stopped by the house. They're married now. Three kids."

"Yes, of course." Her mother almost looked indignant. "Of course I remember the names of your friends. Why, you were *all* friends in high school." Alice Kennedy always had every mother's phone number handy so she could call if Kate and Mercedes weren't home on time.

"But not in the same class," she reminded her mother gently.

"You and Cole were in Debate Club together, seems to me." Mercedes' innocent smile didn't fool Kate one bit.

"One of the highlights of my senior year." Cole actually looked sincere, blue eyes warm with intelligence and charm.

Time to put a lid on the warmth spiraling through her body. Kate would think of the lake. The cool lake. Didn't work. One glance at Cole and she was an ice cube melting under a relentless sun.

Kate turned back to her mother. "Ignacio and Chili are doing me a favor by letting me have the space for the flower stand."

"Can I help at the flower stand?" Natalie piped up.

"Of course not." Irritation sharpened Marie's voice. "A roadside stand is no place for a young girl."

Roadside stand? Kate's new venture had just been redefined.

Cole and Marie locked eyes. Kate and Mercedes exchanged a look. How common were these battles between Cole and his mother-in-law?

"Besides, Cole, I'll be babysitting for Natalie. I'll be home by then." Marie was not giving ground.

Meanwhile, Kate's mother calmly ate her hamburger, seeming to relish every bite.

"We can talk about this later." Cole looked uncertain, a guy backed into the corner. Would he even entertain the thought of having Natalie stay with her mother? Gosh, Kate sure hoped so.

"I am *not* a baby. I do not need a baby sitter." Natalie slumped back and crossed her arms over her chest.

Whoa. Kate resisted the urge to hug the girl. Natalie sure needed somebody in her court. "Want to go get some cake with me?"

Eyes brimming, Natalie pushed back her chair. Together, they went back to the buffet table. Prissy trotted along behind. Cole didn't seem to notice the dog had gone. Playing with his fork, he looked like a man with a lot on his mind.

"Now you be a good girl, Prissy," Natalie warned the dog, extending a hand. Prissy shoved her damp nose into her palm.

"Chocolate or yellow cake?" Kate asked. Cut into generous squares, the two sheet cakes had enormous American flags as a decoration.

"Chocolate."

Kate began to shovel pieces onto plastic plates. "There are laws about working at your age. Trust me, you'll be working soon enough. Maybe something else will come up for you this summer."

Her father used to call a moment like that "chumming the waters."

"Natalie, can you grab that tray?"

While Natalie held the tray, Kate grabbed enough cake for everybody. When Prissy tried to press her nose onto the tray, Kate whisked it away.

"None for you, Prissy. We're not forgetting those oatmeal cookies." Kate was relieved when Natalie hitched a finger through the dog's collar.

When they returned to the table, Cole was talking to Mercedes about her flight. Mercedes looked totally enthralled, like departure times and seat assignments were fascinating. Kate stumbled, surprised by a sudden shimmer of jealousy.

Her sister was home, and nothing had changed. Better get used to it.

"Coming back soon, Mercedes?" Cole asked.

Her mom's head reared up at the question she probably wanted to ask.

"Have to see how things shake out." Her sister was a master of evasion. Glancing up, she held up one hand as Kate slid the tray of cake onto the table. "None for me, thanks."

Disappointment creased their mother's face. "I just hate to have you go."

Kate tried to breathe through the tight feeling in her chest. She set a slice of cake in front of her mother.

"Oh, I'll be back, Mom." But Mercedes said it so quickly.

Mom just stared at her cake. She probably knew Mercedes' visits were only prompted by emergencies.

"Red velvet's your favorite, Mom," Kate prodded, handing her mother a fork.

"My favorite." Teary-eyed, she began to eat.

Kate wanted to stab Mercedes with a fork.

"Everyone having a good time?" Without his chef's hat and apron, Will looked surprisingly hip in jeans and pale blue shirt. The suits he usually wore didn't do him justice.

Will Applegate was probably the type of guy a girl should fall for. Dependable. Compassionate. But was that enough? Not one spark in Kate's body. No heady flush, no tingling in any part of her body. Her hot-man meter wasn't registering. She pressed one hand against the lips that weren't pulsating and glanced up to find Cole studying them. When she caught his eye, he looked away. But his teasing smile stayed. Heat sparked through her body like it was the Fourth of July.

But it was too early for the Fourth and silly to feel like this.

Marie pushed her cake away. "Too much frosting for me."

"Great job, Will." Cole motioned to the happy groups around them.

"We like to think of ourselves as one big happy family at Gull Harbor Care Center." On Will's lips, that comment didn't sound sticky sweet or staged. He was a nice guy. Just not a man that, well, left a girl wondering.

"Prissy!" Natalie's yelp cut the air as the dog chomped down on the plate and whirled it to the ground. One bite, two licks and the cake was gone.

Face reddening, Cole jumped up and snapped his fingers. "You renegade."

Prissy dropped her head but not before Kate saw the frosting on her wide maw.

"Oh, for heaven's sakes." But Marie was smiling.

"We've got to clean you up, Prissy." Natalie grabbed a paper napkin. "You're going to be sick again tonight. Good thing there wasn't much left on my plate."

Prissy stood obediently while the little girl patted at her quivering jowls. *Wish I could be better, Natalie, really I do. Just born to be bad, I guess.* They made quite a pair. The Great Dane regarded Natalie with adoration.

When Natalie finished, Cole pointed to a grassy spot close to the table. "Sit. Over there."

Prissy heaved herself onto the grass and laid her head on her paws. Clearly, she knew she'd been banished.

Cole began to clear the table. Kind of cute, really.

Cute and hot.

Kate's body just had to settle down. Cool off and listen to her head. He was the man working hard to ruin a lot of what she loved about Gull Harbor.

"I'd like to go back to my room now." Marie fussed with the buttons on her bulky navy sweater.

"But you'll miss the performance. Let's just stay for a second."

"Your call," Marie said in a miffed voice that Cole ignored. So he drew some boundaries with his mother-in-law.

Will hopped onto a small stage. A trio of seniors had stepped up, wearing wigs and carrying guitars. "And now I'd like to introduce you to our very own Beatles."

Vintage Beatles music blasted, and three older men strummed guitars and mimed, wigs flopping.

"Bunch of fools," Marie mumbled.

"What are they doing?" Mom asked.

"Pretending they're singing," Kate explained. "Lip syncing. They're having a good time." The crowd sang along and clapped.

"Lip singing?" Marie shouted out. "Don't you always use your lips when you sing?"

"Why don't we sit and listen just a little while?" Cole settled back.

Kate marveled at his patience.

When the number ended, Will took the microphone again. "And now I think we should all remember what Memorial Day is all about. In particular, we honor the men who've served our country. Active duty or National Guard, if you would please rise."

As the national anthem played, a smattering of older men at the various tables stood, hands over their hearts. Those who could stand got up and sang, even Natalie. Her mother's voice quavered on the high notes, and Kate was surprised by the tears filling her eyes. Maybe she was just overly emotional. But that day, she felt grateful and oh, so glad she'd come back to Gull Harbor. Sure, at times the place irritated the heck out of her, but these were her people. Maybe Boston had just been a stop in her life's journey, and it was time to change trains. The thought startled her into all sorts of new possibilities.

When the anthem ended, Marie patted the arms of her wheel chair. "Can I go back now?"

"Sure can. See you all later." Handling his mother-in-law's wheelchair, Cole was all lean muscle and grace.

And nice. Kate hated to admit it, but he was being so darn nice.

Trailing behind her father, Natalie gave Kate a small wave.

"See you next week," Kate called out.

"I should get going, Mom. Have to get back to the house to pack." Mercedes shouldered her Coach bag. Packing might take all of ten minutes, but Mom didn't know that.

"Did you say that you'd seen Cole earlier?" her mother asked as Kate wrangled the walker.

Mercedes exchanged a look with Kate. "Cole stopped over at the house."

"Oh, really." Mom's attention swiveled to Kate.

Not easy but Kate pressed her lips together. Mercedes could explain the plans she had for Breezy Point, but she busied herself rearranging things in her purse.

Oh, well. "Mercedes, want to explain your suggestions?" Kate sure as heck wasn't taking responsibility.

In short, jerky sentences, Mercedes laid out her plan, prefacing it with, "Just an idea, Mom."

Their mother's face pinched with anger. Her eyes swiveled between Mercedes and Kate, whose heart ached. What on earth had her sister been thinking? They were lucky Mom didn't have another stroke.

Mercedes stumbled to a halt with, "I just thought this might be a good option for you."

"For me?" Disgust curled her mother's lip.

This was so rare that she got angry with her oldest daughter. The whole incident reminded Kate of the day Mercedes had told them she sold over one hundred boxes of Girl Scout cookies. Her mother had been so proud until they discovered their father had taken them to every bar within thirty miles of Gull Harbor. He'd pedaled cookies to men who could barely find their wallets and forgot to eat every day. Mom had been furious.

"Sounds like it's more for your convenience, Mercedes Frances."

Mercedes' face paled. Not a good sign when middle names were used.

Reaching for her walker, Alice tilted her head up to Kate. "I'd like to go back to my room now. Please." Tears swam in their mother's eyes.

Kate wanted to shake her sister until every cap in her head

rattled. Seething, she guided her mom over the bumpy grass and then onto the concrete path that led to the side door.

"You leaving this pretty day so soon?" Will quipped, holding the door open.

"Mom's getting cold."

The angry clump, clump of Mom's walker resounded down the hallway. Kate had to hustle to keep up. Mercedes fell back, fishing her phone from her bag. When they reached her mother's room, Kate settled her in front of the TV after checking with Marie about a program they both might like. Kate was relieved to see that Cole was gone. Some kisses and hugs and they were out the door. Her mom didn't cling to Mercedes like she usually did, and she didn't pester her about when she'd be back. Kate should have felt pleased, but a heavy sadness had fallen over her.

"I can't believe you weren't even going to mention this to her. Are you kidding me?" Kate turned to Mercedes after they were in the car.

Lips pouty, her sister stared out the window. She had their mother's delicate features. Kate had her father's full lips and his crazy brows. "You have the best of him," her mother had told her once. Somehow, that was sore comfort. Her handsome dad preferred the Roadhouse to their cozy dining room, where they'd had dinner without him too many times to count.

Driving back to Breezy Point, Kate said nothing more. She could hardly wait to take her sister to the airport.

"It was just an idea." Mercedes' voice made her turn. "I'm in trouble, Kate. Some major clients cut back. Thought I'd snag some new accounts so I didn't cut my overhead. Just dug myself into a deeper hole."

Had Kate ever seen Mercedes look so defeated?

"I took a second mortgage on my townhouse, had to terminate some of my people." Mercedes had always been so proud, the star while Kate was the plodder. Now her lips quivered. Kate didn't know what to say.

When they reached Breezy Point, Mercedes quickly packed her carryon and took one last look around before they got back in the car. Sure didn't seem like she intended to return any time soon. During the forty-minute ride to the South Bend airport, they hardly said a word. Kate snapped on the radio. What could she say? Would she have felt more sympathetic if Mercedes had told her all this earlier?

Hugging goodbye at the airport, Mercedes whispered, "Try to get Mom to see reason, okay?"

"Mercedes." Kate pushed her away. "What part of this don't you understand? Mom said no."

"But it's too big for her. Too much work."

"That's not for us to decide."

Mercedes didn't say another word. Kate watched her sister walk toward the security check with her brisk gait. Was the house issue settled, or was it just beginning? Mercedes didn't give up easy. Kate was getting used to digging in her heels and taking a stand.

Chapter 15

When Cole pulled into the vegetable stand that Tuesday morning, he wasn't stopping to see Ignacio, not really. The sight of Kate Kennedy bent over buckets of flowers made him hit the brakes. Hot coffee slopped onto his jeans. "Damn."

All legs, Prissy scurried to stand and gave him the look. *You really had to do that, Cole?*

"Settle down now. I'm just being stupid." Popping the mug back in the cup holder, Cole swiped at the stain. Bad placement.

Prissy settled down with another side glance. *And you think some of my spots are in embarrassing places.*

While he was messing around, Kate looked up and waved. Sunlight did something glittery to her hair. Cole still couldn't get used to her as a blonde. Kate's honey brown hair had been such a part of her. Sturdy and strong, like her. Reminded him of his old baseball mitt, so soft and comfortable to your hands but holding up really well.

Glancing down, he gave up on the spot and grabbed the bag from the seat. He swung out of his pickup. Prissy leapt down behind him and began snuffling the grass. "Good morning, Kate. Don't eat anything or you'll throw up," he warned.

The dog waited patiently for him to turn away. *Am I not a*

paragon of virtue?

Straightening, Kate laughed. "I'll keep that in mind."

Always a smart ass. "I'm talking to Prissy."

She grinned. "I know." A lot of women used tanning beds or those creams that turned them orange. Not Kate. Light freckles sprinkled across her pale cheeks, turning his legs to mush. Trying to look casual, he shook them out.

"Brought you a present." He held out the bag of cheese curls, pleased when her cheeks colored.

"Thank you. Guess I should keep these sealed until you leave, right?"

His cheeks burned. "Guess so."

They stood there for two beats.

She squinted up at him, nipping at that full lower lip that made him crazy. "I wasn't sure you knew who I was that day. You know, when you stopped to help me on the road."

"Are you kidding? Like I'd ever forget."

"Hmm." She kept working that lip. Suddenly the coffee stain on his jeans wasn't the only embarrassment in that area.

"Looks like you're in business." His eyes swept the stand.

Nodding, she kept working the lip. Full. Wet. He shifted.

"As long as the Kalamazoo guys keep delivering, I'll keep selling. One day at a time." She lifted her delicate shoulders in a blue knit top that hugged her figure.

Cole pulled his eyes away. Kate Kennedy's body had always been a minefield. That much hadn't changed. "Nice sign you've got there." Julio had laughed when Cole told him how he wanted

Kate's Blooms to look, kind of feminine. "A chick sign," he'd told Julio.

Kate's blush softened the stubborn tilt of her chin. "Thanks for asking one of your guys to do this for me."

"One of the perks of being the boss." He watched a cloud pass over her face and wondered what he'd said.

Turning, she set the bag on the counter. Kate's eyes settled on Priscilla, nibbling on the green grass.

"Prissy. Didn't I warn you?" Cole snapped his fingers.

Prissy sat back on her haunches and tried to look innocent. *Just enjoying the late spring color, Cole.*

"My mother might be coming home pretty soon." The teasing light in Kate's eyes dimmed.

"Must be doing better. Glad to hear it."

"She's far from fully recovered. We don't have a restroom on the first floor, which makes it tricky. But I've been thinking…"

Cole knew that look. He'd seen it plenty in high school. Kate's ideas got feet pretty darn fast.

"You mentioned you're looking for someone to stay with Natalie." She licked her lips, and he dropped his gaze to the toes of his new boots. "What would you think of Mom keeping an eye on her this summer? Natalie could help Mom reach everything, stuff like that."

She had his full attention now. "That would sure solve a problem for me. You serious?"

"Of course. You like one of my ideas?" The surprise on her pretty face made him laugh.

She kicked the toe of one sneaker into the gravel. Kate had sure changed. What had caused this uncertainty? Her ex-husband? Cole's fists tightened. He'd like to punch the guy.

"Natalie will love our bookcase. Mom can't go down to the beach, of course, but I come home early. We can hit the beach then." Prissy wandered over, and Kate ran one hand down the dog's back.

How nuts was it to envy his own dog? Prissy closed her eyes under Kate's touch, and Cole totally understood. He'd do the same if given half a chance. "I appreciate your offer. Can I think about it?"

"Sure, but school's over in two weeks, Cole. You better have a plan."

The bossiness was back. "You always were a girl with a schedule. Funny what you forget."

"Sure is." Kate crossed her slim arms under her breasts.

He may have forgotten a lot, but what he remembered about her figure made his body temperature spike like mid-July. He'd been a bumbling senior that night, and nothing much had happened. That wouldn't be the case now.

"How do you and Marie get along?" Glancing up, Kate squinted against the morning sun.

He blew out a breath. "Takes some effort, but she doesn't have anyone else and Samantha hardly ever comes home from California. My mother-in-law's welcome in my home."

He saw the question in Kate's eyes. Knew what was coming and wanted to avoid it at all costs. He got tired of explaining

Samantha's situation. "Haven't been in your house in a long time. But as I remember it, you had a pantry that pretty much became a catch-all after your mom had those cupboards put up."

"I'm surprised you remember."

"Wouldn't take much to turn that pantry into a bathroom. I'd appreciate it if you'd let me do it. Then I'd feel that I was contributing something. You know your mom's never going to let me pay her for watching Natalie. She's like you. Stubborn."

Kate gave him a look, like he was gum on her shoe. "You're not getting the property, Cole Campbell. So don't go getting any ideas about sweet-talking my mother."

His gut clenched. "Good God, Kate. That's not what I intended at all."

Kate studied the pine trees behind them. "Sorry. My sister's left me a little sensitive when it comes to Breezy Point."

Cole wasn't used to seeing Kate so subdued. Like she carried bruises that didn't show. "Why don't I stop by soon? Take a look at it and we can get to work. A good bargain for both of us."

"You might not be telling me that by the end of the summer." Her smile was back. "I'll let you know if there are any problems."

He chuckled. "You always do."

In high school, Kate Kennedy had been a whirlwind — competent, sharp as a tack and good at everything. And she always spoke her mind. You knew where you stood with that girl. Now? He didn't know anymore.

"What's that supposed to mean?" Her hands captured her hips. Full hips, tiny waist.

He had to look up, focus on those eyes. "Nothing." Thank God she hadn't noticed the damp spot on the front of his jeans. "Everything. You were good at everything."

She heaved a sigh, like being competent was a big burden. "Okay, so maybe I was an overachiever."

"Nothing wrong with being capable."

"Capable. How exciting." She twined a length of hair tight around her finger.

"Looks like you and Mercedes are having a difference of opinion. That's all." He wanted to clear the air, as if diesel fumes billowed around them.

Her eyes studied his face, and he shifted. Kate could still make him feel restless. So many layers to this woman.

"My sister and I don't always see eye to eye," she admitted slowly, "but it's nothing we can't handle. I think it's safe to say we won't be giving up Breezy Point anytime soon."

He held both hands up flat. "Honest, I had no idea your family hadn't reached agreement about that property."

"And when we do, it will be my mother's decision."

"I understand totally." No way did he want to step in this pile of poop.

The sun was peeking over the tall trees on the back of the lot and hit her face just right. Prissy started sniffing Kate, pressing into areas that were definitely personal and off-limits.

"Priscilla!"

Prissy sighed and settled into the grass.

Crouching, Kate stroked Prissy's head. "You tell your boss to ease up," she murmured. That did it for the stupid dog. She closed her eyes and rolled over. Kate patted Prissy's tummy.

His skin tingled and Prissy sighed. *Kate's sure got great hands. Just thought I'd mention it.*

"It's not your fault, Cole." Glancing up, Kate pierced him with eyes like toothpicks. "Mercedes might have her reasons for wanting to sell the property, but Breezy Point belongs to my mother. Always has and the old house brings her comfort."

Suddenly, the day wasn't so fresh. The sun, not so bright. "Look, I'm not trying to sell your mom's house out from under her."

Kate didn't look convinced. Jumping up, she grabbed one of the large flats and began arranging the blue and red flowers. Prissy rolled back onto her stomach, sighing with contentment. "Guess I should get to work. Remind Natalie I'll be at the library tomorrow."

"Again, I appreciate you helping Natalie out with the books." Well, heck, might as well come clean. "With everything, actually. Natalie likes you, and Marie doesn't always have the most gentle touch."

"I understand. Thanks." She ran her hands down her jeans. He shrugged out of his jacket. The sun had returned, and man, it was hot.

The main door of the store rolled up with a rattle, and Ignacio waved to him.

"See you later." Cole escaped, Prissy trotting behind him. Ignacio was wearing jeans, but they sure didn't look as good as the ones on Kate.

Cole looked back. Just once.

Once to last him all day.

~~

Reshelving books at the library that Wednesday, Kate ended up jamming Robert Ludlum in with Charlotte Bronte. Where was her mind?

She knew where it was. And she couldn't snap out of it. Maybe she should give up and go home to Breezy Point. But would she just end up on the porch swing, thinking way too much about Cole? Hadn't she done enough of that in high school?

Besides, Natalie was coming in. Time to be a grown up. A role model.

Then Kate spied the book on human sexuality. Wasn't this the non-fiction favorite she and Sarah had spent hours giggling over as sophomores? They'd slide the illustrated book inside a geometry text, turning the pages slowly and studying positions as foreign as congruent angles.

So long ago. Seemed silly.

But the response of her body told her otherwise.

Images of Cole consumed her. The strong thighs in those jeans, the jacket across his broad shoulders. He wasn't some pretty boy who wouldn't get his hands dirty. No, Kate imagined Cole's hands were rough from work, rasping palms that could awaken all kinds of feeling in a woman. Her skin tingled and she tucked "Human Sexuality" back into the stacks.

This foolishness had to stop. Her cheeks burned. That morning at the flower stand, a customer had asked her what the velvety fuchsia flowers were. "C-c-cockscombs!" Kate had blurted out.

The woman's jaw dropped. She plunked the bouquet back into the tub of water as if the flowers were live firecrackers.

Sucking in a breath, Kate tried to explain. "Put them in the sun, and they'll plump out. I mean, grow. Very firm stems. They need to be kept warm and drained. That is, planted in soil that drains well."

Put a cork in it, girl. Tongue-tied and embarrassed, she'd pressed her hands to her thighs to get them to stop shaking.

The customer left with marigolds and geraniums — much safer, their needs simpler. Kate didn't know whether to laugh or cry.

Chili had roared when Kate shared the story. "*Chica*, you are coming into your own."

Now, what the heck did that mean? Had she been dull in high school?

When she found herself jamming a book by Ruth Rendell into fiction and not mysteries, Kate gave herself a good shake.

"Hi, Kate. I'm here."

She wheeled around to see Natalie's sweet face.

"Well, hello. So you made it."

"Uh-huh." Natalie wore a yellow sweatshirt today with her blue jeans instead of one of those exotic tops Marie seemed to favor.

"How did you like Ramona?" Beverly Cleary's heroine had always given Kate a lot of laughs.

"She's really bad, isn't she?" Natalie's eyes sparkled with mischief. Kate imagined the eight-year-old could be quite a handful for Cole and her grandmother.

"How about another Ramona book?"

"Okay. Sure." Natalie nodded.

After strolling into the middle school section, Kate scrutinized the popular series. "Ramona and Her Mother." She moved on. So much that Kate didn't know about that relationship. "How about 'Ramona and Her Father?'"

"Naw." To Kate's surprise, Natalie screwed up her face and plucked out another Cleary book. "Emily's Runaway Imagination" had a horse on the cover.

"You like horses?"

"Sure. I guess." Natalie hitched a skinny shoulder. Her gaze drifted back to "Ramona and Her Mother."

"I loved 'Misty of Chincoteague.'" Only took Kate a couple of minutes to find the gray soft-sided book.

The loveable brown and white pony on the cover brought a smile. "A pony! Aw, he's so cute."

"When I was your age, we all wanted a horse like Misty. I was always sketching ponies on my school papers."

"Did your parents get you one?" Natalie asked, her father's blue eyes blinking wider. Clearly the little girl thought all things were possible for Kate.

"Oh, no." Kate's throat tightened when she thought back to when she was Natalie's age. All those arguments filtering through closed doors. "My family didn't have the money."

"Me neither," Natalie said with resignation.

"You know, a stable just up the road offers riding. At least, I think it's still there. When I was old enough to babysit and had my own money, my dad would take me."

"Lucky duck. Sounds like fun. Does your dad live here too?"

Kate swallowed. "No, my dad's in heaven. He died a while back."

Natalie's warm palm on Kate's hand brought a lump to her throat. "Sorry, Kate."

"Thanks, sweetheart." Kate squeezed Natalie's hand and wondered if losing Samantha had brought this amazing maturity.

Then Natalie went back to leafing through "Misty." Growing up, Kate discovered books provided relief from problems she could never solve.

As she read, Natalie nibbled a fingernail. Kate felt the urge to correct her but ignored it. Cole's daughter seemed so fragile.

"Listen, I might not be volunteering here anymore, not for a while at least. The flower stall is taking way more time than I anticipated." Natalie looked so crushed that Kate hurried ahead. "But I'd still like to work with you and your reading. I mean, we have tons of books no one reads anymore."

"Can I borrow them sometime?" Natalie asked shyly.

"That's why I'm mentioning it."

Natalie beamed. "Great. Tell my dad, okay?"

"Absolutely." Cole could explain the summer plans.

Kate went back to shelving, and Natalie took her books to the front desk.

When it was time for Cole to pick up his daughter, Natalie waved good-bye and disappeared through the glass door. Kate held back. She didn't need one more glimpse of Cole to feed the fantasies that came way too frequently. She'd had the strangest dream last night and he'd played a starring role.

"So nice that she still enjoys printed books." Mildred stood at the door.

"Right." Kate wondered if Natalie had an electronic reader.

When six o'clock came, she helped Mildred close up. Then she climbed into Bonita and headed for the care center to discuss details for the summer.

Tiger lilies grew thick in the ditches along Red Arrow Highway—a good sign. Lately, they'd had just enough rain to coax the orange blooms open. They'd probably have plump blueberries in July. If spring was dry, the blueberries came in late, small and hard.

Traffic had picked up along the old highway, a sure sign that the Chicago people were back. Reaching the care center, she parked and jumped out. Harold sat rocking in his chair at the front door, Chicago Cubs cap on backwards.

"Evening, Kate."

"Evening, Harold. Like the new hat."

He grinned. Kate suspected he understood far more than he ever let on.

Kate found her mother in the dining room, finishing up her pot roast and mashed potatoes. "They give you so much food," her mother grumbled as she struggled to her feet. "Pretty soon I'll need bigger pants. Feel like one of those Christmas geese."

"That's a good problem to have." Kate held the walker while her mother found her balance.

"You're so late today."

"Went to the library after I closed up the flower stand."

"You always did like that library. Nose in a book all the time."

Mercedes was remembered for being a cheerleader, Kate for reading. How exciting.

Her mother flattened the collar of a knit top with wild aqua and pink flowers.

"New top?"

"Click. Click. I've got it down." Her mom made that practiced gesture with her left hand. "Need anything?"

"I've got enough clothes, Mom. Thank you. Thought we might go for little walk."

"Right, because I'm so good at that."

At least her mom could still joke. Matching her fumbling steps, Kate guided her to the side door leading to the gazebo. Outside, they headed for one of the benches under a huge maple tree. The sun was edging over the tall pines, casting long shadows.

"Have you given some thought to having Natalie spend time with you this summer at Breezy Point?"

Her mother sat back with a sigh, like a soldier who'd been in active duty too long. "Yes, of course she's welcome. If she needs a place to go." Pride wouldn't let her mother admit that she herself needed help.

"My flower stand is important, especially now that I don't have a steady job."

"So will you stay?" The eagerness in her mother's eyes took Kate by surprise.

"For the summer, at least. I don't know what I'm going to do come the end of August."

"No sense in those books going to waste," her mother finally said. Then she shrugged with a dismissive look at her right leg and the hand cradled in her lap. "And I suppose I could use some help."

Because Breezy Point had become a touchy subject, Kate had to tread carefully. "What would you think of having Cole put a bathroom in that old pantry? He has carpenters working for him and tells me he can get it installed in no time."

Her mother sucked in a breath. "Don't know if I can afford that, Kate."

"Would be a trade, Mom. In return for your companionship."

The faded eyes brightened. "Well, how nice. Does make sense. Am I going home soon?"

"So they tell me. You can't live here forever, now can you?"

Mom looked so relieved, like Kate was springing her from jail. "I do feel bad for Marie."

"Probably won't be long. We'll let Cole take care of that."

Chapter 16

Contentment swelled inside Kate like warm caramel as she drove home from the flower stand a few days later. Lavender dusted her fingers and she inhaled with a smile. Maybe all those articles were right. The scent of the purple herb was soothing. Offering herbs along with other perennials had been such a great idea. Filling their arms with dill, eucalyptus, and lemon balm, customers spouted suggestions for all kinds of maladies, physical and psychological.

Kate needed both. A weird jumpiness kept her from sleep. And when she finally did nod off, she dreamed she was falling from a cliff. What was that about?

Starting over was a good thing. Every bone in her body told her that. At first, she felt relieved after signing the divorce papers. That chapter of her life had closed. Kate had no hard feelings and wanted to keep it that way. Now she longed for a settled, predictable life with no loose ends.

Pines rustled overhead as she bumped down the road leading to the house. Branches brushed Bonita lightly, and she made a mental note to find her mother's clippers. If she didn't trim them, her beautiful SUV would have scratches.

Her ex-husband's voice played in her mind. "You'd ruin your car because you like the smell of some tree branches?" Brian would never understand.

She was finished with disapproval.

Cole's green truck sat next to a dumpster filled with split lengths of wood. Work on the new powder room must be moving right along.

Running fingers through her hair, she nipped her lips. Shouldn't he be gone by now? Josh she could deal with. Cole? No way.

A table saw was set up on the grass, sawdust mounded below it. She caught its fresh scent as she leaped out and popped the back hatch.

The cool, clear air had thickened, ripening in the June heat and starting to smell like summer. After grabbing a flat of bright pink geraniums, she set it under the peeling blue window boxes. She had so much work to do before her mom came home. She'd made headway with the damp leaves, but weeds were springing up everywhere. As for the house itself, peeling paint had become the norm. Breezy Point had to look cheerful and Kate's list grew.

Maybe Mercedes was right. Maybe this was too much. The house and grounds needed tending. The longest day of the year might be close, but it still wasn't light long enough for her to get everything done.

She'd eased up on her writing. Figured she'd written enough about cancer and COPD. To keep clients, she had to continually feed them copy. Freelancers don't take vacations. Maybe she'd pay for it later, but she needed a break. The flower stand brought a peace she hadn't felt in a long time.

Hollyhocks were springing up around Breezy Point, their

spindly stalks leaning against the white siding. Kate ran her fingers over a furry leaf before going inside. She'd forgotten how much she loved the double pink blossoms and couldn't wait to see them open in July.

Her back and arms ached from lifting flats and pots. As she stood on the back stoop, wondering when she'd get time to paint, weed, and plant, the screen door squeaked open.

"Thought I heard somebody back here." The sun streaming through the birches dappled Cole's smile.

"Hey." The word stuck in her throat. A gray T-shirt clung to a torso that must turn a lot of heads in Gull Harbor. The sweaty red bandana around his forehead wasn't a bad look.

"Glad you're taking care of the place." Kate tore her eyes from the biceps he'd never had in high school. "I'll check the silver later."

"The lady of the house told me where to find the key." His eyes danced with mischief, like Cole knew he was eye candy.

The heat streaming through her body in warm rivulets chilled. She'd had enough of self-absorbed men. Elbowing Brian for mirror time in the mornings had gotten old.

"Glad you're home." Cole swung the door wide and stepped back so she could pass. The man had manners. "I know we talked about the plumbing part of it, but I want to just make sure before I started laying pipe."

Sure. Right. Kate couldn't even look at him as she slid past. On Cole, even sweat smelled good. The annoying liquid heat returned, washing away common sense.

They were quite a pair. Sweaty and dirty. And thinking dirty too. Or was it just her?

Time to regroup. She had to remind herself Cole had plans to change Gull Harbor into one of those cardboard kitschy beach towns she hated. Their vintage storefronts would be replaced by cinderblock buildings with huge windows that displayed boogie boards, seashell curtains, and a slew of printed T-shirts.

Reason slammed her heat like a bucket of ice. The yellow flyers sat in the back of the SUV, but she hadn't distributed them yet. Just no time.

In the kitchen, the clean scent of wood cleared her head, but she was still swimming through a sea of testosterone. Pretty darn intoxicating and very different from Brian, who'd splashed on expensive cologne after his shower. She couldn't pass through the men's department in any store without cringing at that heavy smell.

Nuzzling Kate's hand with her wet nose, Prissy greeted her with a sloppy kiss.

"Prissy. You visiting too?"

The Great Dane's wiry tail smacked the counters with enthusiasm.

Natalie was right behind the dog. "Hi, Kate."

"Like your hair." Kate tugged one of the scraggly pigtails while Natalie beamed.

Cole shuffled his feet. "Hope you don't mind, Kate. But I had no place—"

"Not at all. Great way to get familiar with the place. My mother is looking forward to spending time with Natalie this summer."

Kate watched the girl's tentative smile widen.

Hands on his hips, Cole drank in his daughter like she was water and he was in the desert. Maybe that's how it was for a single dad raising a girl. Kate still didn't know the whole story about Samantha. For a town that held no secrets, Samantha McGraw's story remained hush-hush. She was in California, as Cole had told her. Even Mercedes knew nothing more than that and they'd been cheerleaders together.

"Samantha dropped off the face of the earth," she'd told Kate over the Memorial weekend. "Cole knows the story. I don't have time to keep up with the townies."

But Cole wasn't talking and Kate didn't want to pry. Whatever the situation, Natalie had a dad who cared. He may not understand Natalie, but he clearly adored her.

The longing that twisted inside her took Kate by surprise. After all their planning, Brian's abrupt decision not to have children had blindsided her. Sure, they'd agreed to wait. Get their careers on track. His surprise announcement turned their partnership into a betrayal. The searing ache brought one hand to Kate's chest. Pressing against her heart did no good.

"Hey, Kate, what is it?" Cole pivoted her to face him, hands warm on her shoulders.

She kept her eyes on his shirt. "Nothing. Indigestion, I guess."

"What did you do, girl? Eat one of those hot dogs at the Swirly Top? They haven't gotten any better."

Memories tweaked her grin. What plans did Cole have for the icon where they'd spent so many days? Would the Swirly Top fall to the wrecking ball along with Michiana Thyme? The smile melted from her face.

Cole loosened his hold, and a different type of regret washed over her, bothersome because she couldn't label it.

"Natalie, I won't be finished here for a while, honey. Why don't you…" Cole looked lost.

"Right this way to entertainment central." Kate steered Natalie into the living room. "I'll show you how to work the remote."

But she'd underestimated Natalie. Taking the remote, Natalie clicked a few buttons and settled into one of the faded awning-striped chairs. The blue denim sofa dipped in the middle but that didn't bother Prissy. She climbed right up and settled her long limbs with an audible groan. Dislodging her seemed useless so Kate didn't try.

What about Prissy? Would she be a package deal with Natalie that summer? The dog seemed to follow Cole everywhere.

Intent on the menu scrolling on the TV, Natalie finally settled on a sci-fi show. Spaceships hummed and planets were exploding when Kate returned to the kitchen. Cole stood deep in thought at the pantry door. That manly leather tool belt low slung on his hips brought a shimmy to her stomach. Brian had worked with his mind, not his hands. The change was refreshing.

"Could I show you something, Kate?"

She tried to ignore the way his muscles flexed when Cole motioned to her. Clamping down on the feelings rioting through her body, she slipped in next to him. Even without the shelves, the pantry felt tight. That's the only reason Kate leaned in so close,

close enough to feel the warmth of Cole's minty breath, see the dark bristles brushed across his jawline. So darn hard to keep her mind on rerouting the pipes through the wall.

Dragging one hand through her tangled hair, Kate wished she'd brushed it. With Josh gone for the day, they were alone, just the two of them. Natalie's laughter filtered from the front room while Cole advised her on the toilet placement. He could put the darn thing on the ceiling for all she cared.

When he rotated to face the window, his chest brushed her breasts.

Lord have mercy.

He didn't even blink. "Thought I'd put some shutters on this window. You'll want privacy, or your mother will. Some lighting on either side of the mirror for whatever women do in a powder room."

"Powder our noses."

Cole's nose was strong, with a determined angle.

His eyes fell from her nose to her lips. She moistened them with her tongue, just a reflex. He swallowed then shook himself, eyes focusing on her hair. "So, why'd you change the color?"

"Just a whim. You don't like it?"

"Hmm. Yeah, blonde's good, I guess. Don't be offended or anything but your hair always reminded me of my baseball mitt."

"What?" She didn't mean to squawk.

"Forget it." Cole gave his head a shake. "Well, I… Where was I?"

Kate gulped down a chuckle. "You were talking about the

lighting next to the mirror."

"Yeah. Right." His lips squinched to one side like he was laughing at himself. "Room needs some light. Fine for a pantry but not a bathroom."

"This room was always so dark." Kate's playfulness flattened. Suddenly, she was nine again, when arguing parents were terrifying.

"Hey, are you okay?" Cole's hands gripped her shoulders. "Kate?" He lifted her chin with one finger, his face blurring as she blinked back tears.

"Gosh, I'm… I'm sorry, Cole. Long day, I guess." Her voice trembled, and she swiped at her cheeks. *Really?* "So silly. So long ago."

"Kate? Probably none of my business but…"

Had she ever seen this kind of concern in Brian's eyes? Tears pooled, and the room felt like it was shrinking. Heat jettisoned off Cole's body in waves. Or was she generating it? She felt that one finger on her chin in every nerve ending in her body. When his thumb stroked her skin, she shivered. Cole looked at his hand like it was some foreign object. Then he dropped it to his waist, and she felt the loss.

"I used to hide in here."

Cole's lips had looked luscious until the frown found his mouth. "Hide? Were you playing games?"

She jerked, trying to shake off the past. "Trust me, it wasn't fun. Not with my folks fighting in the kitchen. Again."

There, it was out.

His breath escaped in a hiss. "No. No, that wouldn't be fun at all."

His shoulders twitched like he was going to hug her. She imagined sinking into his warmth, feeling that soft gray cotton against her cheek, his heart thudding in a comforting rhythm. But Cole tucked his hands under his folded arms, like he was locking them in. In the distance, the TV blared and Natalie giggled.

"Gee, Kate. I'm so sorry." His eyes drew her in, so receptive.

"Years of arguing about the drinking and then the silence. That was how I learned they were getting a divorce." She squared her shoulders. Anything to get that expression off his face.

"Katydid, I never knew." His arms came around her.

At first she stiffened, but it felt so good. She softened like the silly putty she played with eons ago, melting her curves against his hard angles. Cole's lips pressed to her forehead, and she squeezed her eyes shut.

"Don't, Kate. Don't go back there. We all should have a magic switch to turn off the past."

What would he want to forget?

"Yeah, I could use one of those. Even after the divorce my dad never quit drinking. It killed him when I was a senior in college. Car accident when he shouldn't have been driving. Sometimes I wonder if that's why I settled on my husband so quickly."

"Aw, Katydid. What a tough way to lose a parent."

She shouldn't nestle closer. She shouldn't drink in his clean scent, more calming than lavender. Their thighs were aligned along with the rest of their bodies. Her body was giving her the green light, while her mind flashed red warning signals. She ignored them.

Apparently you don't have to be swathed in black lace to feel like a trollop. Cole tightened his grip, his lips kissing her forehead, a soft moan vibrating in his chest. In the distance, the TV blared and Natalie told Prissy to calm down.

"What are we doing?"

He didn't seem to hear her whispered words, and she didn't want him to stop.

"Cole?" She looked up just as his eyes fluttered closed. His lips settled and took possession, like a good book where you head straight for your favorite dog-earred parts and heck with the rest. He tasted her slowly, tender skin clinging a bit until he licked it for release. Might as well have been a snake bite, that flick of his tongue. She'd been bitten. Leaving common sense behind, she pressed her body against his so they could fit like puzzle pieces. Well, part of the puzzle, at least. She sighed as he kissed her cheeks, moaned when he tasted her neck with his tongue.

Comfort kisses. That's what she told herself.

"God, you're delicious." His voice was rough, just enough to make her want friction in other places.

She'd gone way too long without sex. Good sex, that is. The kind where you both cared and it mattered.

Head spinning, chest heaving, Kate knew she should break away. She should check on Natalie, although she could still hear her laughing in the distance. She should be ashamed for moving her body against his with a slow, sinuous pressure. Suppressed needs had made her wanton.

This time, she wouldn't take Cole seriously.

This time, she'd be in control.

He groaned against her lips. "Oh, Katydid, we should stop."

"Sure. Go ahead. Stop." Kate pressed closer, rubbing, teasing, lapping up his frustrated growls while she kissed him.

Cole's thumbs skimmed her rib cage, brushing under her soft knit top before scooping down over hip bones that wouldn't hold still. Good grief, it was hot in here. Maybe they should put in a ceiling fan, although she doubted her mother would need one.

With every kiss, every fevered caress, Kate burned through bad memories, reducing them to cinders. And she loved it. Needed it.

Her chuckle came naturally.

"What?" Cole pulled away, a bemused grin tilting his lips.

"What is that cool wetness?" she whispered, patting her upper thigh. My, he must be really excited. His jeans should really absorb better.

"What wetness?" He backed away.

They both looked down. Prissy had joined them, tongue lolling from her panting mouth.

Okay, so Cole hadn't been that needy.

But she wanted him to be.

"Hey, Prissy." Cole patted the dog's head. "Gotta go out, girl?"

The huge Harlequin Dane gave a pathetic whine. Maybe Cole had that effect on all females.

"Beautiful dog." Kate tugged on her shirt and told herself this was a good thing. After all, Natalie was in the front room and this was Cole. She had to collect her thoughts. Her hair was damp along with a few other parts of her body.

Order returned to her life, wagging a warning finger.

Cole whistled, and the dog followed him outside. She didn't much care where the dog did her business. Right now Kate had more serious concerns. Heck, they were right back in Cole's father's pickup truck after that debate competition, parked down near Waco Beach. She brushed both hands up her arms to still the goose bumps.

When he came back in, Cole brought the fresh air with him. Kate was staring out the back window at her father's old tool shed, where her mother now kept the gardening tools.

"Kate, hope I didn't make you uncomfortable."

Was that regret in his eyes? She flicked a tongue over her throbbing lips. The Adam's apple in his strong throat bobbed. Uncomfortable? That was putting it mildly.

Every cell still tingled, screaming *Just one more time* and leaning in his direction.

"Cole, I…"

"Kate?" They both turned with relief at Natalie's voice. She was holding up a book. "You have your very own copy of 'Misty.'" Wonder lifted her voice.

"Sure do. The book was a present."

Mercedes had gotten it for her birthday at a party her parents couldn't afford. "Kid's stuff!" her big sister had said, setting the book aside to study a makeup kit Samantha had given her. Kate had grabbed the book gratefully. Read it by flashlight under the sheets that night.

"Just remember where you got that, Natalie." Cole glanced at his watch. Outside, shadows were gathering under the trees. "We should get going."

"Sorry to keep you. Thanks for all your help, Cole." She was edging him toward the door, as if he were just another contractor, not the man who drove her wild five minutes earlier. Thank goodness Natalie was buried in the book. She didn't seem to notice the sexual tension that hummed in the air like an overtuned guitar.

After throwing some of his tools into a work chest under the kitchen table, Cole snapped the metal lid shut and lifted it. His bicep bulged larger. "We'll be back tomorrow."

"You know where the key is." No way was she coming home until he was gone. Still, she followed him out to the truck, drinking in the cool night air. Maybe the chill would slap some sense into her.

Cole put his tool chest in the back and opened the passenger door. One long leap and Prissy landed in the middle of the front seat with Natalie tucking right behind her.

"Thanks for everything," she told him. Kate's lips still pulsed and she bit down.

"Don't worry, Kate. We'll be finished by the time your mom is home." He circled the back of the pickup.

Would they ever be finished? Really?

They weren't the same people now. Their different feelings about the future of Gull Harbor told her that. As the pickup disappeared down the driveway, Natalie smiled from the window, with Prissy's head crowding her for space. Kate backed up onto the stoop and waved good-bye. "Damn fool."

Was she talking about him or herself?

Going back inside, Kate slammed the door behind her. The kitchen still smelled like wood shavings, but it also smelled like Cole. She pulled the refrigerator open and let the cold blast hit her. A chicken breast left over from the night before sat wrapped in foil next to a bowl of hard-boiled eggs. She grabbed the package and an egg before slamming the door closed. Night was falling, and she really needed a sunset.

Preoccupied, she ate without ceremony on the porch that night before heading down to the beach.

A breeze wafted up from the lake as she made her way down. Her father had put in these railroad ties long ago. Like a lot of the other work he'd done around Breezy Point, the steps were crooked. Any project was always accompanied by a six-pack or two.

When she reached the bottom, Kate kicked her tennis shoes into the tall dune grass and stripped off her socks. The sand felt cool against the soles of her feet as she walked toward the shore. In another month or so, it would take hours for the sand to lose its heat after sunset. In June, sand had a short memory.

Kate wished she had a short memory. High school came flooding back, but this wasn't high school. The casual makeout sessions after a debate victory didn't compare one bit to this afternoon.

She wanted Cole. Wanted him in the worst way.

Unleashed longings battered the common sense she'd pulled around her like a shield.

At the edge of the water, Kate squished her toes into the damp sand. She loved this time of day. Clouds streaked the night sky in elongated puffs of white, like pulled taffy against the rosy glow of the setting sun. Families had packed up and retreated to the cottages for dinner. The shoreline was packed solid and smooth underfoot. Although Kate wasn't a runner, she broke into a rough jog. Tiny stones along the shore bit into her feet, but she didn't edge away. No, she accepted the discomfort, wanting to forget the feel of Cole's lips, the muscled arms and questioning depths of his eyes.

She ran until she had no breath. Gasping, she stopped and bent over, clutching the stitch in her side.

Maybe she was out of shape, physically and emotionally.

Cole Campbell? She needed all her defenses in place. Today, she'd let them down. Revealed more than she'd ever shared with anyone.

Vulnerability wasn't her style.

She'd come home to help her mother and, if she were honest, to recover from the divorce. Gull Harbor was just what she needed. Cole? She didn't want to need him.

Chapter 17

"Come on in." Carolyn met Kate at the door of her cozy bungalow. Crickets sang in the hydrangea bushes below the open railing of a wide porch.

"Love your house, especially this porch," she told Carolyn as they lingered in the open doorway, summer soft in the air. Supported on thick, knotty vines, deep purple blossoms arched over the porch. "Takes so long for a clematis to get that big. What a great place to curl up with a book."

"I often do." Carolyn's quiet smile lit up her blue eyes. "Thought we might sit out here but the mosquitoes can be vicious."

Kate slapped at one buzzing in her hair.

"I'm going to spray in case we want to come out later." Carolyn grabbed an aerosol can from a side table.

Kate scurried inside, where wicker chairs flanked a worn brown leather sofa and earth tone cushions were heaped on the floor. A round coffee table held a cheese tray and a plate of cookies.

"Oh, wow." Kate sank onto the soft leather couch and looked around. From the brick fireplace to the braided rugs on the floor, the house felt homey. "Talk about comfortable."

Carolyn made a face. "I'm probably only about three blocks

from the wrecking ball."

A chill skittered down Kate's spine. Never going to happen to Breezy Point. Not if she could help it.

Phoebe and Chili arrived, bringing Mandy Klavis with them. A pretty blonde, Mandy had been in their class, but Kate hadn't known her well. But she sure knew the Klavis family bakery, famous for their onion rolls and raspberry kolaches.

"You're the girl who dated that hot quarterback, right?" Kate asked.

A quick blush accented Mandy's high cheekbones. "Yes."

"Kevin Corbin? Could we give the guy a name?" Sarah chortled. "Mandy came back last summer, and she's still dating Kevin. In fact, he does some work for Cole."

Cole. Her face felt plunged into an oven. Grabbing a Dolly Madison bar from the plate, Kate took a hearty bite. Never one to resist chocolate chips and coconut, she'd diet tomorrow.

"And how is your flower store coming?" Sarah asked over a cup of hazelnut decaf.

Kate swallowed her mouthful and laughed. "More three eight-foot tables than a store."

Chili shushed her, waving her mug of tea. "Kate's doing great. Aren't we *loco* busy?"

"Busier than I ever expected," Kate admitted. "Had to close up shop early yesterday. Stock ran out again. I'm looking for another supplier for shrubbery."

"You go, girl!" Phoebe pumped a fist.

Chili's dark eyes snapped. "The flowers catch people's attention, closer to the road."

Kate wanted to hug her old friend. "What would I do without you and Ignacio?"

"And Cole." Chili's eyes sparked with mischief.

Opening her mouth to reply, Kate took another bite instead. Best to fill her mouth with chocolate than get into a tussle with Chili about Cole. Cleary Chili and Ignacio adored their contractor.

A knock came at the door. Kate was relieved when the attention shifted to Diana, swirling into the room in a long blue gypsy skirt. The scent of patchouli settled over the room.

"Sorry I'm late. Chicago customer on a buying spree. I wasn't about to tell her I was closing." Diana sat down in the rocker.

"Everyone have a great Memorial Day?" Sarah asked.

"Good crowd at the nursing home," Kate quipped. "Family picnic."

Sarah's eyes softened. "When will your mom be coming home?"

"Soon as she can get around better. We're making some changes, er, in the house…" Kate stuttered to a halt. Damn. Anxiety riddled her just thinking about that pantry. Those crazy kisses had unleashed a yearning that kept her awake at night. She'd been hanging around the care center in the late afternoon to avoid running into Cole at Breezy Point. Her mom even complained about her extended visits.

"Don't you have things to do at home, Kate?" her mother had asked in a querulous tone. "I don't want to find things in a shambles."

She had a point, but four o'clock was still too early for Kate to go home. Instead she drove up to St. Joe, a town a little farther north on the lake. Relaxing with a chai latte on a bench overlooking the harbor, she soaked in the sun and the broad expanse of Lake Michigan. But the soft breeze on her skin only reminded her of Cole's touch, the warmth in his eyes when she'd told him about hiding in that pantry while her parents' marriage fell apart.

"So your mom's coming home soon? Are you putting in ramps? That kind of thing?" Phoebe's questions brought Kate back to her book group.

"She's using a walker now, but we're converting an old pantry into a bathroom. That's critical." Her matter-of-fact tone didn't soothe the annoying ripples in her tummy that threatened to slide lower.

"Who's doing the work?" Sarah asked, oh, so casually.

Kate gave her friend the fish eye, not that it made a difference.

"Cole." The name unexpectedly softened on Kate's tongue. Expressions shifted in the group. "Well, Cole and Josh, his carpenter." Josh seemed to disappear mysteriously whenever Kate entered the house.

"Ah, huh." Sarah exchanged a look with Chili.

Had the two been talking? Probably. That was the thing about small towns. People talked. Kate grabbed another Dolly Madison bar. With her mouth full, she wouldn't be able to stick another foot in it.

"That first floor bathroom will be a big help," Mandy said. "My own mom fell from the roof and broke a leg. The first few days home, she slept on the sofa bed."

"That will probably be the case at our house too, at least for a while." Kate also hoped Mercedes would come to her senses about selling Breezy Point. Just one more battle she didn't feel like fighting.

And then there was Cole. She wished he'd stay away.

But that hope tasted like tin on her tongue.

"Everything will work out." Sarah picked up her copy of "Water for Elephants." Time to get down to discussion.

"How is Jamie?" Carolyn asked Sarah quietly.

Sarah's grip tightened on the book. She did such a good job of hiding her emotions. "We try to Skype on Sundays. Depends on his schedule." Sounded like they were talking about a man who worked at Target, not Afghanistan. Sarah wouldn't want anyone to worry.

"That man, he will be home before you know it." Chili reached over and squeezed Sarah's knee.

Sarah wrapped her fingers around Chili's hand and hung on.

"Why don't we get into the story?" Carolyn opened her book, and Kate smiled to see the multi-colored post-it notes. Yep, Carolyn was a teacher all right.

The discussion was lively that night. Kate felt relieved to dip back into the problems of that earlier era. For a while, they talked about the circus world depicted in the novel. Of course, there was a love story between Jacob, the man who might have been a veterinarian if his parents hadn't died, and Marlena, who was married to the wrong man.

"There's a lot of that going around," Kate mumbled. The words were out, and she could have kicked herself.

"You never mention your ex-husband." Sarah's eyes turned thoughtful. "Brian, right?"

"Might be a reason for that."

"If you don't want to talk about it…" Chili threw an admonishing glance in Sarah's direction.

But Kate had to get comfortable with this divorce. "No, that's okay. I signed the papers. Made it official." Outside, night had fallen and they sat in semi-darkness. This circle of new and old friends felt safe.

"It gets easier," Phoebe piped up.

"Does it?" Kate sure hoped so.

With the hitch of her head, Phoebe added, "A little. With time."

Kate wanted details, wanted assurance. She sure wasn't going to get that from her sister or mother. Her mother never talked about her divorce, as if her husband were still asleep in the room upstairs. "How long have you been divorced, Phoebe?"

"Two years. Past year was easier than the first. Only sometimes, sure, I wish I had someone to be there when I get home. The salon helps."

Kate didn't know Phoebe at all, but tonight, Phoebe didn't look quite as self-reliant as she had come across earlier.

"Don't we have to be our own resource sometimes?" Diana sounded like she was still figuring this out.

Kate knew little about Diana, only that she'd arrived and opened Hippy Chick in Gull Harbor six years ago. Apparently, the shop made it through the punishing winters and that was saying something.

And Diana had dated Cole. That was a story Kate wanted to hear more about.

"How about some wine? Let's turn the lights on. We're all sitting here in the dark." Carolyn leapt up.

Sarah snapped on two brass floor lamps, and Chili leaned over to the pottery table lamp. The bright light dispelled the uneasy mood that had crept into the room.

They trouped into Carolyn's kitchen where their hostess grabbed a box of wine from her refrigerator. A wine connoisseur, Brian would have turned up his nose at boxed wine, but Brian wasn't with her, not anymore. Tonight, that freedom felt wonderful.

"Can I help with glasses?" Kate asked Carolyn.

"To the left of the stove."

As Carolyn poured, Kate glanced at the quotes posted around the room.

"How cute is this?" Diana plucked a heart magnet from the refrigerator. "'Set true love free.'"

Carolyn blushed. "Should we go back into the living room and relax or sit out on the porch?"

"Porch!" the group said with one voice.

Wine glasses in hand, they trouped outside, taking seats on the wicker swing or metal lawn chairs. Carolyn passed out pillows from the living room. The night air remained pleasantly warm. Summer heat had blazed through the cool spring. No sweaters needed, not anymore.

"Here's to summer!" Sarah raised her wine glass.

"Here's to Ignacio's Produce!" Chili's voice rang out strong.

"Here's to Kate's Blooms!" Carolyn nodded in Kate's direction.

"You saw my sign?" Kate felt flattered.

Carolyn merely smiled. "I'll be stopping by. That's a promise."

"Here's to being single," Phoebe said, like she was reminding herself.

"Single!" Phoebe, Carolyn, and Kate roared. Laughing and giggling, they felt like a group of trusted friends and it was summer.

Diana swirled the wine in her glass and lifted it. "Here's to our other businesses!"

"How could we forget, Diana?" Sarah always had a quick save. "Here's to Hippy Chick and The Full Cup."

The recession still lingered. Although there were talks of the housing market picking up, business wasn't booming. On weekends, vacationers crowded the narrow sidewalks of Gull Harbor. Still, For Sale signs were planted in front of homes on the sandy roads that led to the lake.

"A toast for the Chicago people. May they continue to come in droves and may they all need a good hair stylist!" Phoebe said with a raucous laugh.

"To customers who linger," Diana added.

Kate looked down at her worn jeans and pink hoodie with the faded Saugatuck scrawled on it. She could use some new clothes and might just stop at the shop. She'd like to get to know Diana better.

Sarah looked around the group. "What should we read for next time?"

"How about one of the older books?" Carolyn offered. "Like maybe something by Hemingway or Fitzgerald?"

"You just want to get a jump on your lesson plans for next year," Phoebe teased with a wave of her wine glass.

Carolyn laughed along with them.

"Sometimes old favorites are the best." Kate thought back to how pleased Natalie had been to discover "Misty."

"What about a compromise?" Carolyn suggested. "'The Paris Wife' is about Hemingway's first wife, Hadley Richardson. Paris in the 20s. What could be more fun?"

"Paris, huh?" Diana looked as if she wanted to leave tomorrow. "Sounds good to me."

"Want to meet at my house?" Kate was horrified to hear herself offering. Breezy Point was sadly in need of attention, but at least the bathroom would be finished. No need to trek to the second floor and the dated wallpaper.

"Your place is right on the beach." Sarah jumped in before Kate had time to reconsider. "Should we bring our bathing suits? The lake should be warm by July, right?"

"Absolutely. We could even discuss on the beach." Kate warmed to the idea. That way, if her mother still couldn't climb to the second floor, they wouldn't be bothering her.

The girls were all for it. Everyone drifted out to their cars, their good-byes lingering on the night air.

As she drove to Breezy Point, Kate felt content. At first she'd felt like a visitor in Gull Harbor. Not anymore. When she reached home, she didn't go straight inside. The sleepy summer waves lapping at the shoreline below called to her. Instead of going down to the beach, she sat on the top stair, knees pulled up to her chin.

The summer moon cut a path across the water.

The moments with Cole in the pantry rewound in her mind, like a movie on an eternal loop. Would she do anything different?

Well, maybe a thing or two.

The very thought made her restless.

And where did they go from here? In the heat of the moment, had she kissed the boy she used to know or the man Cole had become?

The man who might have plans to change Gull Harbor forever.

Chapter 18

The night before her mother came home, Kate dusted and vacuumed like crazy. Her mom had always been a neat freak. Growing up, Kate and Mercedes were assigned Saturday chores until they took summer jobs in town. Their house always smelled of vinegar, which was used to clean everything, from the windows to the floors. "Keep your house just like you keep your mind. Orderly and neat. Everything has its place," their mom told them.

But that was in the past. Now her colorful new clothes were jammed into drawers or hung lopsided on hangers. Would any of that change when she returned home?

Grabbing the scatter rugs, Kate gave them a good shake outside. The night air felt crisp and cool. Overhead, a million stars pierced the dark sky. Deep in the woods, an owl hooted in round, lonely notes. Down below, the lake sounded restless, waves slapping the shore with a syncopated rhythm.

Or maybe Kate was the one who felt riled up. Dr. Kumar at the care center had warned that her mother would be different now. No surprise. That much was already clear. "The stroke might change your mother's behavior."

Her mom had been so reliable in her routines and habits. Still, the bright clothing and jewelry gave Kate a kick. Alice Kennedy was enjoying herself and high time. Along with her new clothes, her personality had changed. Now the two of them fell easily into casual conversations. They talked about the news—who was divorcing whom in Hollywood or what star had a new baby. Her mother talked about the president, although Kate was never sure which president was under discussion. Details sometimes blurred in her mother's conversations. Still, those talks together felt precious.

Before, Mercedes had been her mother's confidante. Since the falling out over the house, their relationship now was strained. Time would heal that. Meanwhile, Kate enjoyed a piece of her mother she'd never had before.

Folding the rugs over one arm, Kate went back inside, the screen door whapping shut behind her. While she positioned the rugs on the floor, she realized she only wanted parts of the old mom back. Some of the changes? She welcomed them.

Glancing around, Kate felt Breezy Point was as ready as it could be. The new downstairs bathroom sat pristine and perfect, the smell of fresh paint lingering. Cole thought it could use another coat. Thinking about him in this bathroom brought a rush of heat. Her lips plumped, and her body sprang to life. She stumbled from the room, sucking in the smell of that morning's bacon lingering in the air, just as rich and dangerous as Cole's kisses.

From now on, she'd take the stairs to the upstairs bathroom. Good for her thighs, or so she'd read.

Mercedes called three times that night, her sister's way of making up for not being there. "How are things with you?" Kate asked at the end of the last call.

Silence filled Kate's mind with questions. "Mercedes? Are you still there?"

"Yes, I'm here. Not any better, Kate, to tell the truth."

What comfort could she offer her older sister, who always had her life under control? "Things will get better. They always do for you."

"Really? Guess there's a first time for everything."

"I'm sorry, Mercedes."

Her sister sighed. "I know. Have to run. I'm on deadline."

Usually Mercedes' staff was on deadline, not her. Kate rubbed her thumb over the face of the phone.

Sometime around midnight she fell into bed, muscles sore and hands chapped. The smell of cleaning products followed her into her dreams. One good thing about Brian—he'd always insisted they have a cleaning lady. But she didn't dream about buckets, mops or dust rags that night. Instead, Cole and his gentle hands filled her dreams. And what he did with those hands jerked her from sleep, heart thudding like crazy. Staggering out of bed, she threw the windows open wider. The cool fresh air cleared her head, but she couldn't get back to sleep. Finally, she dressed and drove to the vegetable stand early when the sky was still pearly grey. She would pick her mom up right before noon.

Of course, that worked out to be the first day the supplier delivered a huge load of evergreen bushes and perennials. Pots of hydrangeas, forsythia and phlox joined the marigolds and geraniums. Kate needed it, all of it. That was the good part. People were snapping up the shrubs like the popcorn Chili provided free inside.

"I wish I could stay out here and help you," Chili told her, eyes wide and anxious. When she saw the truck, she had rushed out, thinking it might be another delivery for Ignacio. "But it's crazy inside."

"Don't worry. I can manage." Kate pulled her new wide-brimmed straw hat over her face. Sun and Sail had a midseason special on hats, and Kate bought one to protect her skin when she worked at the flower stall. She was already sweating buckets. Mostly nerves, she figured. Ignacio suggested that Kate post a sign directing customers inside to pay when she wasn't there.

Cars prowled the crowded parking lot that had seemed huge a month ago. Some shoppers ended up lining Red Arrow Highway. Downright amazing.

"Guess I better get back." With a wave of her hand, Chili rushed back inside, her ruffled orange top fluttering in the breeze.

The air felt thick with flower pollen and greenery, a reminder of how much Kate had to do this morning. Bending, she began to shove the pots into some sort of order. *One day at a time, one hour at a time.* Kate just couldn't let herself get crazy. That's how that incident in the bathroom had happened. She'd been rushed that day, mindless when she'd ended up in close quarters with Cole. After months of preparing for her divorce, checking each box, suddenly she felt like a kite bobbing high in the spring gusts.

The day before, she'd arrived home at five thirty to find Cole still at Breezy Point. He'd stopped in to install the knobs on the cabinets and drawers, or so he said. What? Josh couldn't do this? But she said nothing, nodding as he leaned against the counter and talked about the aluminum wiring that needed replacing throughout the house. She offered coffee and had been alarmed when he accepted. In the living room, Natalie watched cartoons with Prissy sprawled next to her on the couch. Cole and Kate sipped from their mugs, making small talk.

Did she really know who Cole was? Sure, they'd gone to high school together. Sort of had a history. But that was years ago. Who was he now and what had happened to his marriage that sent Samantha to California, far from her family and friends?

Common sense questions chattered in her head while she battled wild urges every time she got near him. Scared the heck out of her. Gull Harbor was a small town. She couldn't ignore him forever so she'd have to set limits. Get comfortable with him. Comfortable but not cozy. Definitely not as cozy as they'd gotten that night in high school, which she'd apparently blown way out of proportion.

Maybe men didn't have the same kind of memory as women. But could she ever forget? After their heated session on the beach following their victory over La Porte, she could still feel the shocked disappointment when she heard he was going to the prom with Samantha McGraw. Sure, Kate was only a sophomore but she had expectations after that night.

To make matters worse, Kate learned Samantha looked gorgeous at the dance. The white satin band along the neckline of her long black gown accented her cleavage. Samantha had a lot of that. "Like she pointed a flashlight." Mercedes had sounded ticked off. Kate's sister didn't like to be upstaged, even by a sister cheerleader. The yearbook later confirmed Mercedes' description. Beaming, Samantha clung to Cole's arm, looking as if she'd stepped from a magazine. They made quite the couple.

Never had Kate felt so much like the ugly duckling. Dependable on the debate team, overlooked as a possible date.

When Cole graduated and left Gull Harbor, Kate set out to forget the boy she'd adored as long as she could remember. By the time she left for college in Boston, Cole was just an embarrassing memory she was glad to leave behind. College got busy, and eventually she moved on to Brian Bankoff, the man who was "perfect for her."

Lost in her daydreams, Kate didn't notice Cole pull up to the flower stand in his truck. Before she knew it, Prissy was nuzzling her hand and Cole was helping arrange the heavier bushes. Didn't the man have his own work to do?

"Good stock here," he commented with a brief nod.

"The resource Ignacio gave me turned out pretty well."

"Powder room drawers working okay?"

"Perfect." She hadn't even tried them.

"Good choice of color, that apple green." His gaze landed on her face.

"Thank you." She shifted, but his blue eyes didn't lose hold of her lips. Kate would swear she felt them swell.

"Ah, couldn't help but notice that your kitchen needs some paint."

"Yeah, you mentioned that."

"I did?" His forehead wrinkled.

First he wanted to buy the place. Now he wanted to paint it?

"I can do that myself," she was quick to offer. Her shoulders still ached from her housework the night before.

"Josh is over there right now."

"Why?" Was she tired of this invasion of her privacy or just nervous about having Cole around?

"Thought the medicine chest needed an adjustment."

She couldn't be rude to him. She just could not. "That's really kind of you, Cole." He'd always been that way, good with details. The kind of boy who cut his parents' lawn and then trimmed the edges. "But I think that'll be enough for now."

Cole tapped his keys against one palm.

"Well, I don't want to keep you." She turned to the flats of purple and white alyssum Prissy was sniffing with appreciation. A couple was headed toward the booth.

"Come on, Prissy. Time to go." Cole's eyes went to her hat. "Like the look."

"Thanks." She tried to ignore the crazy spiraling of her stomach.

Cole backed away, tripping on a flat of geraniums. A flush burned his cheeks, and she chuckled while he stopped to push the geraniums aside.

"You have these hydrangeas in purple?" a woman asked, a designer bag slung over one shoulder.

"Sure do. The soil is pretty acidic here so they usually do stay blue. More blue denim than blue sky."

The customer crooked her head to one side, and Kate's cheeks turned hot. Was she talking about the flowers or Cole's eyes?

"I mean, you don't need any aluminum sulphate to keep them blue." She had to concentrate. As Kate rang up the purchase, she wondered when she'd gotten so crazy.

Late morning, Kate propped a sign in front of the stand, directing customers inside to pay. Chili had promised to keep an eye peeled. Climbing into Bonita, she headed to the care center. When her phone went off, Kate checked it but didn't answer. She'd call Mercedes back later.

As she drove up Red Arrow Highway, Kate blocked out thoughts of Cole and concentrated on the day ahead. Yesterday she'd spent time with Marianne, the discharge planner, so the paperwork should be ready. Her mother would continue physical therapy at home, if needed. "I can handle my own therapy in the kitchen," her mom had grumbled.

When she reached her mother's room, the beat-up navy suitcase sat at the door. "About time," her mother said, pushing back a wave of blonde hair and trying to rise from the bed.

Kate stopped in the doorway. "Mom, when did you change your hair color?"

"Yesterday. You made the appointment for me, remember? Phoebe comes once a week." Her mother's smile turned mysterious. "She told me blondes have more fun."

Kate's yelp of laughter made Marie turn from her game show. "Sorry, Marie. Mom just took me by surprise." Leave it to Phoebe.

The color made her mother look ten years younger.

"Doesn't she look pretty? I think I'll change my color too." Marie studied her old friend's new look.

Obviously pleased, Kate's mom fluffed her hair. "I wanted to look good when I came home."

Marie sighed. "Glad somebody's leaving this place."

"Looks like somebody's going home today." Will stood in the doorway in a trim gray suit with a bright blue tie.

"Yep. Just have to sign the discharge paperwork. I think we're all set."

"We're always here, Kate, if you have any questions or need anything."

What a super guy. The paperwork didn't take long. Kate scanned the list of safety points and noted that scatter rugs were a hazard. Good grief. Of course. Those rugs would all be tucked into a closet when they reached home.

"Thank you for all your help, Will," Kate said when they finally got Alice into the car.

Smile widening, Will shook her hand, both palms warm on her skin. "Again, if you ever need anything, just give me a call."

"Sure will."

Will Applegate was probably the kind of guy a girl could count on, the kind she could take home to her parents. In high school, he was no doubt head of the math club. As she got into the car and started the engine, she smiled at the very idea.

On the way home, her mom didn't say much, but her eyes brightened as they continued down Red Arrow Highway through

Harbert, a town just north of Gull Harbor. "Will you just look at those beautiful umbrellas?"

Huge hand-painted table umbrellas were displayed in front of shops, just as they were every summer until the August auction.

"The Harbert umbrellas? Mom, they're for the annual fundraiser."

"Fundraiser? Tell me about it."

The vacant look on her mom's face reduced Kate's heart to a pebble. "Local artists paint the umbrellas every summer. Then Harbert auctions them off. Benefits a local charity. We've gone to the auctions, trying to figure out how to buy one but we've always been outbid." Hard to keep her voice steady.

"Well, of course. Kind of nice to have everything be new." Her mother's chuckle coaxed Kate into a giggle. They laughed together. If attitude were everything, her mother sure had it. She'd recover just fine at home.

Colorful flags fluttered from the shops as they passed. "Looks like summer's here." Her mom gave Kate a crooked smile.

"Fourth of July just around the corner."

"Now you're talking like one of the shopkeepers."

"I kind of am now that I work at the flower stand."

"Oh. Right. Good for you, Kate. I think it's great that you're trying something new."

"Thanks, Mom." In the past, compliments had been rare around their house, at least for Kate. Expectations ran high.

Lowering her window, Alice took a deep breath. "Will you just look at those pink geraniums?"

"Haven't gotten around to painting the window boxes yet." Kate pulled in behind a shock of orange tiger lilies. "But I will."

Her mother waved her left hand. "Who cares? The flowers are what count. Thank you, honey."

Kate wrapped the endearment around her like a warm towel. Cardinals twittered in the pine trees while Kate helped her mom from the car.

The beige sedan sat over to one side in the shade. "Can't wait to drive again." Her mom cast a wistful glance in the car's direction.

"I'm sure that won't be long." No way was Kate setting limits on her mom's recovery.

But getting her mom out of the car wasn't easy. The steps loomed ahead, with no railing. Just when Kate was wondering if she'd ever be able to handle all this, Cole roared up. Sun glistened on his dark hair as he jumped out, Prissy right behind him. "Hold it! Let me help you." Relief pulsed through Kate.

"Goodness me. Don't let that dog knock me over!" Her mother cowered at Kate's side.

Cole grabbed Prissy's collar. "Sit." A miracle but the giant dog sat, a surprised look on her face. "Stay." Another miracle. The Great Dane didn't move, looking almost as amazed as Kate felt.

"Prissy's gentle, Mrs. Kennedy. No need to get nervous." Cole's muscled arms bracketed her mother's frailty. "Kate, could you hold the door?"

The screen door squeaked as she pulled it wide, unlocked the kitchen door, and pushed it open. In two shakes, he had her mother through the door and onto the sofa in the living room.

Prissy bounded in after them, abandoning obedience to give the place a good sniff. The cottage was filled with the scent of fresh paint, and Kate opened the windows that led to the front screen porch.

"What is that smell?" Her mother's nose wrinkled.

Kate exchanged a look with Cole. "Cole's converted the old pantry into a powder room. We talked about it a while back."

"Well, I wasn't aware the pantry was old." Her mom's lips tweaked upward. "I thought I was the one who was old."

"Oh, Mom." Kate plumped the pillows behind her mom's back.

"It's an exchange," Cole explained. "I'm relieved Natalie can stay with you this summer."

"Is she coming today?" Her mother sat up straighter.

Cole shook his head. "One of the teenagers in the neighborhood offered to babysit, but just for today. Thought you'd have your hands full."

"I'll be just fine," her mother murmured, eyes flagging.

The warm summer breeze filled the cottage, and her head bobbed. Would take a while for Kate to get used to that sassy blonde hair. Whisking the blue afghan from the back of the couch, she draped it over her mother. Then she crooked a finger and led Cole back into the kitchen.

"I just came to check on the paint job. Hope you don't mind." Cole dropped his voice until it was gentle as the sunshine spilling through the curtains. She wanted to bathe in that light.

"I might have to hide that key in a different place," Kate quipped. Wouldn't be a bad idea. "But thank you for helping us."

"Maybe we should put a railing in on those back stairs. They're dangerous."

We. By that time, they'd wandered toward the powder room. The apple green walls with white trim still surprised and pleased her. But the plain rectangular mirror had been replaced by a beautiful oval edged in shells. Yes, she would have to change the hiding place for the key, but she sure loved this mirror. "Where did you ever find this, Cole?"

"I have my sources." Cole could be a sphinx.

A handsome, hot sphinx.

"Oh, my gosh. So beautiful." The edges of the shells pricked her fingers when she skimmed them.

"Gorgeous." Cole's gaze was pinned to her in the mirror.

Kate's hand fell, and her breath tightened. Cole could do this to her. Just like high school, only it wasn't.

She closed her eyes. "Oh, lordy. We're in the powder room again. But we shouldn't let this happen again." *Not until I have you figured out.*

"We shouldn't?"

"Absolutely." But she melted into his arms like soft serve ice cream.

"Well, maybe we can let this happen." Cole brushed a kiss across the tender spot behind her left ear.

She moaned and sagged into him, clutching his shirt.

"Or this?" Nudging her T-shirt aside, he kissed the pulse beating crazily below her chin.

"I'm so sensitive there."

"I sure hope so." His tongue darted out. Tickled. Teased.

The room started to spin. Groaning, Kate twisted free. Every pore in her body protested when she escaped into the kitchen. Did she hear a dry chuckle behind her?

Turning at the back door, she groped for the knob and yanked it open. Prissy shot up from the floor. "You and Josh did a great job. We can never thank you enough."

Cole got the message, and he didn't look pleased. Was she being ungrateful, not even offering coffee? Without Cole's work, her mother might be confined to the second floor. She would have hated it.

Feelings playing tug-of-war inside her, Kate studied the linoleum.

Cole's boots came into view. "Guess I'll let you girls get settled."

"Girls? Really." Suddenly she felt ornery, like the worst PMS ever.

"Katie, I'll always think of you as a girl."

Oh. Wow. She swayed. Maybe this was heat stroke. His arms fell open, and she wanted to step into them, not the girl from high school but the woman she was today.

But Cole was reaching inside a pocket. "Kate, now that you're home, you probably have an interest in seeing the town's future ensured." He spread some papers out on the counter.

She blinked. "What is this, Cole? Looks like a list."

"Wonder if you'd mind signing this petition allowing tearing down Michiana Thyme." Her gasp brought his head up sharp.

"Now, hear me out."

When he held up one hand, she reached behind her for the door knob.

"Please leave." So that's what this had all been about? He wanted her support?

Embarrassment flooded her cheeks with heat. She stepped outside, where she felt safer. Rays of sunlight sifted through the tall birches. Laughter floated up from the beach, and someone somewhere was grilling. Kate anchored herself in summer, not back in raging passions she didn't totally understand.

"Things change, Kate." Cole had come outside, papers rolled tight in his hand.

"Some things but Gull Harbor isn't one of them."

"If we don't change, we don't move forward," he whispered.

Was he talking about the town or them? "Do things have to move forward?"

With a disgusted shake of his head, Cole whistled for Prissy and climbed into the truck. After he'd roared down the driveway, she dead-headed the geraniums, snapping off the blooms that were past their peak.

The next morning, Kate laid breakfast out for her mother with a note. Then she set out early, the box of yellow flyers on the seat next to her. She'd been so busy lately, no time to do anything with the notices she'd driven up to Stevensville to have printed after the town meeting. Now she passed them out with purpose, stopping at every shop and restaurant along Red Arrow. When she had more time, she'd drive inland and stuff the private mailboxes too.

Against the law but what the heck. She was just mad enough to break some rules.

Chapter 19

Didn't take long for Kate's mother to get her old sass back.

"Don't worry. Mom's feeling great. Yesterday, she even made lasagna." Kate assured Mercedes when she called that weekend. But Kate didn't mention that the kitchen told the tale of what an effort that had been. After helping her mother onto the porch, Kate had returned to clean up.

"Is she able to walk?"

"She manages. Says that using her right hand and leg is the only way they'll get better and she has a point. Keeps the walker right next to her."

When Kate reached Breezy Point the day before, she'd caught her mom scooting from counter to counter without the walker, like she was on a trial run. She was grabbing drawer pulls, the sink faucet, anything to keep her balance. Scared the heck out of Kate. "Mom, what are you doing?"

"You know how picky I am, Katherine Elizabeth. Not that you been doing a bad job, but I like to keep my kitchen just so." She gave the counter another swipe with the yellow sponge.

Mercedes would have to be there to believe it.

"Mom dresses different now and, ah, she looks different too." Just wanted to put that out there.

"What do you mean?"

"She's blonde now."

Made Kate smiled to hear her sister's groan.

"Things better in New York?"

Silence for a few beats. "Things are fine, Kate. I'm working through it." Her sister's uncertainty felt so foreign that Kate didn't know how to respond. They hung up right after that.

Maybe they were both working through stuff. Life had a way of doling out new challenges and sometimes Kate hated it. Every time she thought about that darned petition, she had to slam a door or a drawer. How she hated to be manipulated, especially by Cole. Thank goodness her mom's hearing wasn't that good anymore. She'd never condoned "hissy fits," as she called outbursts.

The weekend after her mother came home, Kate's Blooms got crazy busy. Lines formed. Customers fidgeted. One woman set her flat of bright pink petunias down and quietly walked away. As frustrating as that was, the fast pace kept Kate from overthinking the upcoming week.

While Kate waited for Cole to bring Natalie Monday morning, she wondered if this had been a bad idea. Hearing the sound of his truck, she took a deep breath and went to the back door. Her anger with him still simmered. Over the weekend she'd begun stuffing people's mailboxes with her flyers.

"Kate, someone's coming," her mother called from the front room, where she sat watching a rerun of "Dr. Phil." Her mother used to hate daytime TV. Not anymore.

"Got it," Kate called back. Warm morning air greeted her when she nudged the back door open. Cole helped Natalie from the pickup, and Prissy bounded down behind them, loping toward the door as if she belonged here. Looking at Natalie's hair, Kate found a smile. "Don't you look cute this morning."

Natalie's hair was neatly braided, a red barrette on each end. A red and white striped shirt topped red shorts.

"All set for the Fourth of July?" Kate pushed the door wider.

Natalie mumbled something as she ducked inside with her navy backpack.

"Everything's in her bag, including her lunch." Cole loomed over Natalie like a protective papa bear.

"You didn't have to do that." Taking the backpack from Natalie, Kate knew her mother would disapprove. Feeding people had been her life's work.

"You be good now." Cole gave Natalie a quick hug. Yep, definitely a papa bear.

And disarmingly cute in that role.

"Dad? Really?" Natalie backed out of her dad's arms like a teenager, not a third grader.

"She'll be fine. My mother knows how to handle sass, believe me." Kate leaned closer to Natalie. "Just kidding."

Cole drove away with Prissy looking back dolefully, head hanging out the open window with pointed ears down. Kate ushered Natalie into the living room. Remote in the left hand, her mother pulled her attention from the TV.

Natalie checked the screen. "Dr. Phil? He's a riot."

Mom held out the remote. "Maybe I should hand you the

clicker."

"Maybe you should, Mom." The TV shopping still concerned Kate. At least Natalie wouldn't be ordering new tops every other day.

"Naw, I don't want the remote." Natalie wandered over to the bookcase. "You sure have a lot of books." She devoured them with her eyes, running her fingertips over the worn bindings.

"The porch swing is a good place to read." Kate pulled out her phone and looked at the time. As much as she hated to leave, a shipment was due to arrive in twenty minutes. "Looks like I've got to get on the road. You two have a good day."

Her mother waved her away. "We'll be just fine. Two peas in a pod."

As Kate drove to work, she worried her mother would set down rules. Natalie seemed pretty independent, and she didn't want the two butting heads.

When she got to work, the truck was just pulling up and the driver waved. The morning air felt cool, and she was glad she'd worn a hoodie. By the time the first customers came in at nine o'clock, everything was ready.

By eleven o'clock, she'd sold out of geraniums, along with the philodendron and the maidenhair ferns. The bright pink and purple petunias were holding strong, along with lots of marigolds and zinnias. As she rang up a purchase, she couldn't help thinking how lucky she was. Talking to customers kept her sane. She'd go back to her writing soon, so she didn't lose her contacts on the various blogs but for now? She loved Kate's Blooms. Working with the beautiful blossoms soothed her soul and slowly began to heal her heart.

During a lull right before noon, Chili appeared with lemonade.

"You are a lifesaver." The cool sweetness hit the back of Kate's throat. "Guess summer's finally arrived."

"After the longest winter ever." Chili glanced at Kate's display. "How are you holding up?"

Kate pressed the rim of the glass against her lower lip. "Did I tell you Natalie Campbell is my mother's companion this summer? Hard to say who's babysitting whom. Isn't that amazing?"

"So Natalie's father will be at your house too, no? *Que hombre.*" Chili wiggled her eyebrows.

An ice cube slid down Kate's throat. "We are so different now, Chili. Have you seen his petition?" That last swig of lemonade tasted bitter. She handed the glass back. More cars pulled up.

"Better get back inside. We will pick this conversation up later, *no?*" Chili stabbed a finger at Kate.

"No."

Chili's sassy shoulder twist made her laugh.

Turning, Kate was amazed to find Will Applegate standing there, in a sport coat no less. "Hey, what a surprise. Have you come to buy flowers?"

Will glanced around. "Well, maybe. Looks nice."

"Are you worried about my mom? She seems fine. Did some tests come back or something?"

"No, no, Kate. I didn't mean to frighten you."

"Thank goodness." She eased out a breath.

Will jammed his hands in his pockets and stared around, like he was trying to get his footing. Kate had never seen the man this uncomfortable.

"Are you a gardener?" That would fit. She could picture Will going home to grill and tend to his garden. A real homebody.

"Me? I wouldn't know a daisy from a dandelion, but I have stopped for a reason. I wondered if you'd like to go to the Firemen's Ball with me." His head jerked, like he was surprised by his own words.

"The ball? I'd forgotten about that." Almost all of the men belonged to the Gull Harbor Volunteer Fire Department, and the dance was an annual event.

Caught off guard, she rubbed her dirty hands on her jeans. Will got quiet, like he was holding his breath. She didn't want to hurt his feelings. "That sounds like a lot of fun. How formal is it? Don't know what I'd wear."

"Don't women always like an excuse to go shopping?"

Why not? Wasn't she trying new things? "Maybe some shopping is just what I need. And thank you for the invitation." The ball might draw her attention away from smoldering good looks, broad shoulders, and kisses that never should have happened.

"Well, great. I'll get back to you with details?" Backing away, he stumbled over one of the ties holding the tent up. "See you later then."

Pivoting, he hummed as he walked to his car, careful to shake the gravel from his shoes before getting in. Kate waved as he drove away, fighting the uneasiness in her chest. Her first date in years, but Will seemed like a safe bet.

Chili's music rumbaed on the morning air, all brass and steel guitar. Kate moved to the front of the table and fussed with her snapdragon bouquets.

Just a dance. Not quite a date, right?

After the lunchtime crowd slackened, she ate her ham sandwich in the shade under the tenting Cole had put up. Sometimes she wondered when he worked on his other projects. Chili had mentioned he had a lot of crews. The town was booming, and much of the work was being done by Campbell Construction.

Was Gull Harbor growing in the right direction? Or was he destroying everything that had made her glad to come home? She had to keep circulating those flyers, but she sure didn't want Cole to know.

As she munched, she wondered if Cole would be going to the Firemen's Ball. She could just imagine him swirling someone around on the dance floor of the Whittaker Golf Club.

This bread might be a little stale. She'd have to stop at Mandy's bakery. Kate threw what was left into the trash.

When summer began, she'd closed her booth at two o'clock. That day, she stretched the time to three before propping the Closed sign among the pots.

"I'll watch out for it," Chili assured her.

Kate wasn't ready to go home, so she drove toward the beach. She'd been so darn busy she hardly had much time near the water. That's what Gull Harbor was all about.

After parking in the lot for the public beach, she headed toward the harbor. A gust of wind carrying the sounds and smells of summer reminded her how much she'd missed the water. Yachts and fishing boats were tucked neatly into the slips. Owners fussed on board some of the boats, checking sails or restocking refrigerators. On others, families lounged lazily in the sun. Kate had always wondered what it would be like to own a boat. She grew up with a small blue and white sunfish, and her dad taught her and Mercedes to sail. Some of her friends had ski boats, the kind their parents could use for fishing. Only the Chicago people had yachts, elegant affairs that hosted parties, especially for the holidays like Fourth of July.

Settling onto one of the benches edging the inlet, Kate swept off her hat and lifted her face to the sun. Wasn't everyone supposed to get fifteen minutes of sun a day? Just enough so her freckles didn't go crazy. Sun sparkled on the water, and gulls cawed overhead. She wished she'd saved the crust of her sandwich for the birds.

When she was just a little girl, her dad would take them down to the beach after dinner to feed the gulls with any bread left over from dinner. Mercedes and Kate would tear those slices into bits and stow them in the empty bread bag before heading down to the beach. Of course their dad always had a beer in hand.

Such a long time ago. Kate checked her phone and then the sun over the trees. Strolling back to Bonita, she slid into her SUV and drove slowly up Whittaker until she got to The Full Cup.

"How about a short visit from a tall friend?" Kate quipped as she came through the door.

Cleaning spray and paper towels in hand, Sarah stood at the bakery case. The air was sweet with the scent of cookies and pastries laced with the aroma of coffee.

"Kate, I haven't seen you since book club. How's it going?" Sarah stashed her cleaning supplies on the lower shelf.

"Great. Busy. Mom came home, and Natalie Campbell is spending time with her. Kind of a joint babysitting arrangement."

"I'd say they both win."

"I hope so. Will Applegate just invited me to the Firemen's Ball. Can you believe it?"

"Oh, that's wonderful." Sarah's eyes became distant, shadowed by the past.

Kate could have kicked herself. Of course Sarah had gone to that dance with Jamie every year. Like things weren't bad enough with Jamie across the ocean, risking his life while Kate worried about a dance. Grabbing her friend's hand, she squeezed. "He's coming home to you. It's just a matter of time."

Sarah's shoulders straightened. "I know. You're right of course." A cheerful smile braced her cheeks again.

"But the biggest problem is… I don't have a thing to wear!"

"Hey, girlfriend. Great excuse for a shopping trip."

"I don't have tons of money to spend in the shops." Hard to keep her voice light. A year ago, she wouldn't have thought twice about racking up some plastic damage, as Brian had liked to call it. "After all, I'm not one of the boat people."

"Oh, no. We're not shopping in the boutiques." Sarah waved

away Kate's mental picture. "We have the best resale shop in Southwest Michigan. Second Hand Rose is just up the road."

Kate's shoulders loosened. "Excellent. I can handle that. My, Gull Harbor is full of surprises."

And she was learning to like them. The girl who filled her calendar with times and dates now welcomed the unexpected? Her surprise made her shiver.

Chapter 20

"All she wants to do is sit and read," Kate's mother huffed after a couple days with Natalie.

"I read anywhere, anytime when I was her age." They were having dinner at their farmhouse table. The pungent aroma of marinara sauce rose from the blue seashell platter. Her mom had always been a fabulous cook, but tonight she seemed to have lost her touch. Kate grabbed her water glass. "So, did you use a different recipe for the meatballs?"

"Does it taste like it?" Her mom stopped chewing.

Kate took another nibble. Yep, definitely different.

"The meatballs are…interesting. What's in them this time?"

Her mom blinked. "Brown. I always put something brown in the meatballs."

"Right, you add brown sugar." Kate's heart squeezed. When had her mother ever referred to an ingredient as "something brown"?

"I do?" Relief washed over her mother's face. "Of course. Of course, I do."

What else could be brown? Worchester sauce? Syrup? Fingers numb, Kate pushed her meatballs into a pile of uneaten spaghetti and nibbled on the warm garlic bread.

What had they been talking about? Reading. Natalie and reading. "Aren't you glad she's enjoying our books?"

"Girls that age should be outside. It's summer."

She had a point. Kate had spent every possible minute on the beach when she was growing up. The pages of paperbacks bubbled from her wet fingers. "Okay, I'll try to get home earlier." She'd been coming home later to avoid running into Cole when he picked up Natalie.

"She says she's too skinny for a bathing suit."

Kate erupted in laughter, glad to be talking about something else besides the meatballs. "What? That's crazy. She's a growing girl."

Her mother gave her a stern look. "Don't you remember? She's not a baby anymore. Things are starting to happen."

"Ah. *Those* things. Right." How well she remembered her mother's stilted explanation of the facts of life. "Doesn't matter. She must own a bathing suit, and no one will see her on our beach."

The world readjusted while they talked and everything felt familiar. The same. Kate found herself clinging to the moments when life at Breezy Point was just as she remembered.

That night, Mercedes called. "How's Mom doing?"

"Um, fine, I guess."

"You guess?"

Kate didn't want to alarm her sister. "She just acts a little different sometimes."

Mercedes laughed. "So Mom's blonde now and wears bright

clothes. We can't all be the same all the time, Katie. People change."

Kate let it go. The change ran much deeper than her mom's hair and clothes.

That Wednesday after her conversation with her mom about the beach, Kate came home early. The weather had turned scorching hot, and business slacked off. She'd started to put her seed packets in alpha order when she caught herself. How scary. Did she want to end up like Mildred?

Grabbing her keys, she closed up and jumped in Bonita. Heat shimmered from the road when she turned onto the highway. The whole town was probably frolicking on the beach. Back at the house, her mom was napping on the sofa, the ceiling fan whirring above her. Natalie was sprawled on the porch swing, reading.

"Enjoying that book?"

Tucking one finger into the book by Judy Blume, Natalie frowned. "I think it's mean that they called her Blubber." Her fierce frown looked so much like her father's.

Kate collapsed onto the wicker swing. "That's the point. The writer wants us to see how unkind words hurt people."

"Oh." The frown dissolved. Natalie was processing, wisps of blonde hair curling around her face flushed from the heat.

The leaves of the birch trees outside hung limp and the humid air clung like wet tissue. "How's the summer so far?"

"Okay, I guess. Nothing much to do." Natalie set the book aside.

"Maybe we should go swimming some day. I'll get home early."

"Great. I bet my dad would come too if you asked him."

Kate had been rocking the swing with one foot, and she stopped. That hasn't been in her plan. "Maybe. What would you think about helping us paint some of the window boxes? They're peeling. I'm too busy with my flowers to get to it."

"My dad would probably do that for you." The words came fast, Natalie's eyes bright.

What was this? "Your dad has his own work to do."

Cole got all hot and sweaty when he worked, perspiration beading his forehead, glistening on those muscular arms.

Dangerous thoughts.

Natalie began to gnaw a thumbnail. "Sure, I'll help you."

But even talking about painting on a day like this seemed like an act against nature. Laughter filtered up from the beach below. A boat roared past in the distance, throttle open.

A knock on the back door was followed by the squeal of the screen door and her mother's voice saying a sleepy hello to someone, probably Cole.

Kate swung her body into a sitting position.

"What are you two doing out here?" Cole's shoulders dwarfed the doorway frame. He looked rugged, tired and hot in a way that had nothing to do with the weather.

Kate fought the heat that sizzled through her. The sleeves of his gray henley shirt were pushed up on muscular forearms, jeans low on his hips. Her mouth turned desert dry.

"Daddy!" Natalie flung herself into Cole's arms.

His face brightened. "So how'd your day go?"

"Okay, I guess." Natalie's grip tightened around her father's waist, face tipped up like she couldn't get enough of him. "But I'm glad it's time to go home."

Hands gripping her walker, Kate's mom thumped up behind Cole. "Girl gets bored on a day like this."

"I never got bored, Mom." But Kate had to remember that she tucked in visits to the beach in between her chores like rich frosting between layers of cake. "Cole, I thought I'd come early some days. Natalie and I can go to the beach together. It gets so hot." She brushed back her hair, and Cole's eyes followed.

"Kate said you could come too," Natalie piped up.

Behind her, Kate's mother chuckled.

Cole ruffled his daughter's hair. "Maybe. We'll see."

"'We'll' see' usually means no." Crossing her arms, Natalie pulled away from her father.

Cole looked totally confused and raised one hand to scratch his head. The rich smell of working man rolled over Kate. Fixed her to the spot. Brian had usually arrived home still spiffy in his suit, not even loosening his tie on the way home.

"Why don't you get your things so the nice ladies eat their dinner, okay?"

Natalie and Kate's mom disappeared inside, and Kate was left with Cole. Goosebumps rose on her skin when his eyes brushed over her legs. Her aqua t-shirt was tucked into khaki shorts. That day, she'd noticed more than one male customer checking out her legs. "I was just asking Natalie if she wanted to help us paint the window boxes. But she doesn't have to do this, Cole."

"Won't hurt her to do some painting."

Kate shifted on the swing and recrossed her legs. Cole's eyes followed her movements. Inside, she could hear her mother tell Natalie that of course she could take the book home.

The swing bobbled when Cole sat down beside her. Her chest tightened.

"So, you still doing your writing?"

"Yep, but I'm taking a break for the summer."

When Cole gave her that teenage grin, Kate felt like the years were on fast rewind. "Would you consider writing some articles about Gull Harbor and the efforts we're making to revive it?"

She let the idea sink in, feeling guilty for not thinking of it herself. She'd been too busy posting those flyers. "Maybe. Sounds like a good idea."

"We don't have our own PR person here, you know. Maybe we could go out Friday night. Throw some ideas around?"

Was this a date? Conflicted feelings twisted in her chest.

He licked his lips. She should have offered him a drink, but what she really wanted was to feel Cole's lips melt against hers again, coaxing her, teasing her.

Her thoughts made Kate squirm. Such a slippery slope. "I'm, ah, busy Friday. How about sometime during the week? Maybe when you come for Natalie?"

"Sure. Fine, I guess." He spoke each word slowly, like a brick he was laying down.

Behind his shoulder, she noticed Prissy nosing around in the tall grass.

Cole followed her gaze. "Prissy! Don't you dare."

Shamefaced, the poor dog halted mid-crouch, like she didn't know quite what to do.

Why interfere with nature? Kate waved a hand. "Go ahead, Prissy."

The dog settled back to business with a relieved sigh.

Swinging his attention back to her, Cole grinned. "Why, Kate Kennedy, you getting soft around the edges?"

Heat surged into her cheeks "Not all at. Just have more empathy for the female gender and our needs." Speaking of needs, Kate leapt up and stretched. Too late she felt her shirt lift. His eyes seared her bare skin and she darted inside, escaping, but the heat caused by his attention followed.

Five minutes later, Cole and Natalie climbed into the truck with Prissy. Kate and her Mom watched them disappear down the driveway. "That man's got a thing for you," her mother murmured.

"Don't be silly, Mom." Her stomach clenched and then grumbled. The smell of pot roast filled the kitchen. "Why don't I set the table?"

Her mother thumped over to the crock pot. "Like always, you're just ignoring the point. We should have asked them to stay. With Marie in the care center, those two probably never get a square meal."

"Oh, we can't do that."

Hanging onto the walker, her mother turned. "Why not, Katie? Seems like the neighborly thing to do."

"I just, ah, don't want to interfere. They probably need time together."

Chuckling, her mom turned back to dinner.

Kate began to peel the carrots. How long would it be before Cole found out about the yellow flyers?

"Ouch!" Blood oozed from the cut on her thumb. The peeler clattered into the sink.

"Better watch what you're doing Katie." Her mom still sounded amused.

"Don't I always?" Kate wrapped a napkin around her thumb and pressed. It still throbbed.

Chapter 21

The band passing by in the Fourth of July parade was playing so damn loud. Prissy was having fits. Still, if Cole left her at home, it would be worse. She'd chew up every doorway in the house trying to get to them, and he hated to confine her in the kennel.

"Can I pick up some of the candy people are throwing?" Natalie tugged at his hand.

Cole wished the parade would ban tossing hard candy into the crowd. "All right, but stay close to the curb, okay?" *Note to self: make sure she brushes tonight.*

Natalie whipped out a ziplock bag. She'd come prepared and her secretive smile reminded him of her mother, and not in a good way.

Prissy bumped against his leg. *Don't you think it's time to go home?*

"Take it easy, Prissy. Sit down right here next to me."

Are you kidding me, Cole? We're in a war zone here. People are throwing stuff. And the hands? How would you like to have people feeling you up?

Everybody wanted to pet the big, beautiful black-and-white dog. After all, Prissy was a Harlequin Great Dane. He'd driven all the way to Canada to get her from the breeder after Samantha left. Anything to bring a smile back to his little girl's face. Not many Harlequins in Michigan. People meant well, but Prissy hated to be touched by strangers. Still, she'd never nip or growl. Poor thing was dancing from one foot to the other while Natalie grabbed for the candy thrown from the cars.

The Corvettes passed slowly in front of him, one sweet model after another. Was enough to make a grown man cry. Maybe someday.

"Look!" Natalie was back, the stars on her red headband bouncing when she shook her bag of treats. "Want some?"

"Thanks, but no. And remember to brush your teeth tonight."

She looked so darn pretty today in her red shorts and white top with stars on it. He'd sprayed her with sunblock before they left the house.

"I will." Natalie popped a tootsie roll in her mouth.

"I'm going to check."

She was growing up so fast. Too fast.

The high school band swung past, another horn section blaring. Prissy jerked, and Cole was glad he'd brought the leash. The musicians wore high hats topped with feathers that blew in the breeze. Their red, white, and blue uniforms looked sharp, the red vests glittering in the sun. In back of the musicians came all the local politicians, walking over to the crowd to shake hands.

This was one of those days when he was glad he'd come back to Gull Harbor after college. Not that he had much choice.

"Look, right across the street. Alice and Kate." Natalie pointed.

"Mrs. Kennedy," he corrected her. "It's not respectful to call Mrs. Kennedy Alice."

Natalie glowered up at him. "She told me to. Said it made her feel old as the hills when I call her Mrs. Kennedy." His daughter heaved a dramatic sigh.

Could puberty be any worse than this? Probably yes, from what he could recall.

"Okay, then. Let's go say hi."

The tail of the parade, a pack of Girl Scouts, had just straggled past, handing out cookies. After that, the crowd began to disperse. Keeping Prissy close to his side and one hand on Natalie's shoulder, they crossed Whittaker.

"Enjoy the parade?" he asked as they drew closer to Kate and her mother. Kate's red knit top emphasized her generous figure, although she'd never made a big deal of her body. In fact, she almost seemed to hide it under those sweatshirts in high school, unlike Samantha, who tended to wear her tops a size too small.

Kate's mother leaned heavily on her cane. No walker for her, not when the whole town could see. Like her daughter, she was proud and just looked glad to be there. "Wasn't it wonderful? But your dog sure doesn't look happy."

Reaching out, Alice patted Prissy's neck. Rolling her head, the dog slurped her palm. *Thank goodness you're here, Alice. You don't know what I've been through today.* The two were developing a real thing for each other.

"She hates the noise, but at least she can be with us." He didn't want to go into Prissy's separation anxiety.

"Nice shirt." Kate's eyes swept his shirt that said "World's Greatest Dad," white on navy blue.

"Thank you. Natalie gave it to me." Shirts with silly sayings weren't his thing, but he'd wear a black garbage bag if Natalie asked him.

"You've got good taste," Kate told Natalie, whose broad smile just got wider.

Strolling up Whittaker, the four of them wound up in front of the Swirly Top.

"Want a cone, Mom?" Kate edged toward the screen door that led inside.

"Is a bluebird blue?" Alice laughed. "Guess I'll take a load off." A family left one of the picnic tables, and Alice hobbled toward it.

Grabbing her elbow, Cole guided her. Last thing he wanted was for her to fall. "Why don't you ladies sit down and I'll get the ice cream. How about that?"

"You don't have to do that." Shading her eyes with one hand, Kate stared up at him from beneath her broad-brimmed hat. Color brightened her pretty cheeks.

Leaning toward her, he muttered, "But I want to. Now go sit down. What flavor?"

"Twirls?" Kate glanced at the other two. Natalie was nodding.

"Chocolate and vanilla it is."

Kate could be bossy. If you gave her an inch, she'd take a mile. He remembered that from high school, and she'd only been a sophomore. Red lips pouting, she joined Alice and Natalie at the picnic table. Prissy settled in the protected shade below, head on her front paws. Cole had handed the leash to Natalie.

Inside, the line wasn't too long. Mostly kids. Was it that long ago that he was one of them? Ten minutes later, he was passing out the cones and the four of them settled into contented silence.

Was this a perfect day or what? He stretched out his legs in the sun. A few people stopped to say hi. Sarah Wilkins had her kids with her, along with her mother. Nice folks.

"Aren't they just as cute as the dickens," Alice said after Sarah had walked away. "Good thing her mother helps out."

Natalie had wandered off to talk to some of her classmates at the next table.

"Any word on when Marie will come home, Cole?" Kate asked in a lower tone. When she leaned toward him, he got downright distracted by the scoop neck of that top.

"I… Well, I…"

Alice had her eye on them, looking like she just might giggle.

Cole gave himself a shake. "Don't think that's been decided yet. Is Natalie giving you any trouble?"

He held out what was left of his cone. Prissy took it with one chomp. *About time you remembered that I'm down here.*

"Natalie couldn't be better," Alice chirped.

"No complaints." Kate's eyes slid to her mother. "Of course, Mom thinks Natalie should be able to go down to the beach and we'll take care of that. Hope you're okay with Natalie swimming with me sometimes."

"That would be so cool, Kate!" Natalie's whole face lit up.

"We hit the beach on the weekends." He didn't want Kate and her mother to think that he never took Natalie swimming. The weight of single fatherhood pressed on him.

"Da-ad." Okay, Natalie was giving him *that* look. "The weeks are long, and it's getting so hot."

"I get it. No problem." Being a single parent sucked.

Kate did that leaning thing again, hands tucked down between her thighs. "I'll let you know ahead of time."

Took a lot of self control to keep his eyes on, well, her eyes. She'd swept off her hat, and her long fingers combed through hair that fell past her shoulders. Kate's hair would probably be soft in his hands. Sure smelled pretty whenever he got close enough, but she'd been stiff-arming him lately.

Almost like those kisses never happened. His body wouldn't let him forget.

Her mother snuffled and whipped out a tissue. "Pardon me," she said to no one in particular. "Allergies," she added with a sly smile.

"Mom, you've never had allergies."

"Maybe I have them now." Her eyes flitted across the street to where Michiana Thyme sat in the sun, a huge Sold sign on the side of the building. "Makes me sad to see that place empty."

"I always went with you when you shopped for a dress." Good God, Kate's eyes turned misty.

Her mom snorted. "Not many of those times, that's for sure. But we enjoyed them." They were gazing at that old building like it was the White House.

"Loretta used to keep a bowl of chocolate kisses on the counter."

"Oh, yum. I'd be there every day." Natalie swung her legs with excitement.

"Yes, you would if it were still open." Kate turned toward him, accusation in her eyes. The other two followed suit. Condemned without trial. Wasn't it enough that those yellow flyers had started appearing all over town?

Damn it all. "Gull Harbor hasn't been able to find another shopkeeper willing to take on Michiana Thyme. The place was for sale for two years. You can't blame Loretta for selling."

But they didn't blame her. They blamed him for buying it.

The Downtown Development committee would give their report at the town meeting next week. He sure hoped they'd give him the green light. "We don't want Gull Harbor turning into a Crystal Lake."

"What's happened with Crystal Lake?" Kate turned to her mother.

Cole doubted that Alice knew the facts. Time to explain. "The gambling casino set up shop just down the road from the town and created a fully enclosed community. Guests didn't need the town anymore. Said the shops were outdated, offered stuff no one wanted to buy. Shops closed. Lots of empty buildings. So now the casino is plenty busy, but the town? Not so much." Frustration weighed his words, and he stopped.

How many times did he have to explain this?

"Guess I'll have to drive over and see for myself." Kate's eyes had turned thoughtful.

"I might come with you." Alice looked troubled. After all, she'd grown up in Gull Harbor, married here and raised her kids. She had a lot at stake. Cole hated to worry her, but if someone didn't stop the uncontrolled development from outside investors who could just pull up stakes and leave, the small communities along the lake could become ghost towns, bypassed by Highway 94 and the rest of the world. Gull Harbor had to hold its own and that took planning.

With a distracting stretch, Kate got to her feet. "Time to go home."

If Cole didn't leave now, it would be a while before he could stand up and not give the town a show. He jumped up so fast Prissy's head jerked. She scrambled from beneath the table and gave him the look. *Real nice, Cole. Choke your dog on the Fourth of July.*

Helping Alice maneuver, he guided the group across the street. The summer sun beat down as they strolled to the parking lot behind the bank.

"Going to the street dance tonight?" he asked Kate when they reached her blue SUV.

"Oh, no." Was Kate hiding beneath the brim of that hat?

Alive gave her shoulders a little shake. "Of course she's going. The whole town will be here. Even I might come."

"Mom, really?" Kate helped her mother into the vehicle.

"Well, I suppose I'll be asleep by then." Alice wore a sheepish grin.

Slamming the passenger door, Kate turned toward him. "Thanks for the ice cream. Maybe I'll see you tonight." Smile curving her lips, she started backing away.

Kate loved teasing him. A lot more fun than when she shut him out completely. He had to move slowly. Her divorce was so recent and he remembered how that felt.

"Bye, Alice and Kate. See you next week." Natalie waved as they started back across the street.

Prissy yanked on her leash, bringing him up short. Cole pulled Natalie back just as a car zoomed past. "Thanks, Prissy." If he didn't watch it, they'd get hit by one of the summer people.

His dog threw him a disgusted look. *Trying to get us killed, Cole? Let's keep it together.*

"You are going to go, aren't you?" he heard Alice ask Kate.

Smiling to himself, he grabbed Natalie's hand and gave it a little swing. Oh, yes he was coming to the dance. And he just bet she'd be there.

Chapter 22

Fireworks had been crackling on the beach all day. Kate felt jumpy as she dashed out to Bonita in her lime wedge sandals and the lilac sundress she'd found in her closet. Mixed feelings churned in her stomach. Going to the parade with her mother had been fun, like one of those old Norman Rockwell paintings. The Fourth of July should be a day of parades and ice cream and doing something special. At least, that's what the Fourth had been like when she was little, when her dad still lived with them.

The street dance might be a chance to make new memories in Gull Harbor. She had to get used to going out again. Meet new people instead of the friends she'd left behind after high school.

Who was she kidding? Kate was going because Cole might be there and that defied all reason.

Slipping into the SUV, she rolled down the windows. The sun was sinking into the lake and cool pine-scented air rolled over her. Crickets chirped in the tall grass. Starting the car, she cracked open the moon roof. How she loved driving down Red Arrow Highway with air rushing through the car. Felt like her life right now. Which direction was she headed? She had no idea.

Gravel spun under her tires when she gunned it in the driveway. If she stayed home, her mother would keep dropping comments about Cole. Her mom's health issues seemed to have loosened her tongue. Before, she'd done tight-lipped battle with the vacuum, pounding Swiss steak into submission with a plate or cleaning windows with squeaky precision. Not many words but a lot of work.

Now her mom gave voice to every thought. Absolutely no filter. And she definitely had some foolish ideas about Cole. The playful teasing set Kate's teeth on edge. Why, her mother had practically pushed Kate into going into town that night.

As if she didn't want to go. As if she wasn't hopeful that Cole would be there.

Kate passed Greta's Gifts, the Local Color art gallery, and Tuscany restaurant. At least those three businesses were still in operation. Cole's comment about Crystal Lake scooped a hole in her heart. Sure, she didn't want that, but was his race to tear down buildings the answer? One by one, she pressed damp palms against her skirt. Every time she thought of those yellow flyers jammed in people's mailboxes, her stomach got all jittery.

Music floated on the night air as she parked the car. After applying another coat of Summer Blush lipstick, she walked toward the side street where the dance was held. The tiny white lights strung across the street pricked the darkness. During the summer, it didn't get dark in Michigan until almost ten o'clock. Mercedes and Kate got to stay up later. How they'd loved the extended daylight. Tonight she passed homes with flags stuck in flower boxes. A large bunting hung from the second story of a new bed and breakfast.

Kate's hair was caught up in a ponytail, and the soft summer air brushed the back of her neck. She yanked on one of the spaghetti straps and wondered if she should have worn cut-offs instead with a T-shirt, but she loved this sundress that she left behind when she moved to Boston. Strangely, it suited her more now than when she bought it in high school.

One beer, that was all. Maybe she'd see some kids from high school. Maybe Cole wouldn't be able to get a babysitter for Natalie.

The music throbbed, blurred lyrics spraying into the darkening sky. An electric guitar struck funky chords that reverberated in her stomach. Watching her step on the uneven sidewalk, she hurried along. Drawing closer, she recognized "Surfing Safari," an old Beach Boys tune. During the summer, someone would always bring a boom box to the deserted beach where they partied. The guys would build a fire for s'mores while they popped the tops of beer cans and dug their toes into the cooling sand.

Such a long time ago.

Whittaker Street had been closed for three blocks for the Fourth of July celebration earlier in the day. Now the grills were cooling off and vendors had packed away any leftover food.

The guitar riffs got louder as she approached the crowd. Scanning clusters of strangers, she stumbled and grabbed a light pole. Her confidence wavered. Maybe coming had been foolish. She'd never been great at socializing. Not alone anyway. Suddenly she missed Brian. Missed the certainty of being half of a couple.

But that was all she missed and it wasn't enough. Pushing off from the metal pole, she wove her way through strangers who had probably come from the yachts. Their casually expensive designer clothing wasn't from the Michigan City mall, only twenty minutes away. Absolutely no one that she knew in the crowd and she backtracked to The Full Cup. Just as she got there, Sarah swirled out of the front door, keys in her hand and her boys smacking at each other.

"Cut it out," Sarah scolded the two as she locked up. "Hang onto each other like brothers. Don't want you getting lost."

"You promised we could see the fireworks!" Justin grumbled.

"We will if you're good. Take your big brother's hand," she warned, glancing up. "Kate!"

"Can I help?" What would it be like to have children? She'd never be alone… but then she'd risk having the problems that tore her family apart.

"Think I got it covered, but thanks." Sarah blew frizzy bangs out of her eyes. "The holidays are always so crazy busy. We were just talking to Jamie."

"How's he doing?" Together, they walked back toward the music and the beach, where the fireworks would be set off.

"He's fine, I guess. He never talks about, you know, what he's doing there." Sarah dropped her voice, eyes circling toward the boys. "We still have to schedule that shopping trip."

"I'm ready when you are." Kate wished she were more excited about the Firemen's Ball.

"I'll mention it to the girls."

"Girls?"

"Sure. Chili might want to come. Maybe Phoebe."

"Mom, my shoe." Nathan patted one of his unlaced tennis shoes against the pavement.

Stooping, Kate tied them.

"I'm tired," Justin whined, digging his fists into his eyes.

Kate picked him up. At first he pushed away, looking as surprised as Kate felt.

"You'd make a good mother," Sarah murmured.

"Someday. Maybe." Justin felt warm and solid in her arms.

"Of course you'll have a family." Sarah squeezed her shoulder.

As they walked down Whittaker, everyone greeted Sarah by name. Once upon a time, Kate had enjoyed that same familiarity. Right now, she felt out of place.

"Want a beer?" Kate asked when they came to a stand without a line of customers.

"Do I ever." She took Justin from Kate's arms. "You get the beer while I buy these little guys a snow cone. Sugar them up so we'll never sleep tonight."

Turning, Kate saw Cole right away. No mistaking the broad shoulders and his long, lean body. Cole was standing in a circle of guys. Voices loud and laughing, they'd probably had a few beers. But Cole was in his listening mode. He'd been just like this in debate club, teasing out the opinions for every issue.

When he looked over and saw her, he waved. Her steps faltered, but she pushed on.

Over to the side, people were dancing to "Heat Wave." Some of the children had even joined in, jumping up and down and clapping.

"Two beers, please," she told the guy behind the counter. "Corona light, with limes." She didn't even have to turn to know Cole was moving toward her.

He leaned closer. "So you came."

"Yep." She smiled up at him. "Where's your red shirt?" But he was looking mighty fine in a blue oxford cloth shirt with sleeves rolled up. Looked like he'd gotten dressed up and that touched her.

His relaxed chortle shivered deep into her stomach. "I could ask you the same thing. Not that I'm complaining about that pretty little dress." Cole tipped his beer bottle as if saluting her sundress.

If Kate glanced down, she'd probably see goose bumps rising across her chest. "I decided I didn't want to look like a flag." Cold beers in hands, she turned to find Sarah at her elbow.

"Hi, Cole. How you been? You haven't stopped by lately. Those sticky pecan buns are calling your name." Clutching their mom's legs, Justin and Nathan worked on their cherry snow cones.

"I've been so darn busy, Sarah. It's been crazy. Not that I'm complaining."

"And he's been helping me… Well, us, really. Cole made a bathroom out of the old pantry on the first floor."

"What a good idea." Sarah sounded more delighted than warranted. Then she waved. "Oh, look, there's Uncle Ryan."

A man with short curly hair swung toward them, arms wide. "Where are my two curmudgeons?"

The two little boys giggled as their uncle swept them into his arms. Ryan didn't seem to care about the sticky cherry snow cones dripping all over him. Kate remembered Jamie's brother from high school. He was three years older, a hulkish guy who now had a distinct limp, not that it detracted from his looks.

Sarah smiled up at Ryan. "See? I told you your uncle wouldn't forget." She pivoted toward Kate and Cole. "Maybe we'll see you guys later. We're meeting my in-laws and Mom down on the beach."

With a wave, she followed Ryan but not before mouthing the words, "Dance with him" to Kate.

The thought of being in Cole's arms sent invisible spiders skittering up Kate's arms. "I don't remember Ryan having a limp."

"Motorcycle accident out on Red Arrow. He's lucky it wasn't worse. Kept him from joining the Reserves. Like a lot of us, he wanted to be in the action." Cole's mouth had set.

"Did you want to go to the Middle East too?"

They'd stopped under a street lamp that cast deep shadows and she couldn't see Cole's eyes. "Damn straight. But I have responsibilities here."

"Sure. After all, you have Natalie…"

"And Marie," he added.

"Right, Marie." How well Kate knew how it felt to parent your parent.

"I'm not complaining."

"Didn't say you were." Cole had always been the type who shouldered responsibility and asked for more. That much hadn't changed.

They sauntered back toward the music. No rogue breezes here and she pushed her hair back from overheated cheeks.

"Glad you came." Cole's eyes roved over her as if she were a sticky pecan bun.

"Me too." Why did Kate turn inside out whenever Cole even looked at her? Sometimes life didn't make sense. Will Applegate was such a nice guy. A "catch," as her mother would say, not that Kate was thinking of marriage any time soon.

The band eased into "Wonderful, Wonderful," an old Johnny Mathis tune. The lead guitarist crooned into the mic, and he wasn't half bad.

"Want to dance?" Cole's dark hair looked damp, like he'd just showered. Kate fought a sudden urge to run her fingers through it. Her throat swelled in the most annoying way and she swallowed hard. Taking her beer, Cole set the cups on a planter. The air still felt so warm. Or was it Cole?

She moved into his arms, trying to keep some space between them, but he wasn't having any of that. One tug and she was flat against his chest, breasts sending her signals she tried to ignore. His pale blue shirt felt rough on her arms. She was still ticked at him about the darn petition, but her irritation was steamrolled by a relentless attraction.

Near them, younger couples swayed, arms wrapped around each other. A few gray-haired couples were doing the two-step. One even managed to twirl his wife, and her girlish giggle floated on the night air.

Kate wanted to be them one day. No divorce for her.

"I thought maybe you wouldn't come," Cole said against her hair.

"Why not? It's the Fourth of July."

"Sometimes I think you're avoiding me, Katydid." His jeans were soft against her thighs, not a constant pressure but a brush. Maybe more a stroke. She wanted to close her eyes and enjoy every subtle movement of Cole's body.

He gave her a shake.

"Sorry, what were you saying?" She blinked up at him.

"Nothing. I think it's great what you're doing, Kate."

"Like what? Coming home?"

"To take care of your mom."

"Aren't you doing the same with your mother-in-law?"

"Yeah, but I live here. You came from Boston, right?"

"Boston's pretty warm right now. Ever been there?"

He nodded. "Samantha had an aunt out there. Gone now, but she was great."

The name had kicked the conversation back to serious. "I'm sorry, Cole. About Samantha and everything. Must be hard."

His shoulders shifted. "I try not to think about it." The hitch in his gruff voice indicated he wasn't quite there. Not yet. And damn, the mood had been broken.

"I know that feeling." Her mind flicked back to Brian, but she didn't want to go there.

Cole did. "So I hear you're divorced?" They hadn't talked about personal stuff. Conversations about flowers shipments and Natalie were a lot easier.

"Yep. Signed, sealed, and delivered."

"Didn't mean to pry." Taking her right hand, he cupped it over his heart. Under her palm, she could feel the steady beating, and her own heart joined the rhythm.

"Actually, it's a relief." When had she stopped loving Brian? When had she realized that although he seemed perfect for her, he wasn't? Both goal-oriented, serious students, they quickly settled in with each other. Brian wasn't a heavy drinker, and that scored high with her. Took some time for her to realize that it took more than common interests to keep a couple together. The marriage had seemed sensible and right. But over the years, Kate began to feel boxed into a relationship that felt more like a business partnership gone wrong, not a loving marriage. His surprise announcement about no babies had been the final straw.

"Sometimes it can be like that, I guess."

But he had no idea. How could he? He'd known Samantha forever. They'd all grown up together. She'd know Brian for months and began to hear wedding bells.

Sand gritted under their shoes. In Gull Harbor, everything held a light coat of the pale crystals that invaded the town on windy days.

"Natalie's really enjoying the books." Cole broke into her thoughts. "I've never been much of a reader. Can't help her there."

"She's a great little kid. Kind of like her mother, I guess."

"Only time will tell." Cole's voice flattened with what sounded like resignation.

The band shifted into "Surfing Safari." Like a lot of guys, Cole backed off from the faster rhythm, but he seemed to drop her hands reluctantly.

"I'm thirsty," she announced.

He gave her a relieved smile. Grabbing her beer cup, she sat down on the edge of the planter and he sat beside her.

When she crossed one leg over the other, his eyes dropped and hovered. "Such pretty little shoes."

Now when a man calls size ten feet "little," that's saying something. Skin tingling, Kate tossed back another gulp of beer. "Think I'll take off early next week to take Natalie down to the beach. You could come too, if you want to." Now why had she suggested that? He had his own beach. "I'll give you a call."

Cole's smile was slow in coming. She'd never realized how long and thick his lashes were. Natalie had them too, lucky girl. "Look, Kate, I'm sorry about the petition. I didn't realize you felt so strongly."

"Oh, you'll never know." Misgivings did a slow swirl in her stomach.

"Why do you have an objection to a hotel in that space?" He looked genuinely puzzled.

"Because we ate French toast there as kids? Because Michiana Thyme is, well, a part of our history here in Gull Harbor." She didn't add that Mildred was working on having the building declared a historical site.

People were brushing past, headed toward the harbor. A broad band of stars winked in the darkness overhead. Only in Michigan did you see this many stars.

"Want to go down and watch the fireworks?" She was just about leaping out of her skin, thinking about those yellow flyers.

Had she acted on emotion instead of gathering more information? Wouldn't be the first time.

"Isn't that why we came?" His eyes twinkled wickedly.

"Sure. Let's go."

She was off like a shot and Cole's laugh followed her. When he grabbed her hand, she didn't pull away. At the beach, they found a flat spot up in the dune grass, away from the crowd. She kicked off her sandals, and he took off his loafers. They rested back on their elbows, sand still warm underneath her.

"This is fun, being back for this." The heartache of the past year loosened its grip.

"I'm glad you came home too."

Ridiculous excitement blossomed in her chest.

Gull Harbor didn't skimp on the fireworks display. Colors burst in the skies overhead, big, bright and outrageously noisy. Bright orange chrysanthemums, red rockets, white waterfalls transformed the velvety darkness. The fireworks came with machine gun ferocity, so fast Kate had to catch her breath while the crowd voiced appreciation. Cole kept her hand in his, one thumb brushing lightly over her knuckles.

"Remember the night we went to Waco Beach after winning the debate with La Porte?" Sitting next to him felt so familiar.

His brow furrowed. "I guess. We came down here a lot back then, right?"

"That time was different. Just you and me."

Cole's lips slowly curled into a reminiscent smile. "We got kind of crazy, didn't we?"

"You could say that." After all, he'd been a senior, probably had a lot more experience with crazy kisses than she did.

"You surprised me that day." Reaching over, Cole brushed back a curl that had escaped from her ponytail. "I'd never seen you like that."

"You mean you'd never thought of me like that." A girl who'd climb onto his lap, cupping his cheeks with both hands while she kissed him breathless.

They all clapped at the American Flag unfurling across the night sky in red, white, and blue. "You'd always been so serious, Katydid. I figured I'd let you have too much beer that night. We had that cooler."

She sat up straight. "You mean you felt guilty?"

His jaw shifted. "Course I did. You were only a sophomore."

"I thought you'd ask me to prom." Her admission came out a sigh.

Cole sucked in a surprised breath. "Oh, Katydid. I am so sorry. I was going with Samantha back then."

"Yeah. I didn't get it." Embarrassment heated her cheeks, and she was glad for the darkness.

"I was so young and stupid. Full of myself after winning that competition and way too careless. I'm so sorry, Katydid."

Wasn't she the stupid one, reading way too much into that one night? What did it matter anymore?

"Forgive me?" His eyes were dark, troubled caldrons.

"Yeah. Of course."

"Besides, you were too good for me in so many ways."

Now, that stung. "What?" Jerking upright, she pulled her legs under her full skirt.

"Come on, you have to know that. So smart and confident. We wouldn't have won that debate if you hadn't pointed out that historically head trauma went, what was it you said, 'unreported and untreated' so the numbers the La Porte team was spewing weren't accurate."

"Really? That's how you saw me?" But she'd wanted to be pretty in his eyes, not a brainy geek who was "too good."

His kiss surprised her, but she sank against his chest, crazy for the taste of him. Cole took her face in his hands and she clung to his wrists. Her stomach muscles hurt from trying to stay sitting upright, and her body ached to stretch out on that sand the way it had in high school.

But this felt so very different than back then.

Cole's lips sealed over hers, tentative at first and then more certain. She let herself fall into his crazy kisses. Drank in his heat, the faint taste of his beer. Loved the calloused hands on her skin. The fireworks had stopped. Down in front of them, families were folding blankets and lifting sleeping children. He drew back, surprise sparking in his blue-black eyes. "Katydid, you're all grown up."

"It happens." Felt like the stars were spinning drunkenly overhead.

"I was wondering…" He traced her lower lip with a finger. "Want to go to the Firemen's Ball with me? Will that make up for the prom?"

"Sorry. I already have a date for the dance." She watched his expression turn to disappointment and her own heart echoed that feeling.

Cole's hands fell from her face, leaving a burning imprint. Even in the darkness, she could see his frown. "Hmm. Can I ask who's the lucky guy?"

"Will Applegate. From the care center? Seems nice."

Cole nodded. Was he hurt? Angry?

Why did she have to explain this?

"So are you. Nice, I mean." Kate leaned toward him. Just one more kiss?

"Nice? Give me a break." He pushed up, brushing the sand from his jeans. "Come on. I'll walk you up."

Heads down, they followed the crowd. Disappointment and delight washed over her in troubling waves. Was she terrible for wishing she were going to the dance with Cole instead of Will? When they reached Whittaker, she flitted off into the darkness toward her car. "Good night. See you!"

When she turned, Cole stood there, shaking his head. "Oh, yes. You certainly will."

She shivered all the way home.

Chapter 23

Kate's cheeks hurt from laughing by the time they reached Second Hand Rose, the resale shop on Red Arrow Highway. In high school, Sarah and Chili had been lots of fun. Now? Her old friends were hilarious.

"So what color dress?" Sarah asked, pulling into the parking lot.

"Anything that makes me look like a goddess." Sure. Like that could ever happen.

"Oh, Kate. You *are* a goddess."

"Sarah, you should see the men check Kate out at her flower stand." From the backseat, Kate could see Chili make suggestive wavy gestures with her hands.

Kate's cheeks heated. "Right, while their wives pick out vegetables to cook for supper. Not a lot of single men beating their way to my door."

"So why does Cole hang around all the time?" Chili asked with a sly smile.

"We have business to take care of." Besides, Cole hadn't stopped by since the Fourth of July, almost two weeks now. His parting comment had come to nothing. Had she expected to wake up some night and find him pelting her bedroom window with pebbles? Getting out of the car, Kate squinted at the bright yellow building with a beachscape on the side. "Remember when this place was a jewelry shop? We all bought ankle bracelets." Did the shops change hands continually now? She hated it.

"The artist used crystals in her designs. She told us all sorts of wonderful things were coming our way, remember?" Chili giggled.

"And she was right." Sarah heaved her purse onto one shoulder. "Why do I feel like we're shopping for prom dresses?"

"Remember prom?" Chili wiggled her eyebrows. "Ignacio looked so hot in that bright pink cummerbund."

Sarah and Chili laughed as the three of them piled into the shop. They'd both had dates for senior prom with guys they were dating at the time. Finally, Kate had been invited by Tim Johnson, a sweet guy who sat next to her in Spanish class. A nice time but no chemistry and they hadn't gone to Chicago for the post-prom party. The trip would have been so costly and Tim had looked relieved when she told him she really didn't want to go.

A young girl with springy reddish curls looked up from the counter, flipping her magazine closed. "Hi, can I help you?"

"Are these your prom dresses?" Chili marched over to the rack of long dresses shimmering along the side wall.

"Are you looking for next year?"

"*Chica*, we're way past prom, *no?*"

They burst out laughing, and the girl joined in. "I sort of figured."

"No prom. Just the Firemen's Ball. Kind of like an adult prom." Hangers screeched on the rack as Sarah turned to the task, flipping through dresses in a size that may have fit Kate in high school. Not anymore.

Kate tugged at the waist of her cutoffs. So hard to resist her mother's cooking.

"In your dreams." Kate nudged Sarah into the next size.

"We've had some women come in for that dance." The girl's nametag read "Beth." "My parents always go."

"Will you look at this? Totally hot." Chili held up a black number cut high in the front with hardly any back. The floor-length skirt was a slim tube.

"Way too dramatic. I'm not that brave." Ignoring the look Chili gave Sarah, Kate searched for blue or green, always a safe bet.

Meanwhile, Sarah plucked dresses from the rack with brisk authority.

Kate's discomfort grew. "Are those for you?"

"Of course not," Sarah snorted.

"Sarah, er, I don't think I'd wear those." The low necklines were slipping from the hangers, and side slits would leave nothing to the imagination.

"Why don't you just try on some of these?" Arms full of gowns, Chili raised her eyebrows at the salesgirl.

Kate was being railroaded, but she did need a dress.

"Right this way." Beth led them to the back.

Chili's hand was planted firmly on one of Kate's shoulders with Sarah right behind.

Sweeping a curtain to the side, the girl ushered them into a fitting room with two chairs that didn't match. "Let me know if you need anything."

Sarah and Chili got busy, hanging up the dresses.

"We don't have to find something today," Kate murmured. "I can wear one of my old peasant skirts and top."

"Oh, no, girlfriend. No cotton skirt. Not for Firemen's Ball." Chili shook her head in disapproval.

"Are you and Ignacio going?" Kate asked, and Chili nodded. "Well, what are you wearing?"

"My sister was in a wedding last fall, and she wore a bright pink dress that will suit me just fine. Ignacio is just happy that he doesn't have to wear a tux. Sarah's coming with us."

"No, no, I'm not," Sarah protested, pausing with hangers in hand.

"Of course you are." Chili looked determined.

Kate checked the price tags. The dresses were reasonable. She could buy one just to get them off her back.

Quickly, Chili worked out a dressing room system. She helped Kate with the zippers, and Sarah sat shotgun next to a three-way mirror in the main room. Beth ran go between, grabbing new sizes and finding replacements. "Let me know if you need anything."

Slipping off her T-shirt, Kate reached for a pretty blue gown with a deep ruffle along the bottom.

"Let's leave that one for last." Chili grabbed the hanger.

"But it's pretty. It's like something I'd wear."

"Exactly." Chili fixed her with those deep chocolate eyes.

Kate loosened her hold, and the dress ended up on one of the hooks. "So I'm just a pawn today, right?" She cast a longing look at the gown that hadn't passed muster.

"Right." Chili unzipped the black gown.

"Any progress?" Sarah called out.

"In a minute." Chili held up the dress.

"The backless look is just not me." Still, Kate climbed in. The air vent up above her skimmed her bare back, and she shivered. "What high school girl would wear something like this to her prom?"

"A smart girl. Times have changed." Chili stepped back, giving Kate the same eye she gave to oranges and bananas when shipments arrived. Were they plump enough, firm enough?

Slipping into the black sling heels she'd brought with her, Kate plodded out to do a tight spin for Sarah in front of the mirror. She'd need a shawl with this number.

"I hate those bras that attach around your waist for backless dresses," she muttered.

Arms folded, Chili had joined them. "You don't wear a bra. Not with that material. Just those adhesive cups."

Kate snorted. "That sounds comfortable." She'd gone to way too many business events with Brian, who always preferred black, less on the slinky side and leaning toward sedate.

She'd been his backdrop, she now realized. The crutch for his career. Her shoulders drooped.

"A woman from Chicago brought that dress in," Beth mentioned, while Kate shook herself free of the latest realization about her marriage. "You know, summer people. The back seat of her sports coupe was packed with dresses from her friends in Glen Ellyn."

Sarah's eyes glowed with approval as Kate twirled. "Very stylish. Will seems like a man who appreciates style."

"Will?" Chili's jaw dropped.

"Right. Will Applegate, the care center administrator." Kate turned to face her. "My date for the dance."

"*Aye, caramba, chica.*" Chili fell back, hands pressed against her mouth. "I thought you were going with Cole, the way he hangs around all the time."

"No, Will invited me." Kate skimmed her hands over her hips. Definitely too slinky. "He's been so great with my mother."

"Then let him take your mother to the Firemen's Ball," Chili snapped.

"Cole and I did run into each other on the Fourth of July." Kate made another turn.

"What happened?" Sarah and Chili were totally focused on her now. Beth turned the music down lower. Was she listening too?

"We watched the fireworks. You know, just ran into each other." The shimmy in her stomach must've shown in her face.

"Oh, yes, I just bet." Chili grabbed the top of the zipper and unzipped the dress. "No sexy black dress for Will. No, no, no."

"That's it? You just watched the fireworks?" Sara didn't look convinced. After all, she remembered high school and how Kate had mooned over Cole.

"Yes, we just watched the fireworks." But the sizzle that burned through Kate's body sent her flying back to the fitting room. Cole's kisses, his warm breath on her skin awakened vivid memories that often kept her from sleep.

Blue, she definitely needed to try on the blue. Chili and Sarah were murmuring quietly together when Kate reappeared, kicking out the ruffled hem with one sandal.

"*Aye, caramba.*" Chili put one hand over her eyes.

"It's just not you," Sarah said on a defeated sigh.

"I love this dress." The fabric felt so sleek, the ruffles so soft.

Chili leveled one long, orange-tipped finger at Kate. "We're looking at second-hand prom dresses, but this dress is not for a prom. You've graduated."

Shoving more hangers at Kate, Chili jabbed a finger toward the back and Kate retreated to the fitting room. Yellow wasn't her color, and neither was peach. Dresses flew and the room heated. The air conditioning wasn't turned up high enough. Her face was flushed as she slipped in and out of dresses. One was too ruffly, the next too skinny. Too clingy, too swirly, too dotty, too twirly.

This was like playing Dr. Seuss with dresses.

Beth shuffled the rejects back to the racks and grabbed new options. Although Kate kept the blue ruffled dress as a backup, Chili weighed in for the vampy black number. Her waist hurt just thinking about how that bra would feel. And the thought of Will's hand on her bare skin with that low back didn't turn her on. Not one bit.

A lilac number with a flowing skirt had been worn by a bridesmaid, or so Beth told them. The hem fluffed around Kate's ankles as she came out into the main room. She didn't even make it to the mirror before a quick veto from Sarah and Chili.

Standing in the middle of the store, Kate felt tired and

frustrated. "Maybe we're not going to find a dress today. Nothing's right."

Chili gave Sarah the lifted brow. "Maybe your date's not right."

Hands on her hips, Kate faced them. "Don't start with Will. He's perfectly fine. A very nice date."

Now even Beth was giving her the fisheye.

"Fine?" Sarah echoed in a shrill voice.

"Nice?" On Chili's lips, nice was a bad word.

Swirling around with a loud harrumph, Kate stomped back to the dressing room, where only two more gowns hung from the hook. A long, casual skirt was sounding better all the time, and Diana must sell tons of them. She wore beautiful skirts all the time.

Chili was unzipping the lilac bridesmaid's dress from hell when Beth appeared at the door. "What about this one?" In her hand a red gown glowed with a satiny luster. The neckline made the breath catch in Kate's throat.

Chili's mouth fell open. Behind Beth, Sarah quivered with excitement. "You have to try this on," she pleaded. "It has your name written all over it."

"It does? No. Try Kate Hudson or Keira Knightley. They'd wear a dress like this." Was that her hand reaching out?

"Sorry this wasn't on the rack. A woman from Chicago dropped this off and I just didn't get it out on the floor yet." Beth's eyes clung to the dress, like she wished she had some place to wear it.

The three friends exchanged glances that ricocheted with excitement.

"She wore it to a gala and didn't want anyone else in Chicago to show up in it again, so she brought it here. We get a lot of that." Beth gave a little laugh.

"How much?" Kate flipped the tag over and sucked in a breath. Bargain didn't begin to cover it.

"She said she was writing it off as a charitable donation."

The dress was a steal. Not a reason to buy it but still.

Chili had already unzipped her. "Clear the room, please."

Then Chili disappeared too, leaving her with the dress.

The slinky material slid seductively against her skin. The neckline? Kate slapped a hand to her chest. All she felt was soft skin.

Could she… would she dare wear this?

"We're waiting," Sarah sang out.

"Show time!" Chili's voice joined Sarah's.

Kate shivered. Her stomach doing a salsa, she edged out of the dressing room and down the narrow hall. Sarah and Chili stopped talking.

"Wow," Beth said, her lips a perfect oval.

"I look ridiculous, right? I just can't wear this in public." She turned to Chili and Sarah for confirmation, both hands pressed over her wildly beating heart.

"Can't wear it? Girl, are you crazy?" Chili circled her.

"You look beautiful," Sarah murmured on a sigh of appreciation.

The dress sang a siren song.

Peeling Kate's hands away, Chili aimed her toward the mirror. "Looking at yourself. *Magnifico.* You are looking so fine."

"Hot, damn. Wish it looked like that on me." Obviously Beth tested the merchandise.

Who was this staring at Kate from the mirror? Not the beaten down, recently divorced woman who'd driven home from Boston. Kate moved her hips. The dress followed.

"She'll take it," her friends said in one voice.

Chapter 24

Summer slumped into a muggy late July pocket. The air hung over Lake Michigan like a damp beach towel instead of whisking up to the cottages in cooling waves. Leaves didn't shimmer on the trees anymore. The high keening of locusts slit the airless days. Pick blueberries? Unthinkable.

At the July town meeting, the Downtown Development committee proposed putting Cole's motion to a vote. "Since the entire town will be impacted by whatever happens on Whittaker, the town should vote on it," Billy Cramer announced.

From her seat in the back row, Kate could see that the decision frustrated Cole. He wanted quick approval. Her guilt mounted. One night she took a trip up Red Arrow, stuffing a handful of the remaining flyers in any trash can she found in Harbert and Stevensville. Had her decision about Cole's plans been rash?

Business slowed. People were finished planting their flowers. A Michigan grower made fresh cut flowers available, and Kate put small bouquets together. Red and pink zinnias. Bachelor buttons and marigolds. Sweet Williams and Queen Anne's lace. Customers snapped them up on their way to buy cucumbers and zucchinis from Ignacio.

"How beautiful, Kate." Her mother promptly buried her nose

in a bouquet of zinnias Kate had brought home. Laughing, Kate gently wiped the pollen from her mother's nose, glad she was back in the big bedroom upstairs. Their lives were slowly returning to normal, although climbing the steps took time.

Acting on Cole's suggestion, Kate began to interview some of the store owners on Whittaker. Sarah suggested Sun and Sail, a shop that hadn't been around when she was growing up, but boogie boards weren't around then either.

The owner, Oscar Werner, shrugged when Kate questioned him about the town's strategy for merchants. "What can I tell you? If the town council doesn't start bringing in more tourists, I might not be here next summer."

Kate looked up from her notes. "What would have to change?"

He gave her a wry smile. "You're asking the wrong guy. Ask me about skis, and I can fit you. What fishing lure to use on Lake Michigan? Sure, I'll talk your ear off. But bringing in tourists? I'm no marketer. What we don't need is another gambling casino."

"Got it." Kate left Sun and Sail feeling unsettled and headed for The Full Cup.

"You're going to interview Cole, aren't you?" Sarah asked. "He's the one with the facts and figures."

"I guess." Would any conversation with Cole about Gull Harbor turn into a confrontation?

"You guess?" Sarah's face flushed. "Kate, he's the main driver of progress around here."

"Is it progress, Sarah?" Uncertainty churned in Kate's stomach.

"My word, have you been reading those flyers? Those darn

yellow sheets."

Kate's stomach tightened painfully.

"I don't know what idiot has been circulating them, but obviously it's someone who doesn't know the town. And that editorial in the paper agreeing with the flyer? Another moron. Did you see that?" Sarah slammed a tray of sticky buns into her glass case. Kate felt it clear to her backbone.

"Yes, my mom read it to me. Upset her plenty." She thrummed her numb fingers on the case.

The curls on Sarah's head shivered. "Nathan Petersen no doubt wrote it, our resident complainer. If it's not the poor service at the gas station, it's the lines that need painting on Red Arrow Highway. Always negative. We don't need his kind around here."

Pushing away, Kate turned to stare out at the street. Had her assumptions hurt or helped Gull Harbor?

"Didn't mean to upset you, Kate. I'm just letting off steam. Haven't heard from Jamie for over a week. It's not like him."

"Oh, Sarah. You've got so much on your mind. I shouldn't be making you crazy with my questions."

Late afternoon and the bakery was quiet. They sat and talked at one of the tables, but Kate couldn't share any concerns about her mother. Couldn't mention that yesterday she'd come home to find a frying pan in the freezer on top of the frozen peas.

And then there was Cole. No word from him, and she wished she didn't care.

"Think I'll ask Cole to send Natalie's suit over tomorrow," she told her mother later that evening. "Business has slowed. I close earlier each day."

They'd finished their tuna salad and were sitting on the screen porch, hoping to catch a beach breeze. Even the weeds were wilted. Rain had pounded them in June but now? Nothing.

"Natalie will love that, honey. I can stand up here, directing you with my cane." Her mother gave her a wry smile.

That called for a hug. Their relationship had sure changed.

Before she tapped out Cole's number, Kate sucked in a breath. Amazing how nervous she felt. When he answered, she quickly made her case. "Don't worry. She won't be swimming alone."

Nothing but silence.

"Feel free to come." Kate rested her head against the kitchen cupboards. Was she begging? Sure felt like it. Her entire insides knotted with longing. Maybe she just wanted some closure after those kisses. Wanted some proof so she could believe once again that Cole would wreck Gull Harbor if the town let him.

"Depends on my schedule, but I'll see."

She was being put off. This felt like high school.

The call ended, and she pocketed the phone.

"We're set for swimming tomorrow." Kate leaned into the porch that was still stifling, even though the sun was setting. "How about some iced tea?"

Mom was fanning herself with the weekly *Beacher* magazine "Not before I go to bed. I'd be limping to the bathroom all night." Her eyes slid to the black futon they kept in the corner. "Maybe I'll sleep out here tonight."

"You sure about that?" Kate's gaze swung to the settling

darkness.

"Think someone might come and steal me away? I'll beat him off with my cane." Her laugh was more a cackle.

"You're definitely getting better."

Her mother made a face. "Dr. Jensen says I need more physical therapy."

"I'll arrange it. You have to get used to using that leg again."

"Sure. Like I haven't been doing that already."

A few minutes later, Kate said good night. Upstairs, the air hung hot and heavy. She threw her three windows open wide and flicked on the standing fan she'd picked up that day. Central air, once considered a luxury at the lake, now seemed a mainstay. But Her mother had always resisted the very mention of installing central air. Somehow Kate would have to work that out with Mercedes. After sliding into the pink slip nightgown, she opened the closet door. The red dress flared out at her.

What had she been thinking? When the oscillating fan hit the fabric, it rippled with sensual promise. She closed the door, unable to put that dress and Will Applegate together in her mind.

Once in bed, she tossed fitfully in the stuffy room. The fan only succeeded in bathing her with hot air. Dragging her summer sheet behind her, Kate finally tiptoed downstairs and onto the porch, where the air felt refreshing. A night breeze had kicked up, banishing the muggy heat and she sank onto the futon with relief, careful not to wake her sleeping mother.

~~

The next day, she could hardly wait to get home from the flower stand. "Who's going swimming?" she called out when she burst through the back door. Damp with perspiration, her T-shirt and cutoffs clung.

"Me! I am!" Natalie shot into the living room doorway, ready in a blue striped swimsuit. Her hair was swept up into a ponytail.

Kate followed the scent of chocolate to the plump loaves of chocolate chip zucchini cake laid out on the kitchen counter to cool.

"I don't believe you're baking in weather like this," Kate called out to her mother on the porch. The loaves did look tempting and she brushed the warm tops lightly with her fingertips. Had her mother added any strange ingredients? Maybe motor oil or cleaning fluid?

Natalie licked her lips. "I already tried one, Kate. So yummy."

Mom thumped up behind her with her walker. "What's summer without chocolate chip zucchini cake?"

"Absolutely right, Mom." Kate sliced a piece from the loaf Natalie had tested.

Maybe the meatballs had been a one-time mistake. She could only hope. The first bite of Kate's summer favorite seduced her, warm and richly chocolate. Her mother had rituals for every season. Unlike scrubbing the floors and washing curtains, this was one Kate fully supported. Brian had always been on a diet. The one time Kate baked these sweet, summer loaves, she'd earned a frown and a lecture about calorie count. How wonderful to indulge without silent disapproval.

"Okay, I'll be right back." Kate took the stairs two at a time.

The sky blue bikini from college somehow still fit her. Opening the upstairs linen closet, she grabbed a couple beach towels.

"Want the unicorn or the goldfish?" She shook out the two towels when she reached the bottom of the steps.

"The unicorn."

"It's yours." The colorful blue and green creature had been Kate's favorite. She draped it over Natalie's shoulder on her way to the kitchen. The day before, Kate had blown up a couple of the rafts she found in the work shed. They grabbed them on their way out.

"Be careful on the steps," her mom called out as they left, screen door slamming behind them.

"Mothers always tell you to be careful," Kate said to Natalie. She could have bitten her tongue at the look on the little girl's face. *Think before you speak.* "Grab the railing, Natalie."

Rafts under their arms, they descended and broke through the trees onto the beach.

Out of habit, Kate kicked off her sandals, but the sand was blistering hot and she quickly jammed her feet back into them. "Keep your shoes on, Natalie." The trip to the water was like sprinting across a frying pan.

Kate spread the goldfish towel a few feet from the shore. Everything seemed sluggish that day, even the water. A dull expanse of grayish-blue stretched to a horizon that held not one cloud. Sultry waves stroked the shore. Mothers lolled on rafts close to the children playing in the shallows. Other women wearing floppy hats sat in beach chairs wedged into the wet shoreline, half submerged in the water.

"Time for some sunblock." Kate squirted the lotion into her palm and swirled it over Natalie's skinny shoulders. "Such tender skin. You don't want to ruin it."

"But I want to be tan." Natalie scrunched up her nose, rebellious and cute.

Glancing at her own lightly speckled arms, Kate shook her head. "Trust me, I regret every freckle I ever got on the beach."

"Did you tan a lot?"

"Lived in my bathing suit." Didn't everyone in Gull Harbor? "Before senior prom, I even used one of those foil reflectors to deepen the color. Stupid."

"Did you go to a lot of dances?"

"Some. Not a lot. I was tall and skinny, not exactly man bait."

"Oh, you turned out great."

Kate bust out laughing. "You think so, huh?" So she wasn't a hopeless case? Grinning, she tossed the sunblock onto the fish towel. Natalie was already dipping her toes in the water. Dragging the two rafts behind them, they waded in deeper. Usually this warm, bath-like lake came in August, not at the end of July. When the water was thigh deep, Kate pulled herself onto the raft, landing on her stomach. Natalie did the same. The rafts sagged into the water under their weight.

Letting her hands trail in the water, Kate turned to look at Natalie. "You doing okay?"

"You bet."

"How well can you swim?"

"I took lessons two summers in a row." Folding her hands under her chin, Natalie stared out at the horizon. "My mother used to take me to the beach when I was little. I think I remember that."

Kate struggled for the right words, ones that wouldn't deepen the hurt. "You must miss her a lot."

"Yeah." Such an empty ache in that word. "But she's sick. Dad says that's why she decided not to live with us." Amazing how easily the little girl accepted that.

Sick. That's what her mother had told them, trying to explain the divorce, the drinking. "If he had cancer, I'd stay with him, but he's sick in another way and he won't deal with it."

But a summer day didn't allow such a serious conversation. "Want to go out to the sandbar?"

"Sure." Natalie's carefree grin returned.

During the summer, changing currents continually moved the sandbar. Right now, the shallow ridge of sand wasn't far out. When Kate could see the bottom again, they slipped off their rafts. The water reached Natalie's waist. Kate's toes squished into the sand, her insteps lifting over any rocks. "Watch it, Natalie. Stay where the water is shallow. It drops off fast."

"Look, there's Dad!" Natalie pointed toward shore.

Kate's heart leapt into her throat.

Chapter 25

Cole loped down the steps in a navy swimsuit, a white towel around his neck. Kate sucked in a breath. Dressed, the man was handsome. Bare-chested, he left her breathless.

"Dad! Dad!" Excitement vibrated in Natalie's voice.

Glancing up, Cole waved.

Longing cascaded through Kate's body, awakening memories and deepening them. The way he moved? Cole could have been striding through the hall at Gull Harbor High School. And yet, he wasn't. The man he had become engaged Kate's heart on a different level and left her yearning for him.

At the shoreline, he kicked out of his dockers, waded into the water and did a shallow dive. After a shake of his head, he swam toward them, cutting the surface with precise, strong strokes.

"Let's go meet him," Natalie said.

"Your dad will be here in a second." The emotional onslaught felt so wrong but held Kate's body hostage, like a riptide. She fought it and hoped it would subside.

Natalie threw herself onto the raft and headed toward shore. What to do but follow her? They met Cole halfway, shallow enough so Natalie could stand.

"Hey, Dad, you made it."

"Yeah." Blue lightning sparked in his eyes. "You were on the sandbar?"

"We were careful," Kate said quickly.

Natalie's mouth opened and closed. The flush on her face wasn't from the sun. Maybe she got the third-degree all the time. Darn it, did he have to ruin this?

His eyes circled between the two of them, and his square shoulders loosened.

"I grew up near the lake, remember?" Kate reminded him gently.

"Yeah, I know. But I don't remember that suit." Cole's eyes brushed her and Kate's skin burned.

"Got it in college."

A grin tweaked his lips. "That explains a lot."

The tension had ebbed. Slipping off her raft, Kate submerged herself until she felt the sand against her backbone. After Cole's comment, she figured steam probably rose from the water above her. When she broke the surface, she swept back her streaming hair.

Natalie was tugging Cole into the deeper water. "I want to sit on your shoulders. Can I?"

"Aren't you a little big for that?"

"Daddy? Pretty please?"

Little girls never got enough of horsing around with their dad. Kate knew that much. Cole hoisted his daughter onto his shoulders while she screamed with glee.

Leaving the two of them, Kate returned to shore and grabbed a frisbee from the boathouse. For a second, she stood in the cool darkness, trying to catch her breath. Cole unsettled her in a way that was unexpected and exciting. Nervous energy sent her racing back to the beach where the three of them spread out in the shallow water. They played keep away with the frisbee, splashing each other as much as possible in the process. That was one of the unwritten rules of the game. You had to annoy the heck out of the people playing with you. Watching Cole's muscles ripple under the merciless sun kept Kate in motion, although she had to keep tugging at the darn blue bikini. A pleasant heat began low in her belly when she caught Cole checking her out.

"Natalie, your lips are blue," she commented at one point. Hard to believe anyone's teeth could chatter in this warm water, but Natalie's were.

"Step out, Nat." Cole nodded toward the beach. "Just sit on your towel for a few minutes, okay?"

"Oh, Dad." Shoulders slumped, Natalie dragged herself into shore.

Cole watched her go and then scanned the lake. "God, this feels good. Want to swim out to the sandbar?"

"Sure."

His easy crawl easily outpaced her relaxed side stroke. Kate splashed water his way at every opportunity and he retaliated. Sometimes it felt like they were back in high school. Adult responsibilities fell away and there was only the two of them.

But it had never been this way in high school.

The difference broke her rhythm and her feet scrabbled to find footing.

When she felt the sand below her, Kate stood, wiping rivulets from her face and smoothing her hair. His eyes followed each move, and she trembled.

"I hear you've been asking questions."

"About?" She cocked her head. The sun sharpened the contours of Cole's face and glazed his chest muscles into Greek god proportions. Her eyes slipped from his jaw to his chest and then down, a dizzying journey.

The slippery slope. She forced her attention back to what Cole was saying.

"You tell me. Oscar just said you had questions. Which is a good thing."

"You asked me to write about the town and I am. Found some travel blogs." Partially true. She was on her own fact-finding mission as well.

"Sounds good." Cole's throat worked, like he wanted to say more.

Kate waited and then fell into a comfortable back float, glad she'd polished her toenails bright red. Maybe she'd fallen under the spell of that darn red dress waiting in her closet.

"Look, I'm sorry about the street dance. The beach," he finally said. "Sometimes I can be clueless."

She stood upright. *Really?* "What are you sorry about? I'm not."

Cole's head jerked and his blue eyes darkened to deep water. The last time they'd been this close, he'd taken her in his arms.

Kate wanted to feel every muscle in his chest, his moist breath on her face, the persuasion of his tongue.

Standing in water, she was burning up.

"You're not sorry?" His grin stretched. "Girl, you confuse the heck out of me."

"Sometimes I confuse myself, Cole." *Especially when it comes to you.* They inched closer until she could count the bristles on his jaw.

"I'm sorry because I didn't know you were dating Will Applegate."

"I'm not."

An eyebrow rose. "No?"

"No. He just invited me to the dance. Total surprise. I thought…" *Zip it, Kate.* So much for keeping an air of mystery. With every word, Cole's grin tweaked higher.

Time to forget about the peaks of his dark lashes. Not the moment to study his muscled arms and how they might feel on the skin she was flaunting.

Then it hit her. "Wait… you thought I was making out with you while I was dating Will? That's sick."

His smile faltered. "Not for some people. But, yeah, that's what I thought."

"Don't you know me better than that?"

"We haven't seen each other in a long time. I don't know what to think."

"Ditto. The first time I mentioned the flower stand, you gave me the strangest look ever. What was that about?"

With a toss of his head, Cole stared at the horizon. "Your fancy

Boston education seemed wasted. I mean, you come back to Gull Harbor to sell flowers?"

Dragging one hand through the water, she made an arch. The water rippled out to Cole. "I returned home because my family needed me."

Turning his attention back to her, Cole's eyes burned with sun-like intensity. This was getting too personal. Kate swung one of her hips closer. Cole's hands jerked, like they wanted to grab her waist. His eyes flitted to the shore where Natalie sat watching them. She waved. He waved back, hissing out a sigh between set teeth.

They were so close. She could feel the heat he radiated, or was that her own? "So, what would you do now that you know I'm not dating Will?"

The grin returned, mischievous and quirky—like high school, when they sprayed shaving cream through the vent in Ignacio's locker. "I'd put one hand flat on the small of your back, bring you closer."

"How close?" She could barely get the question out.

"Close enough to kiss you. Soft and then hard."

"I'd like that." She began to tremble.

Cole's eyelids dropped to half mast. "Really? How much?"

"A lot and more." Her fingers tingled, wanting to trace the high arc of his strong nose. "Yeah, I'd like that a lot."

Have you no shame, Katherine?

None whatsoever.

"And if it was dark out… if we were here at night?" He wasn't finished, and she was glad.

"What then?" Her mouth felt like sandpaper.

"Why, I'd slip off that tiny top, Katydid. Kiss you all over."

"All over?"

"Every hill and valley. Lay you out like a picnic on a sand dune. And you can bet I'd take my time."

"But I'd want you to hurry." Her heart was slamming against her ribs.

One eyebrow went up. "Really? Well, your wish is my command."

She gave a choked giggle. "We watched that movie together. 'Princess Bride.' Laughed all the way through."

"Still do. Natalie loves it." A fierce frown had settled on Cole's brow, his chest expanding in an alarming way. "But I'm not laughing now, Katydid."

If Kate lost her footing now, she might drown. *Paralyzed by her thoughts*, the EMS guy would say. *We see this all the time on the beach.*

Reaching out, Cole smoothed back her wet hair. Every follicle of her skin felt his touch. "I'm thinking of all the slow, satisfying things we could do tucked behind a dune, things we never even knew about in high school."

Kate's imagination caromed into every erotic book she'd ever read. Okay, only three but they'd do. "That bad, huh?"

"Worse than bad…but better." Cole shook himself, like a bear waking up from a nap. "And now I want you to go back to the beach while I swim out into the colder water so I don't embarrass us both."

"Sure. Right. Okay. And I'll try not to drown."

He laughed but she wasn't kidding. Body limp, Kate collapsed into a sidestroke. Somehow she made it to shore.

A little while later, Cole joined them and they trooped up to the house. Kate couldn't even look at him. Snapping out the beach towels, she hung them on the clothes lines strung between two birch trees. Cole sprayed sand from their feet with the garden hose.

"Have fun, Cole?" Her mother's voice came from the dimness of the porch.

"Sure did, Mrs. Kennedy."

Kate choked when his gaze found hers and he winked. Natalie was totally oblivious, eager to get inside where Prissy stood, pressing against the screen. Kate still couldn't believe the tolerance her mother showed for that dog, opening the screen door so Prissy could greet Cole with slobbery kisses.

Lips tingling, Kate envied Prissy.

"Natalie, why don't you run upstairs to change back into your clothes?" Her mom beckoned and Natalie scurried inside.

"What the heck? I can never get her to do that without an argument," Cole muttered.

Her mother's laugh hit a surprised, high note. She liked Cole. The realization struck Kate with the suddenness of a summer storm. "And you come inside too, Cole. I got something for you."

Holding the door open for her, Cole sent Kate a smile. Geez, Cole liked Alice too. Would wonders never cease?

"Made some of these small chocolate chip zucchini loaves today. Way too many for us, especially since Kate is always on a diet."

"Mom!" Kate felt more of her feminine mystique melting away.

Her mother laughed again as they trailed her into the kitchen.

"Sure does smell good in here." He sniffed the air.

"I'm a silly fool. Way too hot for baking." Leaning against the counter, Mom propped her cane against the counter next to her. "But I thought Natalie might enjoy a treat."

"Mighty nice of you, Mrs. Kennedy."

"Alice. Call me Alice."

Cole ducked his head. The man seemed too large for this neat kitchen, like a bread that's risen too high.

Swinging open the refrigerator door, her mother grabbed two of the loaves, neatly wrapped in foil. The blast of cold air gave Kate goose bumps. Her shiver wasn't lost on Cole.

"Sure smells wonderful." Cole clasped them to his chest, his gaze on Kate.

By that time, Natalie was back downstairs, wet hair slicked back and a bright blue beach tote over one arm.

"You could stay for dinner." Her mother's offer came out of nowhere.

What was her mother thinking? They had nothing to eat.

"We could order a pizza," her mom said, as if she read Kate's mind.

"Could we, Dad?" Natalie cuddled up to her father.

Kate was relieved when Cole maneuvered Natalie toward the back door where Prissy was already nosing the screen.

"Maybe next time. I promised your grandmother we'd stop in tonight. Better get going."

"Oh, take one for Marie." Mom reached back into the fridge for another loaf. "Sometimes you get sick of nursing home food."

"That's very considerate, Mrs. K-, Alice."

"Maybe next time for dinner." Alice sent a sly look at Kate.

"Yep. Next time." Cole's glance pierced Kate with delicious intent. "Count on it."

Her heart did a back flip. After Cole and Natalie left, Kate cut off a huge wedge from one of the loaves and wolfed it down. While her mother fussed in the kitchen, Kate carried another huge piece out to the screen porch. Settling with a sigh, she savored each bite and wondered when she'd see Cole again.

~~

"But she lost all his manuscripts!" Phoebe's voice probably echoed across Lake Michigan.

"Surely he can forgive his wife," Sarah said softly, one finger tracing the beaded coolness of her glass of sangria.

"When you're Ernest Hemingway, maybe you don't forgive a woman for anything," Kate said dryly. The book group got into a spirited discussion about male authors and their real life women.

This was what Kate loved about the women gathered on her screen porch tonight. They said what they thought. Chili and Sarah had taken the old wicker furniture while Carolyn and Phoebe were seated on the futon. The swing squeaked while Kate rocked.

"Where's Diana tonight?" Carolyn asked, looking around. "Maybe we should wait for her."

"She had to work," Sarah said. "Evening hours are busy for her during the summer."

A pitcher of sangria sat on the side table, sliced lemons, oranges, and nectarines heaped in with the ice. Kate's mom had baked Sunshine Cake, and the scent of nectarines hung in the air. Kate helped sift the flour just so she could keep one eye on what was going into the bowl.

While the group talked, Kate glanced at the clock. Now able to drive, her mother had taken off to visit Marie at the care center. Nice to see her busy and happy, but the agreement was that she'd be home by dark.

The group had been discussing "The Paris Wife," the fictionalized account of Ernest Hemingway's first marriage to Hadley Richardson in the early years, Paris in the 20s. She loved it.

"So anyway, I found it touching." With the warm weather, Carolyn had traded her sweatshirts and sweaters for T-shirts that made her look curvy and cute.

Note to self. Keep the sweatshirts in drawers.

"Maybe everyone's first marriage begins sweet," Kate murmured without thinking. Certainly those first years had been like that with Brian. She could feel the woman's eyes cut to her in the darkness. "I mean, I imagine so."

"Touching and sweet until the husband takes up with his assistant." Phoebe put it right on the line. There was an edge to her words, and Kate didn't want to become *that woman*. The woman who becomes bitter because her marriage didn't work out, although Phoebe rarely complained. If Brian had been unfaithful, Kate didn't want to know. As time passed, though, she wondered. All those nights at work.

Work? Really?

"But here, it wasn't a secretary," Carolyn said, her voice rising. "Pauline Pfeiffer was actually someone Hadley Richardson knew. A friend."

Phoebe snorted. "Right. And Hemingway thought he could have both."

"Didn't I read somewhere that Hemingway always regretted that he left Hadley Richardson?" Chili's forehead wrinkled.

"Maybe we always regret things we leave behind," Kate murmured. The group fell silent, and Kate felt awkward. She held up her glass. "Guess I'm being the philosopher tonight. Sarah, pour the sangria."

"That would be a good title for a book." Carolyn shifted on the futon. "Speaking of the things you left behind, I'm going home next week. Summer break and all that."

"Where to?" Kate asked. She knew zero about Carolyn's background. Her mother's injury and the flower stall were keeping her so busy this summer. She couldn't even think about the fall.

"Santa Fe. My parents retired out there, so it's not really home."

"Sounds terrific. I've heard it's beautiful… and not as busy as Boston."

"Wherever our parents live is always home." Sarah picked at her slice of cake. She hadn't heard from Jamie for three weeks. Kate could not even imagine how that would feel.

"Well, I'd rather visit Santa Fe than Wisconsin. Although northern Wisconsin is beautiful in the summer." Carolyn chuckled. "But all that winter snow gets to you."

"So you chose Michigan instead." Phoebe rattled the ice cubes in her empty glass.

Carolyn shook her head with good humor. "You have to go where the jobs are. Gull Harbor High had an opening."

"Have a great visit." Kate cut another slice of cake. "But you're going to miss the Firemen's Ball."

Carolyn grimaced. "No big loss. Didn't have a date for it anyway."

"Why didn't you say something? We could have fixed you up," Chili yelped.

"Even I have a date to the Firemen's Ball," Phoebe announced, primping her newly mauve hair. "Do you believe that Chili's brother Rafe asked me?"

"Any man would be glad to be your escort." Sarah reached for another slice of cake. "Why, even I'm going to the dance with Chili and Ignacio. Why don't you come too, Carolyn?"

"I'm leaving town but thanks."

Chili turned to Kate. "Okay, how many times have you tried on that red dress?"

"Only once." Kate's face probably looked as red as that wicked satin. "The house isn't air-conditioned. Don't want to stain it before my big night."

"That dress." Chili shook out her hands. "*Tanto caliente.*"

Of course Phoebe and Carolyn wanted to hear about the hot dress. Kate left the details up to Chili and Sarah.

"Sure looks like a designer dress, but we never checked the label." Sarah turned to Kate. "Have you?"

"Of course. Vera Wang. Bless the Chicago people for their good taste." But how she wished she were wearing it with another man.

"Vera Wang?" Reverence swelled in Carolyn's voice. "Hey, I never thought I'd ever know a woman who wore a Vera Wang."

"But what happened to the blonde hair. Kate?' Sarah wailed.

Phoebe sighed. "Not my fault. Kate insisted."

Running one hand through her newly chestnut curls, Kate wasn't about to tell them that Cole had mentioned her dark hair had always reminded him of his baseball mitt. She jumped up. "Did you bring your suits?" She'd sent a text suggesting they all bring bathing suits. The heat had lifted, but it was still July.

Sarah set her empty glass on a side table. "You bet, and the thought of swimming without the boys climbing over me is mighty tempting."

The back door closed. A few seconds later, her mother appeared in the doorway. She was wearing one of her hot pink outfits.

Kate was probably the only one to notice her flushed face in the dim light. "Everything okay, Mom?"

Her mom's smile was still crooked. "Right as rain. Marie loved the piece of cake I brought."

"So do we." Sarah popped the last bite in her mouth.

"Think I'll watch some TV up in my room."

"Night, Mom." Listening to her mother make her way up the stairs, Kate wondered if anything had happened. She'd have to speak to Marianne about the driving. Was it safe for her mother, who had good days and bad?

The group took turns changing in the powder room, and everyone commented about the apple green walls and the beautiful mirror. If only they knew. Ten minutes later, they were giggling like high school sophomores as they tripped down the steps toward the beach.

Dropping her towel, Chili rushed toward the water. With a giddy shriek, the rest of them followed. They ended up on the sandbar, laughing and splashing in the ghostly light of the moon.

Kate thought back to that afternoon with Cole. The sun gleaming off his water glazed muscles and the wicked gleam in his eyes as his confidence grew after she confessed that Will wasn't anyone special in her life, not really. Sleep had been a long time coming that night.

"Here goes the eye makeup," Chili yelped, coming up from the water with hair streaming from raccoon eyes.

"Some of us have a bigger worry than others," Carolyn turned, smiling over her shoulder. Kate didn't think she'd ever seen Carolyn with makeup, only a dash of lipstick.

The night air felt soft and warm. As they cavorted on the sandbar, the group felt like a secret sisterhood, mystical in the moonlight. Kate stared toward the darkened shore. Most of the families were now up in the cottages, putting the kids to bed. The sense of trusted routines made Kate glad she'd come home, but uncertainty pulled at the fabric of her contentment. She'd come back to Gull Harbor wanting her past.

But right now? She was filled with anxiety about what was to come. Plunging into the water, she submerged herself, wanting to leave troubling thoughts behind.

No surprise, Chili was the first one to shed her suit, boldly tossing her scrap of black fabric onto the sand. Didn't take long for the others to follow.

"This is so wicked." Sarah giggled, hands crossed over her chest.

"Wonderful." Relaxing into her sidestroke, Kate couldn't remember when she'd felt this free. How she wished she could block Cole from her mind. As she stroked out to the bar, she imagined his twinkling blue eyes watching her.

And then? What then?

She had no answers, only possibilities that kept her from sleep that night. None of the women knew about the yellow flyers. Had she betrayed them by spurring the community to question improvements that might save the town?

Chapter 26

The remote slipped from her mother's hand when Kate came teetering down the stairs Saturday night in her three-inch sandals. "I look ridiculous, right?"

Her mom brushed a finger under each eye. "Oh, Katie. You've never looked more beautiful."

First time she'd ever heard that from her mom and Kate's throat swelled. The stroke may have changed Alice Kennedy, but sometimes Kate thought it was for the better. "I just hope I don't fall flat on my face." She swished the long skirt of the clingy red gown, grateful for the slit up the back.

"Wait until Will sees that. My, oh, my." Jeopardy droned on in the background, but her mother wasn't listening. "I like your hair brown again, Katie. That blonde? Just not you."

A thunk to the heart. "You mean good for you and Mercedes but not for me?"

Her mom leveled a look, eyes suddenly clear and sharp. "I mean every child is different. Your hair always reminded me of the brown velvet dress I wore when I met your father."

"You never told me! I've never seen that dress."

"You can't hold onto everything." A quick clearing of the

throat. "But the color? That I'll never forget."

Her mom smelled of almond shampoo when Kate bent to hug her. "Thanks, Mom."

When the back doorbell rang, Kate ran to get it with short mincing steps. The dress wouldn't allow more. Only Will would ring the bell instead of just knocking on the door and calling out, like everyone else in Gull Harbor.

"Evening, Kate." Will's blue eyes widened when she pushed the screen door open. "Aren't you s-something?"

Enough to make the poor man stutter? Kate's laugh tickled her throat. "You're something yourself in that baby blue sport coat." The khaki slacks and red tie made his outfit conventional. Nice, but so Will. So proper.

"Maybe I should have worn a tux." His eyes swept her one more time, two red dots appearing high on his cheeks.

"Trust me, this is not a tuxedo event. Come and say hi to Mom."

In the living room, her mother chatted with Will for a few minutes, and then they were out the door on their way to the Whittaker Country Club. A summer rain had left the air moist. Maybe she should have used more hair spray on her long curls.

When Will pulled into the parking lot, Kate's nerve deserted her. She froze, gripping the edge of the front seat in his sensible white sedan. How could she walk into that ballroom dressed like this? Why did she listen to Chili and Sarah about a gown that was sexier than sin and so not her?

At least Cole wouldn't be here. The thought made her both

relieved and sad. After that scene at the beach, would he ask someone else? Her mind spun. Downright juvenile, the doubts spinning through her head.

Music was playing when they swept through the door. Will treated her as if she were made of glass, offering his arm and looking everywhere but at her. Was he embarrassed to be with her? Kate's spirits sagged. One of her crystal chandelier earrings kept getting caught in her hair, and she wanted to rip it out. She'd overdone it. Chili motioned them over, and Will steered her in that direction.

"Oh, *chica*." Chili held both hands to her cheeks. "You look so beautiful."

"Gorgeous." Sarah's eyes sparkled. Was she wearing that blue and green dress from Second Hand Rose? The one they wouldn't let Kate buy?

Ignacio raised an eyebrow. "Don't ever wear that to work, okay? Guys will drive right off the road."

Will and Ignacio knew each other, which made things easier. After the guys left to fetch drinks, the girls began to dissect who was with whom and what they were wearing. Although the band had been playing something slow and dreamy, they broke into "Old Time Rock and Roll." The fast beat drove people from the dance floor to the auction items, and the three women got up to follow the crowd. This year, proceeds from the fundraiser would buy new hoses and a replacement microwave for the firehouse. Some of the local artists had donated paintings to the silent auction and Kate studied them.

"I'd like to have a dune scape for my office." Kate scribbled her name on a couple of the cards. Sarah and Chili became quiet, and Kate turned to face them. "What?"

"Which office?" Sarah asked. "Do you mean the one in Boston?"

"You can't be serious." Chili slapped the heel of one hand to her forehead.

What could Kate say? She set down the card. Her office? No image came to mind. Not the home office at the condo Brian now fully owned. Not the dining room table at Lisa's before she left for Michigan. Kate felt like a balloon that had been released into the air. The height felt dizzying.

Could Kate go back to Boston? Did she want to? Her mom was definitely feeling better physically. Still used a cane but she'd made peace with it. Her mind? That was another question. Kate tried not to ask Natalie too many questions about what happened during the day. When she found a jar of strawberry jelly in the oven, Natalie insisted she'd hidden it there herself, playing a game with Kate's mom. Hard to picture but easy to accept.

Chili clutched Kate's elbow. Sarah's eyes were focused on the door and Kate wheeled around. Perfect. Chills rippled through her body, leaving her nauseous. *Would the floor please swallow me up?* In the door stood Cole, looking heartbreakingly handsome. He filled out the tailored suit, but the bolo tie was the kicker, along with those western boots. Her mouth went dry and her pulse speeded up. On his arm, Diana glowed in a halter-top gown that looked like water when she moved. "Holy smokes."

"*Aye, caramba*," Chili whispered.

Felt like Kate's heart had been carved right out of her chest.

"Here you are, Kate." Will tapped her elbow. "Want to dance? I just put in a request."

The band began to play an old song called "Lady in Red." Kate felt numb as Will led her to the floor.

"What? You don't like it?" His eyes searched her face, and somewhere she found a smile. After all, this wasn't his fault.

"I love this song. Very thoughtful, Will." She wasn't going to spoil his evening.

Blocking out the sight of Cole and Diana making their way across the floor, Kate closed her eyes. Humming off key, Will brought her closer. She tried to relax, to let the music move her. Will was such a nice guy, so sincere and great with older people. A good man.

She peeked over his shoulder. Chili and Ignacio had settled at their table with Sarah, and she sent a little wave their way. Ryan, Jamie's brother, joined them with his date.

Then Will swung her around, and Kate came face to face with Cole. They were staring straight at each other over the shoulders of their partners. Cole looked as surprised as she felt.

"Anything wrong?" Will pulled away.

Could he feel her heart galloping like a herd of runaway ponies? "No, of course not. Everything's fine."

But Kate knew right then. Knew she wanted to be in another man's arms. Because she loved that man. For the second time in her life, she loved Cole Campbell. No matter how many times she tried to swallow, she could not ease the ache in her throat that shifted to her heart. Her high school crush was a paper cut compared to the machete lodged in her heart tonight.

Every time Cole smiled down at Diana, the blade sank deeper. It wouldn't matter if Diana wore an outrageously sexy red dress or a paper bag. Men would always be attracted to her because she was the real deal.

Kate felt counterfeit. The girl who tried too hard.

Cole bent his head to hear something Diana said. They moved away.

"You all right, Kate?"

She jerked. Blinked furiously before she glanced up. Bless his heart, Will looked so concerned. "I just need some… water." If she'd said *air*, they would be outside in a heartbeat. Alone. The last thing Kate wanted.

Will led her back to the table. She was so relieved when he didn't place his hand in the small of her back because that was her favorite sexy move.

How would she get through this night?

"You two look great together." Sarah reached over and squeezed her hand.

"Ladies' room?" Grabbing a small beaded bag, Chili shot to her feet.

Oh, yeah. "Excuse me, Will? Be right back."

Will smiled and turned to Ignacio. Such a great guy.

Perfect. Will should be perfect for her.

Except that he wasn't.

She'd made that mistake once before by choosing Mr. "Perfect for You." No way would she ever do that again. Without the feelings that electrified her just looking at Cole, what was the point? Attraction couldn't begin to cover how she felt about the man. His concern for her mother, tender care of Natalie, sexy smiles and the kisses she felt straight to her toes. The list of Cole's good points left Kate weak with longing.

Thank goodness the ladies room was empty. Chili waved a manicured finger in Kate's face. "Don't you go cozying up to Mr. Administrator."

"Will's such a nice guy." Kate put both palms on the cool sink and leaned forward. Was she going to be sick?

Tsking, Sarah grabbed Chili's fingers. "Will is a fine man. Admirable."

The disgust on Chili's face told Kate just what she thought of that.

Opening her bag with shaking fingers, Kate took out a small brush and ran it through her hair, forgetting the can of hairspray she'd used earlier. The brush snagged. "What a mess."

Taking her shoulders, Chili rotated Kate to face her. "Yes, it is a mess. You keep pushing Cole away. Why?"

"He's with Diana, for Pete's sake." Her voice wobbled.

"She's a red herring!" Sarah's words exploded like a firecracker.

"A what?" Kate's brush clattered into the sink.

Scooping up the brush, Chili jabbed it at her. "You know. Like that book we read in the group, right?"

Sarah nodded. "The thing is," she began softly, "we sort of

fixed those two up tonight. Cole had to come to the dance because he's a fireman. Chili suggested Diana. They're still friends, and she wanted to come."

"Why?" Kate's legs gave out, and she plunked down on the tufted dressing table bench. "Why would you do that?"

Chili's jolly chuckle rippled through her body. "If he didn't come, he would not see you in that dress, right?"

"And he had to see you." Sarah was nodding again. So they'd both been in on this?

One hour ago, Kate would have given anything for Cole to see her in this gown. Now? She felt so confused.

The door flew open, and Diana whirled in on a wave of perfume. Her silver sandals skidded to a halt. "What's this? You planning the next book club meeting?"

"You two need to talk." Chili circled the air between Kate and Diana. "Diana, you explain please, yes?"

With that, Kate's two friends swept out of the room. The door whapped shut, leaving a thundering silence.

"Did they clue you in?" Smoothing her long blonde hair, Diana met Kate's eyes in the mirror.

"Kind of." Kate's head spun.

"Just so you know, I have no designs on Cole. But when he asked me to come as a friend, who was I to say no? Besides…" Whipping out some gloss, Diana coated her smile in luscious pink. "Now Will? He's kind of cute."

"But he's with me!" What the heck?

Bringing out a hand mirror, Diana surveyed herself from every angle. "Come on, Kate. Do I look like I just fell off a turnip truck? I practically get heat stroke every time you and Cole look at each other. If you're going to openly lust, at least hand out spoons so we can lap some up. I'm definitely in the line of fire and so is poor Will."

"Poor Will?" Was it that obvious?

"Cole's done nothing but talk about your flower stand tonight. I like your bouquets but there's a limit. Know what I'm saying?" The smile she gave Kate was wisely wicked. "I just asked the band for a ladies' choice. Will might not be with you for long."

"Be kind to him. He's a great guy."

Diana's smile softened. "Hey, I could go for a great guy, one who wasn't crazy about another woman."

Hmm. What's that about? No time to ask.

Grabbing her purse, Kate pushed back out into the room. Her chest felt like a blender, anger, disbelief, and relief whirling inside. She'd been lovingly sabotaged by her friends. Women like this were hard to come by.

When she returned to the table, everyone had left for the buffet, except Will. "Hungry?" he asked.

"Sure." But once back in her seat, plate laden with food, Kate could barely swallow. Slices of ham sat uneaten, along with the scalloped potatoes. Instead, she nibbled on her salad. Felt good to bite down on the crunchy cucumbers. Two tables away, Cole sat with Diana and some guys she recognized from his construction crew. When Diana caught Kate studying them, she smiled.

How could Kate be mad at her for coming with Cole? After all,

Diana had been so open and honest.

Dessert was chocolate layer cake from Sarah's bakery. "I told them to cut big pieces so now eat." Sarah pushed a chunk toward Kate, who sank her fork in for more than a small bite. Didn't chocolate cure everything?

The band began playing "Beautiful World," a ladies' choice, and Diana approached the table. "Mind if I steal your date?"

Will flushed. Almost looked like he'd refuse.

Swallowing the cake made Kate's throat ache. She'd need the Heimlich if she weren't careful. Grabbing her water glass, she took a big gulp. "Of course not. Will, this is Diana Palmer, a friend from my book group."

Always a gentleman, Will got to his feet. "Well, of course. I'd like to hear more about the book group."

Sarah and Chili became very quiet, like they were waiting for the other shoe to drop. Will led Diana to the floor and Kate went back to her cake.

"Isn't this a ladies' choice? You know, where you ask me to dance?" Cole's voice tickled her ear.

Turning, Kate inhaled his soap and her fork clattered to the table. Chili and Sarah broke into giggles. All the way to the dance floor, Kate felt the heat of Cole's hand on her back, incinerating her common sense.

Cole led her to a dimly lit corner near an open set of French doors.

"Warm in here. I need some air." He swirled her into his arms.

He needed air? She was burning up. "I'm hot too."

"So I noticed. Where'd you get the dress?"

"Like it? Fire engine red."

"Right, five-alarm fire. The slit's not bad either." She felt Cole's chuckle deep in her chest. So did her breasts.

Why fight this? The man was a luscious armful, and she wrapped her arms around his shoulders with a sigh. Barely moving, they molded their bodies together. Bad idea. Or good? Cole groaned.

Over his shoulder, Kate could see Diana talking to Will, lips close to his ear. The man was laughing. Will hadn't laughed all evening, and Kate smiled to see him having fun.

"Having a good time?"

"Uh, huh."

"You looked like you might snooze off during dinner."

"You were watching me?" Her indignation quivered with pleasure.

"Like the way you eat your cake. With passion." Cole wiped one corner of her mouth with a finger.

Her stomach dove into free fall. "But you're here with Diana."

Smug was the only way to describe that grin. "And you're here with Will. Diana and I are old friends. Besides, Sarah and Chili set us up."

"So I heard."

His eyes deepened to navy. "Don't you think we should get together?"

"And do what?" Her lips had turned numb.

Cole chuckled. "Oh, I can think of lots of things."

"Blueberry picking? Natalie and I have that on our list."

"Not quite what I had in mind. I'm tired of waiting."

The urgency in Cole's voice struck a chord. "Me too," she whispered. Was the room spinning?

"Want to step outside?"

The music had ended. People were returning to the tables, except for Diana and Will, who were still having an animated conversation. Will was nodding, head close to Diana's luscious blonde hair.

"I have to remind myself I came with a date."

Cole's glance slid beyond her shoulder. "Our dates seem very involved."

"At least they've moved to the edge of the dance floor, but they are our dates."

With a frustrated growl, Cole took her elbow. "You are an honorable girl, and I am an honorable man. So no trip to the car tonight. I like to walk on the beach. Might just amble down your way tonight. Do you still wander along the beach at night?"

"How did you know that?"

Cole threw her a mischievous grin. "Sometimes I see you pass our house. In fact, I watch for you." He was playing with one of her curls.

He watches for me?

She could hardly breathe. "Think you might be walking down my way tonight?"

"Could be. Going to be wearing that dress?"

"Maybe."

"Not for long." Cole coasted both hands up her back on a heated mission and she gasped. He chuckled before pulling away. "Later."

Somehow, she made it back to the table. For the rest of the evening, she couldn't even look at Chili and Sarah. The pent-up energy as she waited for the evening to end frazzled her nerves. Somehow Kate resisted her friends' repeated efforts to drag her off to the ladies' room.

"Is Cole ready for the vote next week?" Chili asked.

"Don't know. We didn't talk about it." The question jerked Kate back to reality. Would she be sad or glad at the outcome? Her interviews with shopkeepers had shown her a different side of the issue. Maybe Gull Harbor should control their own destiny and oppose support from outside the community. If anyone tore down Michiana Thyme and repurposed that space, maybe Cole should be the man to do it.

Thank goodness they didn't stay long after that. Will seemed preoccupied on the way home. "Do you know Diana Palmer? She a friend of yours?"

"We're in the same book club. I told you."

"Oh, right. I guess she owns a dress store?"

Even in the darkness, Kate noted the flush working its way up Will's neck. He wouldn't be able to stop in at a dress shop as easily as the flower stand. "Do you have a mother or a sister?"

He glanced over. "Yes. Both."

"Diana's shop has nice gifts."

Kate had no clue if Hippy Chick sold racy lingerie or Italian pasta. Let Will find out. Everyone should light up like a Christmas tree for someone. That wouldn't be her and Will. He seemed to realize that too.

When they reached the door, she gave him a quick hug. "Thanks for inviting me."

Will squeezed her for a second, as if she were a relative he was seeing off at the train station. "Great evening. Give my best to your mother." He whistled all the way to the car.

Kate couldn't wait to get inside.

She sure hoped her mother was asleep.

Chapter 27

The sultry whisper of waves met her when Kate tripped down the steps and kicked her flip-flops into the dune grass. All had been quiet up in the house. Kate had considered wearing the red dress down to the beach, but she maybe she'd need it again someday. A girl could hope. Instead, she opted for cutoffs and a T-shirt. No bra tonight.

Following the light rain that day, the sand felt cool underfoot. Feeling downright wanton, she waded into the water, lifting the hair from her shoulders. A breeze whisked across the lake's surface, not strong enough to whip up any whitecaps. Definitely not forceful enough to cool her heat. The moon slipped out from behind a cloud and rippled across the surface toward her, as if it were lighting the way. She wanted to dance on the brightness. Had there ever been a night so beautiful?

Hearing a rustling behind her, she turned. Dressed in only a pair of cutoffs, Cole tossed a blanket onto the sand before wading in and wrapping his arms around her.

"No bolo tie?" she whispered, putting an ear to his thudding heart.

"No red dress?" A chuckle rumbled from his chest to hers before he lifted her chin and fitted his lips so perfectly over hers.

Such tenderness. Such sweetness.

Erasing past hurts.

His hands scooped Kate from behind, fitting her against him. The kisses became longer, hotter until she couldn't catch her breath.

Then he pulled away, chest expanding with a deep breath. "Want to walk a bit?" In the darkness, she couldn't read him, but the surge of heat in her body answered the question, at least for her.

"No. Not now. I just want you."

"Katie Kennedy," he murmured, pulling her back into his arms. "You always did know what you wanted."

But I didn't always get it.

Tonight, she was taking it. No walking home with lips bruised, body throbbing, and mind left to wonder. Tonight was all or nothing. From the look in Cole's eyes as he led her to the blanket, it wasn't going to be nothing. She loved this man like crazy. Maybe she always had. Desire pulsed through her veins like heated syrup.

Eyes burning, he pulled her down and she sank onto him.

"Aw, Katydid," Cole whispered, burying his nose in her hair. "So beautiful."

"Okay, does my hair smell like your baseball mitt?"

"Man, you've got a memory like an elephant. Nope, better."

When she looked into Cole's eyes, Kate saw tomorrow and the day after that. Smoothing back wisps of her hair, he cupped her chin, closed his eyes and kissed her. Scooting closer, Kate tightened her arms around his neck. Felt like she wanted to crawl inside him.

She loved him just that much. When he skimmed his hands over her hips, every muscle in her body tensed.

Her teeth chattered with nervousness. She felt grateful for the soft light of the moon. His hands and words calmed her. "So beautiful, Kate. So very beautiful."

She bit back words like, "hogwash" and, "You're crazy." The look on his face stopped her. For him, she was beautiful. The light burning inside her swelled big as the moon. His hands were gentle as she'd always known they'd be.

"What's this?" He chuckled when he palmed her breasts and felt no bra.

"Just me," she whispered, nudging him back so he could have a better look, see and feel it all.

Oh, my. So wanton. And crazy in love.

"Never *just you*, Katydid. Every part of you is special. You should know that."

His kisses didn't stop with her lips. That was just the beginning. Moaning, pressing, exploring, they tumbled, losing clothes along the way. Their kisses were deep and their hands, slow. She slid down his body like a moonbeam, lips glancing off angles, tongue flicking while he moaned.

"My, oh, my, you must work out." Kate squeezed a firm bicep that was easily twice the size of hers.

"Just working, ma'am," he drawled, the accent making her smile. "Could do some work for you if you like. But I like inside jobs the best."

And he proved it.

"Oh, my, construction man," she moaned. "I could find a job or two for you."

Cole swallowed her next moan, hoisted her gently as if she were the thistle that blew in the breeze. They sank into mindless heat, pleasing each other with the slow pace of a first time. He laughed at the sand in her hair. She exalted in his hard, lean muscles. She felt grateful for the darkness and the gentle swish of the dune grass with only the moon to watch.

"Am I too heavy?" she asked, when he lifted her into a position that amazed her.

"What do you think?" His teeth gleamed through a wicked smile. He showed how that the position could be, well, quite nice.

Kate wrapped her legs and love around him tight. In the end, she felt him pulse clear through to her spine. She'd been moving toward this for such a long time. She knew that now. *I love you. I love you.* The words sang in her head.

But she kept them locked in her heart. For tonight.

"Where'd you learn all this?" she asked him later much later, when every nerve in her body had met its match and they'd reluctantly found their clothes.

"Not telling." He stroked a thumb down her chin. "Look, I know this sounds corny, but it's never been like this."

She swallowed. "You don't have to say that, Cole." That comment cost her, but he'd been married to a beautiful woman.

Sitting up and reaching into the sand, Cole tossed stones out across the lake. "You just don't know. I'm not a guy who runs around, Kate."

"But there was Samantha."

Cole sucked in the cool lake air. "Look, I don't like to talk about this."

"I noticed. Fine if you don't want to."

"Yeah, well, I definitely don't talk about it around Natalie."

"I understand." *But I want to know. I have to know.*

Cole skipped another stone across the water. "No secret that Samantha was always a party animal. Guess I was drawn to her wild streak. We got crazy in college, like everyone else. Then her drinking got out of control. And she began mixing some other stuff with it. Dangerous stuff."

Kate remembered Mercedes saying with respect, "That Samantha can sure hold her booze." Maybe there was a limit for everything. Watching their father had taught Kate that.

"Everyone loved Samantha. I felt lucky when she married me. Thought she'd settle down. Thought once she was a mother, she'd see how much we needed her sober." Cole's chin tightened. "She went into treatment twice and was furious with me for insisting."

"The drinking's a sickness. You know that. Cure's not easy." Kate thought back to her dad and what her mother had told her.

"The first time Sam came out of rehab, she lasted a month. The second time, a week." His mouth twisted. "Her recovery was going in the wrong direction and so was she. Along the way, she found pals to feed new addictions."

"Oh, Cole." She stretched both arms around his chest to hold the pain.

He stroked her arm slowly with the flat of his hand. "So we

split up. She left for California. Leads a pretty wild life out there, or so I hear. We divorced two years later, and I made sure I got custody. By that time, she had a police record. Samantha can visit Natalie, but only when I'm with them. She came back once after I sent her the plane ticket. Marie still had the house so it was easy to supervise. I don't even know if Natalie remembers that visit. Samantha was jumpy, distracted. Made a lot of trips to the rental car I got for her. Whatever she needed was probably stashed in the glove compartment."

Kate cinched her arms tighter, feeling so helpless and understanding the pain.

"The second time we made plans, she called when we were waiting for her at the airport. Gave me a bogus story about a friend needing her, so she wasn't coming. Probably sold the ticket. Had other uses for the money. If she ever visits again, I won't tell Natalie until Samantha walks through the door."

"Poor Natalie." How Kate's heart burned for the little girl. "It's an illness. Cole. She didn't choose it."

The next rock Cole tossed out nicked three waves before it sank. "Well, neither did we."

Pulling her knees into her chest, Kate dug her bare toes deeper in the sand. "I understand but doesn't knowing how hard it is to kick the addiction help a little?"

Cole turned and studied her, jaw shifting. "You're talking about your dad?"

She nodded.

"Sorry, so sorry." His arms felt warm and comforting because he knew. He understood the hurt and the pain that were so hard to explain to other people. Smoothing back her mussed hair, Cole whispered, "You're so beautiful, Katydid, so understanding and wise."

She pulled back. "No one has ever called me that."

"Well, they should have. But I'm glad I was first to tell you that you're wise. Don't let it go to your head."

She socked him playfully in the arm.

"Wish I could have been first for a lot of things with you. Want to take a walk?"

"Sounds good."

Hand in hand, Cole and Kate walked along the waterline toward Gull Harbor. The tragedy of Samantha echoed in Kate's head. She knew addiction could wreak havoc in people's lives. Wasn't her own family proof of that? Their father's drinking had brought pain and disappointments they still couldn't talk about openly.

Although the beach was deserted, sun tents sat ready for the next day, buckles, shovels and inner tubes heaped alongside.

"How about you?" Cole asked, snugging her to one hip. "What happened to your marriage? How could any guy let you get away?"

Quiet for a second, she struggled for the words to explain something she was just beginning to understand herself. "Brian was perfect for me. Everybody told me that. We were both serious about our studies and had plans for the future. The type of people who made lists and checked things off. We were two people made for each other."

Cole started laughing.

She poked him in the ribs. "It's not funny. I thought that's what I wanted. The house, the cars, the success. His dinners with clients became vacations with clients. Somewhere along the way, we lost each other. I wasn't surprised when he told me children weren't in the plan. Never had been."

His quick intake of breath cut the air like a knife. "Wow. So who asked for the divorce?"

"I did," she admitted. "It's so hard to explain to people. No, he didn't abuse me, but he'd rather read the stock reports than talk to me. His dad had been like that. Guess we believe what we want to believe."

"Guys aren't always honest, Katydid. Don't blame yourself, okay?"

Cole's shirt smelled like the beach when he folded her into his arms. She wanted to stay there forever. Almost told him that she loved him right then. Her heart ached with the weight of her feelings.

One kiss and the spark ignited. Much deeper than chemistry, their words had given each other so much comfort, they had to seal it with their bodies. When they reached a deserted stretch with no houses, they shed their clothes in the pitch darkness and ran laughing into the water to make crazy love on the sand bar.

Much later, after Cole gave her one last, reluctant kiss at the back door, she wondered if that had really happened. Had *they* happened? Her aching body gave her the answer as she crawled into bed. The sheets slid deliciously on her overstimulated skin. *Yes. Yes, that had happened. Yes, I love him. Yes, he must care for me too.*

But as Kate drifted off to sleep, those darn yellow flyers flitted through her thoughts and dreams. In her dream, she chased them down but could never retrieve them all or the message they carried.

A few days later, the town voted down the motion that would have allowed Campbell Construction to tear down Michiana Thyme. Mildred set the wheels in motion to declare the building a historical site. Where that would end up, no one knew. Kate felt both relieved and terrified. What would Cole do if he ever found out the campaign to oppose his project had started with her?

Chapter 28

The day was hot and Cole was late. They were going blueberry picking with Kate. Next to him in the front seat, Natalie hummed along to the radio while Prissy panted. They'd both been a lot happier lately with Kate spending time at his place. The past two weeks had been crazy. Kayaking, sailing, lots of sunset picnics on the beach, and today, picking blueberries. Not easy with their work schedules.

He was making up for lost time.

Kate seemed to feel the same way.

"Why are we going blueberry picking?" Natalie poked her head around Prissy.

"Because Kate thinks it'll be fun."

Natalie settled back. "Everything with Kate is fun."

Cole chuckled. His daughter was right.

When they reached Breezy Point, Kate was sitting on the back stoop wearing the shortest white shorts he'd ever seen. Not that he was complaining.

She looked up and waved. The sun bounced off her caramel curls, or "mitt curls," their personal joke. Felt good to have their own jokes – kind of like high school but better. Now that she'd given up on being blonde, he was relieved. He liked the Kate he used to know.

Loved her. He loved her. Cole jammed the truck into Park so fast both Natalie and Prissy gave him a look. "Sorry, sweetheart. You too, Prissy."

"Good thing I always wear my seatbelt." Natalie had hooked an arm around Prissy, who snuffled and shot him an accusing glance.

Fine, Cole. Let me fly through the windshield just because you're in heat.

Waves of hot and cold pulsed over Cole, like he was stuck in a car wash.

But he liked it. Loved it. Loved her.

He loved Kate. Smiling, he turned off the truck and sat there for a second.

"Dad?" Natalie nudged him with her elbow.

Prissy swung her head his way and blinked. *Snap out of it, Cole. Stuff happens.*

"You're late." Kate stood. Her tiny blue tank top got his attention and he climbed out. Natalie and Priscilla scrambled down from the passenger side.

"I want to say hi to Alice." His daughter dashed for the back door with Prissy galloping behind her.

"Mrs. Kennedy," he called after her, but Natalie wasn't listening, so he gave Kate a kiss. "Um, strawberry jam?"

"On a toasted English muffin. Like we had last Sunday at your house."

"Yep, that was good. *You* were good." The woman was so delicious. Arm in arm, they went inside. "Sorry I'm late. Had a million things to do."

"That's okay. My whole day's open. Chili's sister is visiting from Mexico, and she wanted to sell flowers. Do you believe it? Anyway, I'm on vacation today. Not that I don't like the flower shop. I just don't want it to be forever."

"How's the writing coming?" They'd reached the kitchen, and he pulled her into the powder room, just for old time's sake. Natalie was talking with Alice out on the screen porch.

Kate snuggled into his arms. "You're so bad…"

He shushed her with a kiss. Flattened her against the wall with his entire body. Life was making one thing clear. He could not get enough of Kate Kennedy.

"No fair. Not around mothers and children." Pushing him away, she ducked under his arm and escaped.

"What about the dog?" he called after her.

"Her too."

Natalie came running into the kitchen with Prissy's nails ringing on the linoleum. The two of them look like they were up to no good. With this group of women, he felt totally outnumbered.

"I want to stay here with Alice today."

"What?" Kate gave Natalie a puzzled look. "But we're going to pick berries. For pies."

Alice joined them, putting a hand on Natalie's shoulder. "Natalie says we're having a girls' day today, but I do need those blueberries for a pie. So you two just get going." She shooed them with her right hand, which was finally responding to therapy.

Something didn't feel right. He exchanged a look with Kate. "What is this?" He tried to stare Natalie down. Did no good whatsoever. Even Prissy looked away, her pointed ears twitching.

Natalie crossed her arms over her chest. "I don't think Prissy should be out in the sun."

Well, she had a point there.

"Take some water." Turning, Alice opened the refrigerator door, and Natalie grabbed two bottles. Then she slammed the door shut but not before Cole saw the can of sink cleaner sitting on the top shelf.

"Is that a…"

His daughter shoved an icy water bottle into his hand. "Better get going."

"Yep, time's a wasting. Those berries will all be picked." Alice began shooing them from the kitchen. Then she stopped. "And Cole, I'm so sorry the vote didn't carry for your project."

Amazing how what seemed so important in early summer now appeared to be another opportunity. "Not a problem. I have another idea." Kate had paled a bit. "Hey, what is it?"

Her curls bounced when she shook her head. "Nothing. Let's hit the road."

The phone rang just as they got to the back door. "Mercedes?" Alice said, voice lifting. She made a hand motion that they should leave. "You've got news? What is it? Tell me."

"Later." Kate was dragging him out the door.

"Don't you want to talk to your sister?" he asked, but Kate shook her head. He thought she'd plow right through that screen door. "What was going on back there? Kate, I swear I saw a can of cleanser in that refrigerator."

Kate shrugged. "Happens all the time."

The pieces began to come together. Natalie had changed this summer. Not only did she adore Kate, she loved Alice too. She'd probably do anything for the older woman.

"So your mom's still not totally connecting the dots?" Twisting the bottle open, he took a big swig of water.

Breaking off one of the pink hollyhocks blooming next to the back door, Kate stuck it in her hair. "Life is what it is, Cole. I try not to think of the person my mom used to be and love the woman she is now."

"She's a trip."

"And she's still my mom. I kind of like her quirky. She doesn't give so many orders."

"That's my girl." Cole kissed the tip of Kate's nose and opened the passenger door. The days were gone when she'd make a big deal out of the dog hair coating the seat.

Once on Red Arrow, he headed north and rested a hand on her knee. Habits had formed so quickly with Kate. "Missed ya, babe."

"We were together last night."

"I miss you even when you're with me. Know what I mean?" He laughed while Kate drank half that bottle of water without taking a breath.

~~

Under the bright sunlight, blueberry bushes waited, heavy with ripe berries. Had Kate ever felt this content? Cole drove down the bumpy road and parked. Jumping out of the truck, Kate sprinted for the counter where the girls were handing out buckets. Armed for berry picking, Kate and Cole walked into the rows. Not even noon and the sun was merciless.

"Feels like an inferno in here." Cole wiped his brow.

"Yeah, but smell those berries. They're huge this year." When she glanced back, Cole was checking out her white shorts, not the bushes. "Get back to business, mister."

"Yes, ma'am. Whatever you say, ma'am."

Kate gave him the look and Cole grinned back. The man was so sexy without even trying. Sexy and sweet. Closing one hand gently over a plump cluster, she tugged. The berries came off easily, and she released them into the bucket. "I feel like a little girl again when I'm picking."

"I'm glad you're not a little girl, or I'd be in big trouble for what we've been doing." Snatching at the very top branch, Cole grabbed some berries and promptly popped them into his mouth.

"Quit that. Fill the bucket." But she did steal one. Was anything as tasty as a berry warm from the sun? The sweet flavor exploded in her mouth.

Cole laughed at her as if she was still the uptight sophomore and he was the skinny senior, too big for his britches. Seeing him this carefree made guilt pull her up short. His vote had not passed, and she had to come clean about that. She wanted no secrets between them.

The two of them worked in silence while the sun bore down. She was grateful for the water bottle, but soon, it was drained. Sweat beaded on Cole's forehead. Whipping out a hankie, he tied it around his forehead. Oh lord, he was so handsome.

"What is it?" He dropped another handful into the bucket that was filling up fast.

"Nothing." How could she explain that what she'd done in June made no sense to her in August? She hadn't trusted him to do the right thing.

Setting his pail down, Cole took her in his arms and coaxed her with his lips. His kiss tasted warm and sweet as the berries. If only she could redo this summer. Go back and revise the parts where she'd messed up.

"I love you, Kate Kennedy. You know that, don't you?"

She pushed back, dizzy with happiness. "You do? Really?"

He nodded and came in for another kiss. She didn't mind the sweat. Didn't mind the dirt. Still, Kate's conscience pricked at her bubble of contentment.

"I love you too, Cole, but…"

"*But?* Really, there's a *but?*" He stumbled back.

"You won't love me when you hear this." Her heart squeezed so tight it hurt.

Hands on his hips, Cole waited.

The sun beat down and Kate squirmed in the heat.

"Those yellow flyers? I wrote them and stuffed them in every mailbox in town." Her words came double time. "I-I thought I was doing the right thing."

Cole dropped his head, alarming at first. Then his shoulders shook.

She leaned closer. Saw his lips twitch. "Are you laughing at me?"

Cole ran a hand across his face. "Aw, babe. I'm sorry. Did you think I didn't know that? Who else would go off half-cocked and run off flyers when the lights hadn't even cooled in that meeting hall?"

"And you didn't mention it? You let me suffer?"

"'Suffer'? Is that what you call it. Girl, I'm suffering now." By that time, Cole had her firmly in his arms. A mother and her daughter peeked around the bushes. Kate and Cole were making such a fuss.

"What are they doing, Mom?" a little girl asked.

"I do believe they are having an argument. Let's go to the next row, Marcia."

Kate's world had wobbled out of focus. Maybe she was getting heat stroke.

He loves me. Even though I've been an idiot.

Cole gave her a little shake. "Say it!"

"What? Oh." She settled into his warmth. "I love you. Have loved you since that La Porte victory, you terrible boy. Making me crazy and then taking another girl to prom." Laughing, Kate hurled the words onto the heavy August air, making sure the woman who'd started picking in their row heard. She looked up and frowned at Cole.

"That's it." He grabbed both buckets in one hand and towed Kate toward the checkout. "We're going home to tell your mother."

"Tell her what?"

"Why, we're getting married of course."

"We are?"

"Damn straight. Give you thirty seconds to think about it."

When they reached checkout, he jammed the pails at the woman at the register, who weighed them and poured them into a cardboard flat. Dazed, Kate followed behind, watching Cole set the flat of berries in the back of the truck. Hit her then that every day of her life, she wanted this man coming through her front door.

"You don't want to wait?" she finally squeaked out.

"For what?" Cole opened the truck door. "Kate, I've been waiting for you a long time. Maybe forever. The waiting stops now."

He was right. Kate kissed him before she climbed into the truck.

Her mother looked startled when they burst through the door twenty minutes later.

"What? No berries?" She checked their empty hands.

"In the pickup," Cole told her. "We've got news, Alice. Wanted you to be the first to know and I probably should ask permission."

Natalie poked her head under Alice's arm. "News?"

Cole squatted until he was eye level with his daughter. He was so good with Natalie and Kate knew he'd be just this patient with their children too. "What would you say if Kate and I got married?"

"My wish came true? I just knew it!" Natalie threw herself into her dad's arms and Prissy began to bark.

"Mine too." Her mom lifted one corner of her apron to her eyes. "You've both made me so happy."

"Aw, Mom." Kate gave her a good hug.

With a sniffle, her mother hugged her back before turning to Cole. "Now show me those berries."

Later when Natalie and her mother were working in the kitchen on the pies, Kate and Cole rocked gently on the porch swing. The day before, she'd been painting Natalie's nails. Now she shook the nail polish and began to paint her toes. The look of concentration on Cole's face made her nervous.

"Let me, okay?" He held out one hand.

"Really?"

"Sure. This might be a skill I need to master." Looking so pleased with himself and hotter than heck, he stroked her toenails with the bright pink polish. And she had this to look forward to for the rest of her life?

After he'd finished and the polish had dried, she dashed upstairs. "Turn about is fair play," she said, returning with a scissors.

"Whoa, what have I gotten myself into?"

"I think you could use a trim." Lately Cole's hair had gotten shaggy.

"You and Natalie. She's been trying to send me to the barbershop but I'm so busy,"

Draping a towel over his shoulders, Kate began to snip.

"Thought you liked my hair long." He was definitely uneasy and she stopped.

Was she overstepping her bonds? "I'll leave it long if that's what you want. Guess I wanted my high school buddy back."

"You sure you're ready for a change? Things can't be the way they were, Katydid." He grabbed her wrist. "That isn't possible. You can't repeat the past."

"I know that. Humor me?" Blushing, she laid the scissors on the table. "Maybe I'll always want things the way they were. Got to work on that."

He leaned closer to whisper against her lips. "We'll work on it together. Now grab those scissors and finish what you started. Long hair is too hot in the summer anyway."

"I like you hot."

"We'll talk about that later."

Epilogue

The guitarist played Pachelbel's Canon and this all seemed so right while Kate waited her turn. In front of her, Natalie showered hollyhock petals in a wide arc as she walked toward Cole. Trotting alongside, Prissy nipped at the falling flowers, a pink boa around her neck. Chili, Sarah, and Mercedes stood grinning on one side of the minister in their hot pink gowns. On the other side, Ignacio, Ryan, and Josh lined up behind Cole. Finally it was Kate's turn and she had only one goal, one person whose eyes coaxed her forward. Her groom's smile stretched wide as the beach. The casual ceremony felt perfect. A September lake whispered approval.

The sun had started its descent, orange rays streaking the skyline and silence fell over the group clustered around them. This was their moment, the moment Kate had been moving toward ever since she saw Cole Campbell in the hall on her first day of high school. Clutching a bouquet of bright pink calla lilies, she squished her bare toes into the sand to stay steady. The white crepe tiers of her short gown from Second Hand Rose fluttered in the breeze.

She blinked back tears of joy. Had Cole ever been more handsome? Wearing a black tuxedo jacket with jeans and a bolo tie, he was everything she'd ever wanted. And she'd come home to him here in Gull Harbor. Felt like the whole town had come to watch them "tie the knot," as Cole teasingly told her. Phoebe and Carolyn stood high on a dune with Diana, their faces suffused with color from the setting sun…or was that hope radiating from their smiles? After all, if Kate could reclaim her high school dream, maybe they all could.

Settled in their white wicker chairs adorned with bows, her mother and Marie whispered with excitement. So much had happened that Kate's head spun. Mercedes had come home, possibly to stay. With the town's blessing, Cole was repurposing the former Michiana Thyme building into a new town hall, and Samantha was threatening to visit.

All would be well. Life moved on, that much Kate had learned, but one thing was certain. She'd found the man to stand by her and share whatever came their way.

"Thought you were never going to get here," Cole whispered, kissing her cheek and threading her arm through his.

"Oh, Cole, I'm so glad I came back home. Back to you." Smiling into his blue eyes, Kate felt a warm flood of shared memories. Together, they'd make more.

They both turned to the minister and the future that lay ahead.

THE END

Other Books by Barbara Lohr

Man from Yesterday
Always on His Mind
In His Eyes
Late Bloomer
Still Not Over You
Every Breath You Take
Christmas Dreams and Santa Schemes

Best Friends to Forever
Marry Me, Jackson
Steal My Heart, Trevor
Christmas with Dr. Darling

Windy City Romance series
Finding Southern Comfort
Her Favorite Mistake
Her Favorite Honeymoon
Her Favorite Hot Doc
The Christmas Baby Bundle
Rescuing the Reluctant Groom

About the Author

Barbara Lohr writes sweet contemporary romance. The *Man from Yesterday* series is set in Gull Harbor, Michigan, where the boy you left behind might be the man you want forever. The charming, small beach town actually exists but under another name.

Best friends are worth a second look in her Best Friends to Forever series. She takes readers to the South with this series, which takes place in Sweetwater Creek.

In her *Windy City Romance* series, the Kirkpatrick family and friends are based in Oak Park, Illinois, a suburb of Chicago. However, these adventurous girls take readers on exciting jaunts to Tuscany, Guatemala and Savannah. They travel wherever their hearts take them.

Family often plays an important role in Barbara's stories. "No woman falls in love without some family influence, either positive or negative." She feels strongly dark chocolate should be an essential part of the food pyramid. Good food often figures in her work. She lives in the South of the United States with her husband and a cat that insists he was Heathcliff in another life. Visit her Facebook page and be sure to sign up for her newsletter for new releases, great giveaways and a fun group of readers who enjoy Barbara's work. She loves to hear from her readers!

www.BarbaraLohrAuthor.com
www.facebook.com/Barbaralohrauthor
www.twitter.com/BarbaraJLohr

Acknowledgements

Many thanks to Romance Writers of America and Central Ohio Fiction Writers. The loops and forums of writers who address writing and publishing issues are also invaluable to me. A huge thank you to my readers, who participate on my Facebook page and have been so supportive

For my daughters, Kelly and Shannon, when we shared Judy Blume and Madeleine L'Engle together, we never saw what lay ahead. Keep those reading lamps on over your beds. My grandchildren, Bo and Gianna, bring me such joy and will probably appear in quite a few of Mama B's novels. To my husband Ted, words aren't adequate to thank you for your love and support, especially when my computer crashes and you have to provide tech support. May we have many more wonderful years together that include trips to Leopold's for ice cream.